MAGIC LANCE

MAGIC LANCE

MYSTERY & ADVENTURE IN THE NEW WEST

HAL SIMMONS

CLEAR LIGHT PUBLISHING
SANTA FE, NEW MEXICO

©2008 by Hal Simmons

Clear Light Publishing
823 Don Diego, Santa Fe, NM 87505
web site: www.clearlightbooks.com

All rights reserved. No part of this book may be reproduced in any form by any electronic or mechanical means, including information storage and retrieval systems, without permission in writing from the publisher.

This book is a novel, a work of fiction. All names, characters, happenings, incidents and locations are a product of the author's imagination and are not to be construed as real. Any resemblances to actual persons, businesses, places or operations and activities, past or present, are purely coincidental.

First Edition
10 9 8 7 6 5 4 3 2 1

Library of Congress Cataloging-in-Publication Data

Simmons, Hal, 1938-
  Magic Lance : mystery & adventure in the new West / Hal Simmons. -- 1st ed.
    p. cm.
  Summary: "Set in Western mining and ranching country, Magic Lance is a novel of intrigue, romance, suspense and personal transformation. Conflicting dreams of Indian casino operator Lucky Joe, who is buying up ranches to create a Native American state, and the small-time rancher Lance Burnett, who refuses to sell, have unforeseen and violent consequences"-- Provided by publisher.
  ISBN-13: 978-1-57416-094-9
  ISBN-10: 1-57416-094-x
  1. Ranchers--Fiction. 2. Ranch life--Fiction. 3. Indians of North America--Fiction. 4. Casinos--Fiction. I. Title.

PS3619.I5594M34 2007
813'.6--dc22
                                                                          2007029411

cover photo by Marcia Keegan
Cover design by Marcia Keegan and Carol O'Shea
Book design, typography, & production by Carol O'Shea
Lance design by Ronald Kil

To Fritz and Lois
and to Marc, Peggy and Lade

ACKNOWLEDGMENTS

In most creative efforts there is the creator, but there also are others involved who influence and mold the work in varying degrees. These persons deserve acknowledgment for the important part they add to the creative work. In the case of the *Magic Lance*, editors Carol O'Shea and Lee More offered significant suggestion, correction and editing to the original plot and form.

Publishers Harmon Houghton and Marcia Keegan have somehow stayed the course in the world of quality book publishing and distribution, while so many others in the same field have vanished.

Plaudits for the cover of *Magic Lance* go to Santa Fe artist Ronald Kil and designers Carol O'Shea and Marcia Keegan .

My personal thanks are extended to a limited group of backers who agreed to read the earliest drafts on this book and make comments before the ink was dry, allowing important changes to be made before advanced drafts were submitted to editors. My thanks to Ina Simmons, Howard Bryan, Nan Griswold, Jill Simmons, Charles (Lade) Ladenberger, Peggy Ladenberger, Susan Garza and Tony Hillerman.

CHAPTER ONE

The dream of instant riches was never more evident than when Hernando Cortez arrived in Mexico in 1519 with eleven ships. He found gold in incredible abundance, possessed by a people of relative military weakness. The gold was seductive and hypnotic. It was taken by force of arms.

The success of Cortez's venture became a dream of countless explorers for centuries to come. The gold and silver lay hidden. It was up to those with ambition and spirit to find it and possess it.

Recognizing that the lure of instant riches was irrepressible, the Spanish Crown decreed that a *quinto*, the royal fifth, of all mineral riches taken from the New World would be paid to the Spanish government as tax. This requirement sounded reasonable in Madrid. In the frontier regions of the American Southwest, avoiding *el quinto* was a risk of doing business.

Those adventurous souls who ventured into the wilderness of New Spain, seeking the fabulous cities of Cibola, and gold and silver they hoped would equal the spectacular treasure finds in Mexico and Peru, were the most aggressive and fearless souls of Spanish culture. They feared no law, feared no foe, and feared no fate. They were apostles of both the material world and the Faith. They willingly sacrificed their lives for both dreams, and their daring and courage inspired lives for generations to come.

By the twentieth century in the American Southwest, the easy gold and silver veins and placer locations had been found, mined, and mined again. Still, the dream of instant riches remains, and the hope of a new find, or the re-discovery of an earlier find that had been lost, burns in many hearts.

Lance Burnett and his wife Jan held hands as they entered the abandoned silver mine entrance. It was late summer and hot. A cool stream of air flowed from the mine, as though it was Nature's air conditioning system. Jan winced as they moved slowly into the tunnel. They had gone but a few steps when a bat sped past her face. She dropped to one knee and screamed, slapping her hands at her hair to make sure it didn't lodge there.

Lance laughed. "Just a bat. They eat bugs."

Jan was not amused.

"This is horrible," she said. Lance paid no attention. He pulled her along the mine tunnel, flashing his light ahead and around the back and ribs of the mine.

"It may have been a hundred years since anyone's been in this thing," Lance said. While he was intrigued with the newly discovered mine drift, he also was wary. Perhaps, he had thought, this was the lost Spanish mine his father told him about years before. That mine had been lost centuries ago and remembered as legend and wishful thinking. Its location was rumored to be not only on the Three V Ranch, but on at least a dozen other ranches in the area. The legend of a lost silver vein also had a downside. Although he himself did not believe in spirits, Lance gave some thought to the curse that was said to abide with the mine, perhaps placed by the original Spanish miners who worked it centuries before the Americans arrived. Whether the curse came from the Spaniards or from Indians who wished to discourage future miners, or from storytellers, it was said that

MAGIC LANCE

whoever sought the riches of the mine would find danger and death instead.

The day before, Lance had been scouting for a possible water line route that would use a PCV pipe above ground. The line would transport water from a windmill almost a mile away, over a rock stretch, along the side of a hill about twenty feet above a dry arroyo bed, and finally to a galvanized steel water tank in a flat area next to the arroyo bed.

As he dropped into the arroyo and approached the proposed location for the tank, Lance was surprised to feel a slight breeze of cool air on the side of his face. He made his survey measurements and was about to continue down the arroyo to the gravel road when it occurred to him that it was strange to feel a cool breeze at one spot on a hot day.

His curiosity aroused, he went back to the same stretch of the arroyo and proceeded for some distance. Thinking the earlier experience must have been his imagination, or a brief climatic fluke, he turned back down the arroyo, this time walking closer to the base of the hill. When he saw his own footprints made earlier in the sand, he decided to retrace them. At a place where there was a concave curvature in the hillside as it reached the arroyo bed, and only in a five- to ten-foot section, he again felt the cool breeze. He scrutinized the hillside next to the arroyo. There were two piñon trees growing on an earthen dike. The dike was covered with side oats gramma and three awn grass, along with four-wing salt bush and a thick growth of Apache plume bushes.

Lance licked the index finger of his right hand and stuck it in the air. The coolness was not strong enough to indicate a flow direction, but it definitely was cooler than the air in the surrounding area. Lance approached the piñon trees and peered through their thick, dark green, needle-covered branches.

He observed nothing unusual. He was about to abandon his exploration when he thought of the earthen dike. While it initially seemed to him a natural feature, it was almost too symmetrical when compared to the chaos of the rocky hillside. As he walked along the dike, he noted it was flat on top, where the piñon trees and Apache plume and four-winged salt bush grew, and then flared off and slanted down as it merged with the arroyo. Perhaps the spring run-offs, when the high mountain melting snows sent torrents of water plunging down the normally dry arroyos, molded the dike in that spot. When he was even with the area where the dike ended in the arroyo bed, he decided to work his way through the salt bush and piñon trees, and see if he could find an explanation for the cool air that seemed to be coming through the piñon boughs.

It was only after weaving and bobbing through the piñon boughs that he saw the entrance of the mine. It was about four feet high and six feet wide. Just inside the adit, or mine opening, the drift expanded to about eight feet in both height and width. It appeared a portion of the back had collapsed, reducing the size of the mine entrance. From the arroyo, and the opposite hillside, the entrance was completely obscured by the two piñon trees. From above the mine entrance on the hillside, a narrow ridge of sedimentary rock blocked the entrance from view by anyone walking above it. Lance kneeled down, peering through the adit into the silky blackness of the mine drift. Without a light, he had no desire to proceed further.

When he returned to the ranch house later that day, he could hardly wait to tell Jan of his find. He invited her to accompany him the next day, with a strong flashlight, to explore the mine. To his knowledge no one had ever discovered a mine on the Three V Ranch. He had passed the area many times and never felt a cool breeze or seen the mine entrance behind the piñon

MAGIC LANCE

trees. On horseback, a person would be too high to feel the breeze. Except for a couple of months during the summer, it would not be hot enough to feel it at all.

Jan told him she was not eager to go into an abandoned mine. The thought of it frightened her. She recalled warnings she had heard all of her life about the hazards of abandoned mines: bad air, rock falls, unexpected shafts, getting lost, and a host of unknown dangers.

Nonetheless, the thought of possible treasure, should the mine contain silver, or even gold, intrigued her. And while she did not admit it, the thought of remaining by herself outside the mine, while Lance went in alone, was as undesirable as going in with him. Lance was over six feet tall, and although he weighed almost two hundred pounds, he was considered lean by his friends. Jan was proud there was no fat on his muscular frame and that he would not hesitate to protect her from any threat. Somewhat reluctantly, she opted for being with Lance. Perhaps they would encounter something of value—something to offset their persistent shortage of money and the tension it was causing between them.

"Are you sure you want to go into this thing?" Jan asked, as she and Lance inched along the floor of the mine. "What do you think we might find?"

"There might be a silver vein in here. We're in the boundaries of the silver belt."

Were it not for the strong hand of her husband, Jan knew she would run back to the daylight. The closeness and dampness of the rock and the impending blackness reminded her of a tomb. It was like being buried alive.

Lance was fascinated by the tunnel construction. When they arrived at some set timbers that supported the back of the mine tunnel, he paused to run his hand along the old wood. They ducked as they passed under the timber support, and bent down as they pressed through thick spider webs farther into the tunnel.

"Lance, I don't like this," Jan said. "This is horrible." She looked back to the tunnel entrance and could not see even a modest suggestion of light.

"We'll just go a little further," Lance said. He flashed the light around the tunnel.

At about the time he decided to turn around, Lance spotted what appeared to be a narrow wooden box, four feet long, situated at the seam where the rib or side of the mine reached the mine floor.

He focused the flashlight beam on the box.

"What's that?" Jan asked.

"Looks like an old box. Maybe an old treasure chest," he added teasingly.

"Can you open it?"

"Let's see," Lance said, passing the light on all sides and along the top of the box.

He focused on the end, where a crude wooden handle was attached. He looked at the other end of the box and saw a similar handle.

He tried to lift up the wooden plank that formed the top of the box, to see if it had hinges or moved. It did not. He put his boot on the end of the box and tried to push. There was no movement. The box was solidly seated in the rock that composed the floor of the mine.

"Lance, look at that," Jan said, pointing to a symbol on the rock rib above the wooden box.

Lance shined the light on the symbol. It was a carving in the rock that looked like the outline of a Valentine heart, but with a gap in the outline at the bottom near the point.

"What is that?" Jan asked.

MAGIC LANCE

"I have no idea. Maybe some miner was heartsick over his girl friend."

"Is it a heart?"

"It looks like it," Lance said. "But what about the gap at the bottom? How come they left a gap?"

Lance flashed his light around the ribs and back of the tunnel. There were no other symbols in view. His interest returned to the wooden box. "Let's see if we can pry that out. Maybe it's a tool box, or something like that."

Lance took out the hunting knife strapped to his belt and pushed the blade into the crack that separated the top plank from the side of the box. The wood was desiccated and he worked for a time to force the blade into the crease. Realizing the box was tightly closed, he forced the blade into the seam all the way to the hilt. Then, using the blade as a lever, he pried the top plank up. It moved an inch, then an inch more. When he had a couple of inches of space, he flashed the light through the opening and put his eye close to the wood.

"What do you see?"

"Looks like rocks," Lance said. "Could that be silver ore?"

Lance pulled again on the wooden handles on the ends of the box. Nothing budged. Then he sat on the mine floor and used his boot heel to kick it, to jolt the box free from its tight fit. Then he moved to the other end, sat down, and kicked it. Then he kicked it from the front, loosening it.

Lance stooped down, grabbed hold of the handles and tried to lift the box out of its compartment. It did not release. He started kicking it again from all angles.

He sat on the mine floor and repeatedly kicked it from all different angles.

"Let me try it," Jan said, stooping down in front of the box and grabbing the handles.

Neither she nor Lance realized that the last kicks had jolted the box from its centuries-old entrapment. Instead of trying to muscle the box out of its setting, Jan wiggled it back and forth. Suddenly the box released from its hold. She was about to say how coordinated she was when with a thunderous roar the entire side of the tunnel rib crashed down where she was stooped. Instinctively, seeing the rock slab collapsing upon her, Jan dived to her right. Everything cleared the falling rock slab except her right foot and leg above the ankle. The pain was unbearable.

Lance was standing slightly to one side. The edge of the falling rock slammed onto the mine floor an inch in front of his toes. For a moment he was stunned. Jan's terrifying screams shocked him.

"What happened?" he shouted, swinging the flash light to and fro. The crushing power of the falling rock slab, the deafening roar of it striking the mine floor and the rising dust cloud disoriented them.

Jan screamed in agony and desperately pushed on the rock slab with her free foot to try and pull her smashed foot out from under it. When her efforts failed, she lay back helplessly on the floor of the mine.

"Help me, Lance. Help me."

Lance leaned down and tried to get his hands under the slab to lift it. His efforts were as futile as Jan's had been. The rock slab weighed hundreds of pounds, perhaps a ton. There was no way to move it.

"Oh God, this hurts," Jan murmured. Then she lost consciousness.

Lance momentarily was stupefied. He placed his hands and the flashlight up next to the top of his head. Then, setting the flashlight on the mine floor, he put his hands under the slab again, and tried with all his strength to raise it. It was hopeless.

MAGIC LANCE

Lance considered his options. Either he had to lift the rock slab, or he had to dig into the floor and allow Jan's foot to drop into the dug-out space.

His first thought was the long steel pry bar in the back of the pickup. "I've got to get to the truck," Lance thought. Jan lay unconscious. He could not bring himself to leave her. Nor could he save her with his bare hands.

Thinking of the desperateness of her condition, he ran along the tunnel to the mine entrance, toward the pickup truck parked under a stand of Arizona walnut trees.

A spare tire, five-gallon water can and heavy-duty tire jack lay haphazardly on top of the steel pry bar. Lance struggled to remove the pry bar. Finally, with a few curse words for support, he was able to slide the bar free. He raced back to the mine at a reckless pace. When he reached the support timber, his felt cowboy hat was the only thing that prevented a head concussion. Stumbling on toward the fallen slab, his feet skidded to a halt just as he reached it. He flashed the light around the tunnel and to the spot where Jan lay. To his surprise, she was trying to sit up, leaning back and propped up on both elbows. Her eyes were wider than he had ever seen them.

"Lance! On the slab!"

Lance scanned his light over the surface of the slab. Not three feet away, and not three feet from Jan, were two huge, black tarantulas, moving slowly, their hairy, bent legs scuttling across the rough rock surface.

"Be still," he said. He inched forward. As he closed on the tarantulas, they veered away from him, directly toward Jan. She screamed and fell on her back.

Lance cupped his rough, calloused left hand. He swept it across the slab, picked up the tarantulas and slung them against the rib of the tunnel.

"They're gone!" He breathed a sigh of relief. The higher danger of Jan's entrapment surged back quickly in his mind.

"I'm going to get you out of here," Lance said as he leaned down and kissed Jan on the cheek.

"Oh Lance, this really hurts."

"I know darling. I'm going to work as fast as I can. I have to be careful, to make sure I don't hit your foot. I'm going to be very careful. Just hold on, and I'm going to get you out of here."

After positioning the flashlight, he jammed the bar under the rock slab and tried to lift it up. The slab did not budge. His only chance, Lance decided, was to gouge out a portion of the mine floor so Jan's foot could drop down. The steel bar was heavy. He had to concentrate to make sure he did not strike her foot. As he drove the pry bar into the mine floor, he thought of the double jacks, the early miners who worked in the silver mines, driving steel into the mine face for blasting holes. While one man held and turned the drive steel with his hands, his partner slammed the steel with a sledgehammer. The slightest miss would mean a partner's smashed hand.

The work was slow going. After a ten-minute effort, Lance dug a hole about the size of a grapefruit to one side of Jan's foot. He paused a moment to review his progress and shine his flashlight beam on Jan. Her eyes were closed. He could not tell if she were conscious or even breathing. Nor did he have time to check. His only chance was to get a hole dug that would allow her ankle and foot to drop down from the rock vise that held her tight. He resumed his work. As he dug, he realized that along the mine floor, where it met the rib, there was a shallow water drain carved in the rock floor about eight inches wide. In the drain, a dark green moss grew. He realized it was the combination of the drain and the moss that buffered Jan's foot and ankle from being crushed even worse than they were.

MAGIC LANCE

Lance drove the steel into the mine floor, then used his hands to scoop out the crushed rock pieces and toss them to the side. At one point, he took a brief rest to catch his breath and allow his hand muscles to rest. It was then he heard what he thought was a loud cracking sound, farther back in the mine. The sound was indistinguishable, like a wood timber crack, or rock falling. Lance stopped all motion; his breathing stopped. For a moment he switched off the flashlight. He strained his ears to listen in the silence of the mine. While listening and hearing nothing, he imagined something was crawling on the back of his neck. Instinctively, he slapped the spot with his hand. Then he flicked on the flashlight. There was nothing on his neck or hand, but to his horror, he saw a tarantula crawling on Jan's blouse, right between her breasts, heading toward her neck. Instead of sweeping the spider this time, and without thinking what he was doing, Lance grabbed the tarantula in his bare hand and squeezed it to death. As soon as he realized what he had done, he shook his hand violently and scraped it with his left hand to rub the crushed remains off his right palm and fingers. A feeling of revulsion surged in his stomach and he flashed the light in all directions to see if any more black furry creepers were coming toward them.

As Lance resumed his digging with the steel bar, he thought of the curse and the early miners' stories of the Tommy Knockers, those dwarf-like creatures that live in the mines and cause many strange things to happen underground in the eternal dark and silence. Were the Tommy Knockers and the curse closing in on him and Jan?

The hole under Jan's foot expanded. Ten minutes later, Lance had gouged enough of a depression in the mine floor that her leg and foot dropped down and he was able to pull her away from the slab.

Once she was free, Lance dropped to his knees and put his face next to hers, with his hand on her chest. She was unconscious but breathing. It was weak.

Lance imagined his wife's high cheekbones, perfect complexion, grey-blue eyes and sensual lips. Now her mouth was turned down at both corners and dust and dirt covered her face and hair with a layer of fine grey powder, giving her a ghostlike appearance.

Lance considered his options. He could drag Jan along the mine floor, out to the pickup, or he could try a fireman's carry. On further examination, he saw her foot was swollen and covered with dirt. There was no blood, but when he gently nudged her sock down, he saw that her foot and ankle area were dark purple. He lay down next to her, pulled her arm over his head and struggled to his feet, picking her up on his shoulder. The trip out of the mine was half-walking, half-stumbling. Jan's slender five-foot, seven-inch frame was a burden Lance barely noticed. At the pickup truck, he eased her onto the front seat, allowing her to slump over on her side. He gently arranged her legs and feet on the floorboard.

He knew she needed immediate medical help. He also knew the nearest medical help was in Sierra City, thirty-five miles away.

As Lance scurried to the driver's side, he turned and looked back toward the mine. He wanted to make dead sure he was not being followed.

CHAPTER TWO

There was so much money coming in, they no longer counted it. They only weighed it.

Lucky Joe leaned back in his swivel chair, fingers interlocked and resting on top of his barrel chest. He was de facto chief executive officer of the Magic Lance Casino. He didn't run the operation day to day. The casino professionals did that. He was the liaison between the tribal gambling committee and the casino professionals.

The liaison job paid well. One hundred and fifty thousand dollars a year. And that did not count the per capita tribal payment of seventy-five hundred dollars per month. That amount was tax-free. With a wife and two children, his income was close to thirty-five thousand dollars per month, not counting benefits.

Social circumstances had changed in the past fifteen years for the Grey Piñon Tribe. Once a lower economic class in America, its members now were nouveau riche. The allocation of gambling rights to Indians under the federal Indian Gaming Regulatory Act a quarter century earlier changed things in a way few expected. From being among the dispossessed, the Grey Piñons now collectively were among the wealthiest one per cent of the population.

Stories and family photos handed down from his mother and father, and especially from his grandmother and grandfather, of the old lifestyles and the inbred poverty of the 1900s were hard for Lucky Joe to imagine. Although he remembered growing up poor, he had not felt poor; in fact, in those early days, when life was primarily confined to the reservation, he remembered his traditional Indian lifestyle with a sense of pleasure and pride. For the past decade, so much money had flowed into tribal bank accounts that the only problems were generated by tribal members jockeying for position within the tribe.

During the last few years Lucky Joe moved up the tribal power ladder. To an intangible degree, his rise was based on family connections; he preferred to credit his own strengths and leadership abilities, special personal attributes, hard work, discipline and perseverance. It was not chance that opened the way for his rise in the tribal system, he thought. It had to be that unique collection of qualities in himself. Obviously he was chosen by higher powers, and he appreciated the selection. Deep inside he felt he deserved it. He was confident other Grey Piñon members were fortunate he had been chosen. He thought that someday he might even be chosen to fill the role of cacique his grandfather now occupied, the top chief of the Grey Piñon Tribe.

Being the chosen one, at least in his own mind, he could rest easy in his swivel chair, his fingers interlocked on his chest, listening to the sounds of the Magic Lance Casino.

Later that evening, Lucky Joe walked to the main floor to observe the night's operations. The casino atmosphere was a stark contrast to his traditional culture. The architects and decorators had tried to connect with the spirit, and reflect in form and color something they vaguely understood. If appearances counted, they had caught some of it, Lucky Joe thought. In the deeper levels of his heart, however, he was a stranger in the halls of the Magic Lance. Yes, the gold, brown and beige of the Anasazi rock walls melted attractively into the rich earth tones of the marble floors and carpet. And yes, large Indian pottery with Native American designs sat in nichos in the high walls of the entryway. But in Lucky Joe's opinion, the architectural and decorative efforts were overwhelmed by the garish blinking lights, the ringing of the slots, and the milling hordes of gamblers moving from one slot machine to another, one blackjack table to another, one aisle to the next.

All these people, Lucky Joe thought, all these people. Where do they come from; why do they bring their money here and rhythmically, constantly and hypnotically drop it or stick it in a Wild Cherry, or a Double Diamond, or a Four Leaf Clover. He looked at a row of players sitting on chairs before the quarter slots. A good number of them were seniors. A guy who looked like a truck driver sat before a slot at the end of the row. Lucky Joe wondered how long he had to work to make the money he was dropping in the slots, voluntarily giving it to the tribe, at odds so fixed the outcome should be obvious even to the simple-minded.

Lucky Joe wrinkled his nose as he looked at an ashtray crammed with cigarette butts, squeezed into the narrow space between two slot machines. He looked for a casino employee to get the ashtray emptied. While the air-conditioning system was designed to handle heavy cigarette smoke, such a constant volume was added during all hours the casino was open there was no way to eliminate it all. Lucky Joe checked out two casino guards dressed in crisp white shirts, black ties, tailored pants and black boots. They passed by him deferentially and disappeared through a door at the north end of the casino. They were lean and well-groomed.

Lucky Joe looked at himself in the full-length mirror along the wall leading to the restaurant. Lucky Joe was not lean. His chest was round and excess weight bulged over his belt. His best physical attributes, he thought, were his thick black hair, smooth complexion, and bowling pin upper arms. And at six foot two he was taller than most other tribal members.

As the end of his work shift approached, Lucky Joe felt a creeping mental and physical fatigue. He returned to his office, resumed his restful position in the swivel chair, leaned back and interlocked his fingers on top of his chest.

Suddenly, outside the office, two men shouted at each other. There were sounds of scuffling, grunts and groans. Lucky Joe jumped to his feet and ran toward the open door. A security guard appeared, holding a middle-aged, diminutive tribe member in a hammer lock, pushing him into the office.

"What's this!" Lucky Joe exclaimed.

"He said you sent for him," the guard said. "Drunk as usual."

The man stopped struggling. His head hung down.

"I didn't send for him, but I'll take care of this." The security guard released his ward, partly relieved to be rid of the man and partly irritated, suspecting nothing disciplinary was going to happen to him.

Lucky Joe showed the man to a chair in front of his desk.

"So, Louie, how is it?"

Louie rubbed his hands together. Lucky Joe put his face up close to Louie's. The man's eyes were bloodshot. If exposed to an open flame, his breath was potent enough to ignite.

"My luck hasn't been so good," Louie said.

Lucky Joe walked to his chair behind the desk and tapped some keys on the computer.

"You owe a hundred and fifty thousand," Lucky Joe said.

Louie nodded his head.

"You're not our top debtor in the tribe, but you're in the top ten," Lucky Joe said. "Are you proud of that?"

Louie shook his head.

MAGIC LANCE

"The devil's got you. Too much drinking. Too much gambling." Louie nodded.

"What are you going to do about it?" Lucky Joe asked.

"I don't know. I've got to wait for my luck to change."

"You're luck isn't going to change, Louie. Nobody can drink as much as you do, and gamble as much money as you do, and handle it. The odds don't change."

Louie slumped a few inches deeper in the wooden chair. His eyelids almost shut.

"I'm going to put the Magic Lance off limits to you, Louie. You're a debt problem, and now you're a security problem because of your drinking."

"How can I get my luck to change, if I can't play."

"We're going to put a hold on half your per capita. That's three thousand, seven hundred and fifty dollars per month." Lucky Joe ran a quick calculation on his calculator. "Even with no interest, that's going to take you over three years to pay off."

"I've got a lot of debts. I can't live on thirty-seven-fifty a month."

"What can you live on?"

"I need at least five thousand."

Lucky Joe ran the calculation. "That'll take five years to pay off, even with no interest."

"I'll try to do it," Louie said.

Lucky Joe pulled out a legal pad and was making some notes when a third man entered the room.

In the circle of tribal leaders, the person most influential in Lucky Joe's life was this man of slight stature, a crooked left eye, coarse black hair still shiny that stuck up like porcupine needles, missing digits on the fourth finger and pinky of his right hand, a left-leaning stance, penetrating black eyes, and a smile that communicated more of a threat than a light-hearted spirit. His tribal name was unknown to many tribe members. In his presence, he was called El Segundo. In his absence, the "El" was dropped, and he was referred to simply as Segundo.

Skipping formalities, Segundo walked right up to Louie.

He did not raise his voice, but the tone was embedded with threats.

"You disgust me," he said in Louie's face. "We have given you a dozen chances. Treated you with kid gloves. And how do you repay us? By threatening our staff. Like we owe you some special treatment because you are Grey Piñon. You deserve stricter treatment because you are a Grey Piñon. We hold you to a higher standard. You are a disgrace to the tribe. I will not tolerate you in the casino any longer. You are banned. Do you hear that? You are banned."

Louie lowered his head and scooted down in the chair, trying not to look at the old man, trying to avoid the verbal arrows that pierced his heart.

"Look at me, you little worm. You are going to lose your entire per capita. You are not fit to come into this establishment again."

"Lucky Joe Cruz told me I could pay it off."

Segundo's eyes flashed to Lucky Joe.

"He told you right. You can pay it off, at seventy-five hundred per month. That's final."

Segundo grabbed Louie by the arm and jerked him from the chair. He called the security guard standing outside the door.

"See that this man does not come back into this casino," Segundo said. "Not now, and not ever."

After Louie was taken away, Segundo dropped into the chair Louie had occupied. A smile ripped across his face.

"That's one less problem." The encounter invigorated him.

"When are you going to take charge of this operation?" he said, turning to Lucky Joe. "With the gambling compacts com-

MAGIC LANCE

ing up for renewal with the state, decisive leadership is crucial. We need steel backbone. The tribe's interests are paramount."

Lucky Joe Cruz felt a sinking in his stomach.

"We need to have a serious talk," Segundo said. "But not here. Meet me at the honored place by the river in fifteen minutes. You are the subject matter."

CHAPTER THREE

A sandstone ridge ran parallel to the river across from the Grey Piñon village. At one place north of the village, the ridge formed one bank of the river. At a salient point, children occasionally jumped or dived off the cliff into the river, a drop of about thirty feet. This was not sanctioned by the tribe, since several boys had been injured and two killed when they struck underwater obstructions. Nevertheless, in each generation, on hot summer days, there was an irresistible urge to show one's prowess or to impress young ladies by jumping or diving off that ridge, into the flowing water. Even the foolhardy did not try it in dry years. In wet years, when the river was running full, there were a few adventurers. Most who took their chances came out unscathed, or with only sore backs and strained limbs. Their successes encouraged followers. Then disaster would strike. A diver would be seriously injured or killed, and the diving and jumping would cease for a few years.

Downstream the ridge curved away from the river, leaving a sandy bank between the base of the ridge and the river's edge. The river once curled against the ridge and cut a swath out of the base, leaving a rock overhang twenty to thirty feet above the sand bank. Under the overhang was the honored place for the Grey Piñons, a place of sacred rites, of war meetings, of ceremonial gatherings. A fire pit was in the center. On the ceiling of

MAGIC LANCE

the rock overhang, fire smoke of several centuries blackened the sandstone.

When Lucky Joe arrived at the parking area above the ridge, a whiff of piñon smoke swirled in the air. It reminded him of childhood days, attending tribal dances at the honored place and at the village plaza, hardly sleeping the night before, juiced with anticipation. He stepped and slithered down the rock steps cut in the sandstone ridge. A low fire provided sufficient light for him to find his way in a place he knew well. As suspected, although he did not know how Segundo could have reached the site before him, he saw Segundo seated on the plastered adobe bench near the ridge base. A fire flickered in the pit.

For several minutes, Segundo sang a chant. Then he sat in silence.

Lucky Joe gazed into the night sky, packed with twinkling stars. The chant and the place moved his thoughts away from worldly things.

"There are important matters to be considered," Segundo said finally. "Things that appear solid are not always solid. This matter of the casino and the money it produces is one of those things. Money has led many of the people astray. The old ways are being forgotten. Our sons and brothers are misled. They think money will buy everything. It is coming to an end. The materialism of the white-eyes has offered a false road. We must maintain another way. We must offer a new way, which happens to be the old way, that takes our sons and brothers back to the truths of the past."

Lucky Joe had prepared himself for being fired from his casino liaison job. Hearing Segundo speak of more lofty subjects was a relief.

"The Magic Lance produces money beyond all expectations, but if it is not checked, it will ruin our way. Already, people are starting to leave the pueblo, converting to a culture that is foreign to them, maintaining blood ties to the tribe only for the benefits of the Magic Lance. When the casino is gone, our people and our way will be gone. What the Spanish and the English and the churches and missionaries and the U.S. government could not do, the Magic Lance will do for them, destroy the people, destroy the spirit, destroy our way."

"It is something that concerns me," Lucky Joe said, hoping to keep Segundo focused elsewhere. "We all have become dependent on the money. The spirit has been set aside. If the money is withdrawn, I fear there will be little left."

"We understand each other," Segundo said. "So we must act." Lucky Joe nodded his agreement.

"The money that is shown in the tribal accounts is just ink-on-paper," Segundo said. "However, having been given this temporary advantage, we must take advantage. We must strike in the limited amount of time we have. The ink-on-paper must be converted to something else. Something in harmony with the life of the tribe. Land! We must move quickly to convert ink-on-paper to land. And the lands of our fathers."

"I have the plan," Segundo said. "You are the one I have chosen to carry it out. We must sacrifice ourselves. Our personal interests must be set aside."

Lucky Joe gazed into the dim light, adjusting his eyes to the subdued light of the piñon fire in the center of the pit. The flames projected dancing shadows on the concave surface of the sandstone ridge. He was flattered Segundo had chosen him for an important role, especially since he had anticipated being fired.

Segundo was a man to whom Lucky Joe listened and a man for whom he maintained a certain level of fear. Segundo, as war chief, was the de facto political leader of the Grey Piñons, not the governor whom the tribe held out to the public as its leader.

MAGIC LANCE

Segundo had behind-the-scenes power, understood by all members of the tribe. Tonight, what he said was what Lucky Joe already had considered. The Magic Lance was a shadow on the wall, an illusion that produced phenomenal amounts of money, money that had transformed tribal members from the downtrodden poor to financial moguls. Yet there was something foreboding about the shadow, something insubstantial, something out of harmony with what Lucky Joe thought was real.

Lucky Joe was uplifted when he heard the old man speak. He was uneasy about a lifestyle based on wealth, wealth totally dependent on a giant casino with flashing lights, a steady stream of tourists, construction workers, sales people, truck drivers, government employees, tribe members, senior citizens, ringing bells and cigarette smoke.

The two men sat in silence for a time. Lucky Joe let his mind be still, thinking of nothing, awaiting the plan Segundo seemed ready to announce.

At last, Segundo began to describe the plan.

"It has not been so long ago," Segundo said, "that your ancestors roamed over much of the land in this state. There were rough boundaries with other tribes, but unless there was raiding or trading, those boundaries were respected. Now we are confined in this matchbox reservation. Our land is only a token of the past. The white-eyes' houses come right up to the reservation fence lines. Before it is over, they will overrun our few remaining acres. We are honored with an opportunity to correct that problem."

Lucky Joe shifted his feet and scratched his neck. He drew in a deep breath of piñon smoke.

"There are times," Segundo continued, "when ranchers do well, and there are times when ranchers do poorly. For the past decade, while we have prospered, they have been doing poorly.

The conservationists have been our ally. They already have eliminated many small ranchers from making a living on the land. Those who remain have city jobs to support themselves. Big ranchers are a mixed bag. Many of them have incomes from other sources. They will not be so easy to handle."

"I am not following you now," Lucky Joe said.

"I have been doing my homework," Segundo continued. "I have been reading government statistics, the census of agriculture. I know the acreage of private land in the state. I know the number of farms and ranches. I know the amount of federal land and state land, and the acreage of the cities, the lakes, the national monuments, the state parks. Yes, and even the Indian reservations. I know what they raise and what they grow, and I know what they sell, and how much they get for it."

"Even with the wealth of the Magic Lance, there will not be enough money to buy the developed areas. But with the help of our Indian brothers, with the other casinos, we may have just enough to buy up the private land outside the cities and the developed valleys."

Lucky Joe was attracted to the idea of buying land. He immediately envisioned a vast area owned by Native Americans. At the same time, the idea struck him as far-fetched. It was much too big a thing for them to handle.

"We must be quiet about what we are doing," Segundo said. "If word of our plan gets out, the price of land will skyrocket and resistance will build quickly. It is an operation which must be done quickly, and it must be done quietly, like war planning. We will be the war party that fights the greatest battle of all time for our people. Our young men have been dormant and cowed too long. It is time for war. It is a war that must be won before the other side knows there is a war. We have the money to do it, the ink-on-paper. It is only a question of whether we have the will to do it."

MAGIC LANCE

The idea was of such magnitude, Lucky Joe cringed at the thought of attempting it.

"For the moment," Segundo said, "you and I are the only two people who must know of this. I emphasize this," Segundo said. He stood up and approached Lucky Joe. "Do you understand?" he asked, only a short distance in front of the younger man.

Lucky Joe resisted saying yes to a set-up question. He gave a nod. Although he was considerably bigger than Segundo and towered above him, the old man frightened him. The chief's persona in Lucky Joe's mind was a mixture of tribal tradition, personal respect and youthful dread, imagination, piercing black eyes and porcupine hair.

"I will lay out the plan for you in the next few weeks," Segundo said. "Eventually, this will involve all Indians in the state. It will take all of our concentration and energy and courage to do it. We cannot defeat the white-eyes in traditional ways. We have to engage them in their own system, using the laws they used against us for so long, and buy their land with their own money. It will be fair. They took our land and paid us nothing. Now we will take their land, and pay whatever they ask. Is that not fair?"

Segundo picked up an aspen twig and drew some abstract figures in the sandy floor of the honored place. He resumed the chant he sang earlier.

Lucky Joe sat in silence.

"I have decided that the first place the tribe will buy," Segundo said, "is a piece of land along Quail Run Creek down near Sierra City. It adjoins the national forest and takes in three or four miles of river. There's only a small house on the property. And a young couple who don't have much. They run some cattle on their own land, and on a government grazing lease."

"Why that place?" Lucky Joe asked.

"It is the gateway to Forest Service land that was the favorite hunting ground of Wild Horse. And it contains the hot springs that was the resting and healing area of our tribe for centuries. That one location is the cornerstone, even if all else fails. It is the key tract in the plan. It will be our first step. If we can get that land, it will ignite the tribe's spirit. It will be the showpiece for our entire effort. With it, we will set the pattern for what will follow."

"Who owns the place," Lucky Joe asked, "and how much do they want for it?"

"The man is named Lance Burnett. He has a woman. I haven't made any contact with them yet. But whatever they want, we will pay it."

"That's strange," Lucky Joe said with a laugh. "Our source of money is the Magic Lance. The name of the man who owns the key piece of property we want is named Lance."

Segundo sat on the adobe bench and leaned against the sandstone wall, rubbing the side of his face with his deformed hand. "Yes," he said pensively. "I hadn't thought of that."

The old war chief spent several minutes drawing figures in the dirt with the aspen stick and singing his chant. "Yes, I never thought of that. The match of a name. Is it an omen?"

"An omen?" Lucky Joe asked.

"Is it an omen?" Segundo repeated, half to himself and half to Lucky Joe. "And if an omen," he said in a whisper, "for whom—and of what?"

CHAPTER FOUR

As he left the mine area, Lance called the Sierra City Medical Center on his cell telephone, giving Dr. Geoff Romero advance notice of what happened. Members of the medical staff awaited them when they reached the hospital. They stabilized Jan's foot and ankle, then lifted her onto a gurney and wheeled her into the emergency room. Occasionally she seemed conscious, but after a few moments lapsed into a state of semi-consciousness. She was in shock. Dr. Romero spoke briefly with Lance and examined the injury. It was serious but treatable, he told Lance. A call had been made to Dr. George Dixon, an orthopedic surgeon, who would shortly arrive and take over treatment. Within minutes, Jan was on her way to radiology for X-rays. From the initial clinical exam and the history, it was probable she had multiple fractures, Dr. Romero said. Dr. Dixon would make the next call.

Lance listened. Dr. Romero observed his glazed eyes. He told Lance to go to the waiting room. They would report to him as soon as they could. Dr. Romero placed his hands on Lance's arms, turned him in the opposite direction, and gestured with his head and eyes for a nurse to accompany him down the hall.

As he sat in the waiting room, Lance replayed the mine incident. What caused that rock slab to fall? Could it have been braced by the wooden box? The side of the mine fell after Jan lifted the box out of its tight fit. He could still hear her desperate screams. Everything went bad after they encountered that strange heart symbol on the mine rib. It was too much bad luck to believe it was just bad luck. First the slab falling, then the tarantulas, running into the mine timber, the cracking sound back in the mine, then the lone tarantula crawling up Jan's blouse. Lance got up and went to the men's room to wash the residue of the tarantula off his hands. Anxiety arose as he thought of the curse—that danger and death pursued whoever sought the riches of the mine. What else would explain that quick sequence of events?

The rock fall reminded Lance of dangers associated with living in an isolated location. The ranch was little changed from what it must have been in the late 1800s when a German settler named Jim Brandenburg founded it. The ranch stayed in the Brandenburg family until purchased by Lance's grandfather in the 1940s. It was inherited by his father in the 1990s. Lance, the youngest of three children, was the only one who had an interest in staying on the ranch. His brother Marc was a mechanical engineer. His sister Peggy was a nurse. Both left the Three V for college and never returned.

Lance, however, loved the open range life. He loved cattle, hard manual work, not having a boss, working outdoors, horseback riding, hunting, fishing and the solitary life of an owner-operator. He was a State Aggie. When Lance got his agricultural degree, his ambition was to return to the Three V. By then, his mother and father were ready to move to Sierra City. Due to his father's low back and heart problems and his mother's arthritis, they felt a need to be close to medical facilities. It was agreed in the family that Lance would have use of the ranch in return for operating it and making the mortgage payments and taxes. If he ever made a substantial sum of money, he would consider paying his mother and father some rent. To date, he had paid no rent.

Living on the ranch, with his mother and father gone and his brother and sister only occasional visitors, Lance was lonely. It was a normal weekend for him to leave the ranch house on Friday afternoon, drive to Sierra City and go straight to the Silver Spur, a bar and dance hall frequented by local farmers and ranchers, but also by half the single young people in Ladenberger County, and a few married ones who didn't let family connections interfere.

Despite Lance's eagerness to find a young woman and companion, two years at the Silver Spur had not produced the type of woman he was seeking. There were plenty of women. Lance was a lean, handsome man, tall with wide shoulders, strong calloused hands and a wide smile. He didn't smoke or chew. On a given night, he did drink a quantity of draft beer and the more he drank, the better the ladies looked to him. But Lance was cautious of becoming permanently connected to a woman who was not what he envisioned as an ideal wife. To the best of his ability he tried to follow advice given to him years earlier by the family physician: "Don't make love to any woman whom you do not wish to marry."

Lance wanted someone moral, attractive, sensual, talented, smart, loving and loyal. And he wanted someone who wanted him. The lounge ladies were fun for a dance and flirting, but he developed no relationships with any of them outside the confines of the Silver Spur.

He met Jan unexpectedly. One afternoon at the Sierra City library, Lance was browsing through history books dealing with life in the state's silver belt, which stretched from Beetown in the north down to River Crossing in the south. Sierra City was right in the middle. While standing in one of the book aisles, he glanced down to an open area at the end of the row. There was a beautiful woman seated on a child's chair, her hips overlapping both sides of the seat. She had a five-year-old girl on her lap and she was reading to a half-dozen children about first grade level. Lance meandered to the end of the aisle and stood watching. Gaping was the way Jan later described it. She noticed his interest and nervously shifted her position on the chair. He noted her anxiety and casually walked by, glancing at her all the way. Their eyes met for a moment, but she never skipped a sentence. Lance selected a history book, then hung around the library check-out desk for half an hour until Jan ended her reading session. She came by the desk to talk to the librarian. Lance surprised himself when he went right up to her and complimented her for taking the time to read to small children. She thanked him but quickly left the library.

Lance asked the librarian, whom he had known all his life, who Jan was. He was told she was the new first grade teacher at Sierra City elementary.

"You aren't the first to ask," the librarian said.

Lance knew almost from that day that Jan Murphy was the woman he wanted to marry.

In the hospital waiting room pondering recent events, Lance acknowledged to himself that Jan was having a hard time adjusting to life at the Three V Ranch. Almost daily, she told him how much she missed being with people and her classroom kids. There were parts of ranch life she liked, she said. She was especially attached to Pepper and Nugget, the ranch cattle dogs. Jan treated Pepper more like a child than a dog. Lance assumed that if Jan could have several children, the kids would take care of her loneliness, give her plenty to do, and eventually grow up to love the ranch as much as he did. True, after seeing what happened with his own brother and sister, he knew it was not auto-

MAGIC LANCE

matic that ranchers' children would love the land and its lifestyle the way he did. But in spite of difficulties, Lance knew Jan was the woman for him, and that she would make a fine mother as soon as those children arrived.

This mine accident was serious. He understood that. Getting by in an isolated setting, when you have health problems, is not easy to handle. He had seen injuries ruin other ranch families. In the one-family operation of a small ranch, if either the man or woman was disabled and the other had to take care of the disabled partner, it made ranch operations next to impossible. At some point, Lance slid down in the chair and went fast asleep.

The next thing he remembered was someone jostling his shoulder. His eyes opened and he saw Dr. Dixon and Dr. Romero standing over him.

"She has a serious group of fractures," Dr. Dixon said, "and some impingement of nerves and blood vessels in the ankle area. Hopefully, she'll get full use of her foot back. It's going to take time. She's going to need a lot of rest and rehabilitation for at least three months."

"You can go see her now," Dr. Romero said. "She's been asking for you."

Lance did not say another word on his way to the recovery room. Jan lay on a gurney with an IV in her arm. Her right foot and ankle were wrapped and still showed considerable swelling.

Lance took her hand. Jan squeezed his.

"The doctor says you're going to be all right. You're going to be all right. You need some rest and rehabilitation, but you're going to be all right. And I love you, Jan."

Jan's eyes were watery.

"How do you feel?" Lance asked.

"Not too good."

"You'll feel better when we get home. These hospitals scare me." A tear ran down her cheek.

"Jan, what's wrong? Are you all right?"

"Lance, there's something I have to tell you."

He moved his face close to hers. "What is it, sweetheart?"

"Lance, this whole thing is too much for me. Living so far from town. We're so isolated out there. I'm scared every time you leave the house. I'm scared."

"That's more or less what ranch life is," Lance said. "You have to be strong."

"I know that now. I guess I didn't really know it before. I'm so lonely and isolated out there. I miss my job at school, and I miss my kids and all my friends at school."

"Jan, we better talk about this later, when we get back to the house. I know you're in a lot of pain, and you're under a lot of stress right now."

"Lance, I can't take the ranch life any more. All the isolation and all the money problems. It's not working for me. It's not ever going to work for me. I've made up my mind. I love you Lance, but I'm not going back to the ranch. I've thought about it a long time and I'm never going back. I'm so sorry."

CHAPTER FIVE

If a horse had kicked him in the face, the effect could not have been more devastating. Lance did not know what to say. Short of breath, he told Jan they would talk about it later, when she felt better. He knew she was weak and under the influence of the anesthetic and he did not wish to engage her in a controversial subject. After holding her hand for a while, and changing the subject, Lance became quiet. He sat in a chair at the end of the bed staring at the ceiling. In the quietness of the hospital room, Jan closed her eyes and fell asleep.

Lance stood next to his wife for several minutes, his mind swirling. He placed his hand on his forehead and let his head drop. For several minutes, his mind was blank. He had no idea how to respond to Jan's announcement that she was not going back to the ranch. Everything in his life was out of harmony. A relationship he assumed would last forever now was threatened. After a period of hesitation, he concluded Jan's sleep would last and he could leave the hospital. Outside, an array of sparkling stars filled the night sky. From the hospital, Lance drove to the Silver Spur, intending to have a single beer before returning to the Arc de Triumph Motel on the north side of Sierra City.

There were times during their year of marriage that Lance knew Jan was longing for her former urban life. He thought it was a wish that would fade as she became used to the outdoors.

It was hard for him to imagine that given a choice, any person would not prefer life in wide-open country, free of pollution, traffic, crowds, crime, the noises and frustrations of the city. Yet he knew Jan was serious. Had he made a major miscalculation? Jan would not be the first young lady to fall in love with the romance of the ranching life, only to experience a rural isolation and loneliness. Yet there were many women who adapted and who loved it. Lance was sure Jan would be one of those. Had he misread her? Was her desire for her own career stronger than he thought? Was it possible she had found someone else? He thought of the young music director at their church. Jan seemed to talk about him a lot, and he kept encouraging her to join the choir.

Once inside the Silver Spur, Lance moved to an open bar stool and ordered a draft beer. He surveyed the crowd, looking into the mirror that covered the wall behind the bar. In his single years, the expectation of meeting some gorgeous woman was what led him to the Silver Spur. Tonight, after a year of marriage, he had no such expectation; his interest was in the bubbles on the beer foam. He needed time to turn things over in his mind.

He downed the first beer and ordered a second. Hardly had he grasped the fresh cold mug when the smell of perfume encircled him.

"Hi, neighbor," said an energized voice. Lance turned to his right. Up close were two of the best-looking female eyes he had ever seen. They belonged to Judy "Lightning" McClain. Lance's spirit lifted instantly.

"Well..." Lance could think of nothing to say.

"We just dropped in for a drink," Lightning said. "I saw you here by yourself and thought I'd say hello."

"I'm glad you did. Jan got hurt this afternoon. Broke her foot and her ankle. I've just come from the hospital."

MAGIC LANCE

"Oh, Lance, I'm so sorry. I didn't know. What happened?"

"The weirdest thing. We were in an old mine tunnel, and part of the rib came down. Fell right on her foot. I didn't know if I was ever going to get her out of there."

"Lance, that's terrible. How is she?"

"Dr. Dixon thinks she's going to be okay. It's going to take several months though. I'm not sure what we're going to do."

"Whatever I can do, I want to do."

"I'm going to stay in town for awhile, till she gets out of the hospital."

"I'll send Lupe over tomorrow to your place," Lightning said. "You tell me what you want him to do, and I'll tell him."

"Well, that's appreciated, but I can get out there part-time. I'll take care of things. I may need to take you up on it later."

"And, excuse me," Lance said, in a change of tone. "Would you like a drink?"

"Yes, I suppose so." Lightning moved around to get up on the adjoining bar stool. In doing so, the back pockets of her skin-tight jeans rubbed against Lance's right leg. A wave of excitement went right up to the back of his eyes. Lance's attention was attracted to a leather belt Lightning wore, covered with red, white and blue Indian beadwork. Although Lance had seen Lightning several times before, she had never been this close to him. The things that intrigued him from a distance were even more intriguing and inviting up close. Lightning radiated an energy with her blue eyes and a vibrant skin tone. When she smiled, the corners of her mouth rose elegantly, revealing perfectly aligned, gleaming white teeth. When she turned her head, her silky blonde hair seemed to float in the air. Lance also gazed at Lightning's long, graceful fingers capped with fingernails painted blood red. He was not surprised Big Bob McCoy would hire a woman of Lightning's outstanding looks.

"How're things at the Cascade Ranch?" Lance asked. "You able to keep Mr. McCoy at a distance?"

"Big Bob is not an easy man to keep at a distance. But they don't call me 'Lightning' for nothing."

Lance flashed a wide smile. Bob McCoy was one of the biggest landowners in the state, and his limitless wealth from oil, banking and insurance gave him an economic advantage few ranchers enjoyed. One of those advantages was having the money to employ people to run his properties, including the Cascade Ranch. While not certain, Lance thought Lightning ran the household aspects of the ranch headquarters. Randall "Scooter" Jones was the operations foreman. Lance sometimes thought that Lightning and Scooter were the two people who really owned the Cascade Ranch. Big Bob McCoy came in about once a month in his twin jet. He landed on a specially built runway that allowed his jet to taxi within fifty yards of the house. Everyone bowed and scraped when he was there, but as soon as the jet soared into the sky with Big Bob on board, life returned to the former routine in which Lightning and Scooter ran the place.

Since his ranch property adjoined a sliver of the Cascade Ranch at Quail Run Creek, technically Lance was a boundary neighbor. He knew Lightning from a few chance meetings in town and once at a brief encounter at the river when he was watering his horse and Lightning came riding by in a pickup driven by Scooter Jones. All were short encounters but he remembered her well. What he remembered about her was her beautiful face and a figure that was the talk of the county. It also was known that Lightning was not interested in local hicks. Her taste was for the young business tycoons who often accompanied Big Bob McCoy. Locally she most often was in the company of Scooter Jones.

MAGIC LANCE

Notwithstanding that big-city attitude, having a woman that gorgeous sitting next to him on a Silver Spur barstool was a pleasure Lance rarely experienced.

"Do you think you can run things, with Jan in the hospital?"

"I think I can handle it. If the price of cattle holds up." In his opinion, the price of cattle was invariably low, and the spread between what the rancher got and what the public paid at retail got wider every year. "Tell Big Bob that if he really wants to get rich, he should buy a meat packer."

"Oh, I think he's already about as rich as they get," Lightning said. Then, giving it a thought, she added, "But if there's another dollar to be made, you can bet Big Bob's going to be first in line and he's going to make it."

The bartender slid a glass of Cabernet directly in front of Lightning. She picked it up, looked straight into Lance's eyes, and took a long drink.

"You ever think of working for a large operation?" Lightning asked.

"Like the Cascade? Not me. I like running my own show."

"It can pay pretty well. You're a lot more talented than the people Big Bob has working for him; Yours Truly being an exception, of course."

Just as Lightning was about to say something that would go with a smile and charming tone of voice, a large man in a Western shirt stepped between the bar stools, looking straight into Lance's face. The man's head, wide shoulders, thick neck and muscular arms seemed to hang over Lance like a bird of prey.

For a moment, glaring eyes caused Lance to straighten up and pull back. Without a word being said, the man turned his back to Lance. He said something to Lightning that Lance couldn't quite understand but that seemed to be a reproach. With no hesitation or argument, Lightning obediently turned

HAL SIMMONS

loose her wine glass, spun round on the bar stool, stepped down to the floor and walked away, the big man following immediately behind her. When she was several feet away, she leaned out from behind the man's frame, winked at Lance, smiled and rolled her fingers in a goodbye gesture.

Women and barroom confrontations were so common to Lance that he barely blinked. He laid no claim to Lightning McClain, and he was not eager for a confrontation with Scooter Jones. Lance recalled one story he'd heard that Scooter Jones beat up a young bank officer from the First State Bank of Sierra City for having made the mistake of inviting Lightning to dinner when she came to town for a charitable fund-raising event.

Lance turned back to the bar, studied people in the mirror, and re-lived that sensual brush of jean pockets against his leg. Lightning McClain clearly was a woman of charm.

Ten minutes later, Lance finished his second beer and was fishing in his pocket for money to pay the tab, when in the bar mirror he spotted an old high school classmate approaching. It was Earl Wallace. Lance spun around on the bar stool just as Earl came up to him.

"They're letting just anybody in here tonight," Lance said.

Earl jumped on the bar stool recently warmed by Lightning and ordered a drink. He shook Lance's hand and slapped him on the back.

"Boy, does this place have distinguished clientele," Earl said. Lance looked to his left and to his right, indicating the compliment couldn't be directed at him.

After some minutes of good-hearted conversation, Earl admitted he had come to the Silver Spur half-looking for Lance.

"It's business," Earl said. "You don't know it yet, but you're in demand."

MAGIC LANCE

"I'm in demand?" Lance said. "That's usually what they say when the sheriff's looking for you."

A country Western band took over from the recording system and added decibels to the background. From the corner of his eye, Lance saw the Scooter Jones group get up from their table and head for an exit. As the group departed, Lightning was the last person in line. As she departed she placed both hands behind her back, palms out, on top of the pockets of her skin-tight jeans and wiggled her fingers in Lance's direction.

CHAPTER SIX

Lance was both embarrassed and pleased that Lightning had given him some provocative attention. That's what he used to come to the Silver Spur to get, and he rarely got it from a woman of Lightning's caliber. She is a high-priced woman, Lance thought, and while he was not looking for a woman, it was flattering to attract her interest.

Earl Wallace twisted a glass of bourbon in his fingertips and gazed at the soft, warm, golden brown liquid, dancing with the ice. Earl liked the easy lifestyle, Lance thought. Ever since they played high school football together, Earl's desire to get the most he could from the least expenditure of effort had been a trademark. Lance gave him credit for consistency. Today he was chubby but not obese; poor skin complexion, hair slightly oily, cigarette breath, with clothes that would look good on someone who was forty pounds lighter. Lance thought that after you knew someone for two or three years his habits and mannerisms usually receded from your thoughts and you would more or less accept him for what he was, the good and the bad included. With Earl Wallace, you always started from square one, re-evaluating him every time you met, and in sum there always were more negatives than positives. Nevertheless, Earl was someone Lance had known for enough years that he was easier to talk to than a stranger, as long as you maintained your guard.

MAGIC LANCE

"So, who says I'm in demand, if it's not the sheriff?" Lance asked.

"To be honest about it, I'm not sure," Earl said. "But I know you're in demand. And the interested party has cash money."

"Must be the credit card sleaze. They send me offers like mail confetti."

"No, it's not credit cards. You don't think I'd deal for those greedy-guts, do you?" Earl laughed and took a swallow of bourbon.

"All right, so who says I'm in demand?" Lance looked back to the door where Lightning departed, with a faint hope she might return.

"What I know is that there's something called the Religious Land Trust. They want to preserve the West. And for God knows what reason, they're interested in your eight hundred acres, and the government grazing leases. And mineral and water rights if you've got any."

"They want the Three V?" Lance said. "Who the hell would want the Three V? That's a strike against them right off the bat."

"That's exactly what I told 'em. But they said that's the place they want. They told me to get a price."

"Who the hell is the Religious Land Trust?"

"I was contacted by a guy who said his name is Lucky Joe," Earl said. "At first, I didn't take him serious. With a name like that, I thought he was a horse jockey. And this Religious Land Trust sounds like one of those land conservancy groups, except it's not religion like we think about it. I mean, it's not Christian, or anything like that. I think this Lucky Joe guy may be a front for some Indian powwow group. You ever heard of any guy being named Lucky Joe? Doesn't that sound kind of weird to you?"

"Never heard of him. Is he from around here?"

"I really can't tell you much more. I'm sworn to secrecy. Plus, I don't even know much more. But from the looks of this guy, I don't think he's a Catholic priest or a Baptist minister, or anything like that. If you really want to know, I think he's an Indian chief or something. And a rich one. Got a big diamond ring, drives a new, four-wheel-drive, Ford Expedition. A big one. Talks like he's got money. Said he would pay cash. I'm supposed to get a figure from you. He didn't know I was a friend of yours." Then, taking on a pensive look, Earl added: "At least, I don't think he knew that."

"Well," Lance said, polishing off the final brew in his beer glass, "tell Lucky So-and-So that if he wants the Three V, he just ran out of luck. Not for sale."

"I kind of thought that's what you were going to say. So I prepared him for the worst scenario, and tried to get him interested in another place over in Seep Springs Canyon. He said he'd be willing to look at that too."

"When you see him again, ask him what church he's representing. I'd like to know."

"I'll do that, but somehow this guy doesn't seem like a religious type. I'm not sure what he does seem like, but I can't picture him in a collar. Maybe he's on the Jesus Road."

Lance slowly turned his big mug on the bar, debating whether he wanted a third. The bartender gave him a high sign, and Lance ordered one more, and a second bourbon for Earl.

"Lance, you know all about small towns. Everybody knows everything."

Lance looked at Earl, waiting for something to follow.

"As you may know, I manage the Desert Palms Apartments for the Lindseys," Earl said. "And it came to my attention that someone named Jan Burnett leased one of those units last week."

Last week. Lance's eyes stared into the mirror, looking right into themselves. Last week. Jan rented an apartment last week. That was before the accident.

"You sure that was last week?"

MAGIC LANCE

"That was when she came in. I think the lease starts the first of the month. I wasn't sure if that was you, or what."

"Well," Lance said, clearing his throat. "Jan wanted to work on a project here, and it seemed like commuting from the ranch every day was going to be too much, so we decided it would be better if she had a place to stay here in town temporarily. We're going to try it for a while, with me coming in, and her coming out to the ranch, and see if that works. It's not going to be a long-term thing. And now this injury thing."

"Oh, yeah. I heard about the accident," Earl said. "Not trying to get nosey. I just thought you might be coming in town, and that might impact whether you had some interest in putting the Three V on the block."

"No, no, that's got nothing to do with selling the Three V. It's not for sale. Tell ole Lucky that the Three V is an unlucky place. Just ask Jan. He's better off over in Seep Springs. Who's selling out over there, anyway?"

"Jack Peterson's spread. His wife can't handle the place, now that Jack's gone. It's an estate sale. If you're not selling, you got any interest in buying? The Peterson place is a great buy."

"How much do they want for it?" Lance asked, still in a mild state of shock.

"It's a thousand acres, and they're asking six hundred and fifty thousand. Six hundred and fifty an acre is too high for cattle ranching, but these places aren't selling for cattle operations any more. You know that. That's nothing new."

"So, if I got six hundred and fifty dollars per acre for my eight hundred acres, that'd be . . . how much?" Earl pulled out a hand calculator from his shirt pocket, and ran off the calculation.

"Says here, five hundred twenty thousand, cash money." After waiting a moment, Earl asked, "Is that a figure you might have some interest in?"

"Not for sale. Hell, the re-finance mortgage is almost that much."

In his mind, Lance scrolled through recent developments. Jan secretly rented an apartment a week ago, before the accident. She says she is not going back to the ranch. Lightning tells him he is better than anybody Big Bob has working for the Cascade Ranch. The Religious Trust is offering cash money. His monthly mortgage payment is past due. And Lightning has the best body he's ever seen.

"Let me know if the Poor Little Brothers of the Windfall buy the Peterson place," Lance said, shoving thirty dollars across the bar. He slapped Earl on the back, feeling a layer of flab where muscle used to be during their football days, slid off the bar stool, and headed for the motel.

He could still feel those two blue jean pockets rubbing against his leg.

CHAPTER SEVEN

A stack of pancakes, with sausage patties on the side, and a miniature pitcher of maple syrup were set before Lucky Joe. He lifted the thick mug of steaming coffee for a sip before he contemplated the breakfast.

As they did eighteen hours a day, the sounds of the Magic Lance Casino permeated the coffee shop. The casino sounds were the aural atmosphere. No one who worked in the gambling establishment heard them any longer.

Lucky Joe cast a glance at his grandfather's breakfast, which was the same as his own. Alfredo was a tall, thin man, thin as a straw. He wore traditional Grey Piñon tribe attire, a Western shirt, blue jeans, low heel Western boots with rounded toes, and a leather tooled belt with silver concho buckle with a spider web turquoise stone in the center.

Although in his eighties, Alfredo had few wrinkles in his face. His eyes were muted black and his long, narrow face was like a lance blade on top of his slender body. His straight hair now was mottled grey. It was tied in a ponytail, with a red and silver bandanna wrapped around it.

Although Lucky Joe was thinking only of getting plenty of butter and maple syrup on his pancakes, he stopped short and inspected the meals of his wife Rachel, his daughter Andrea and his son Rick. When finally all was to his satisfaction, he exhaled, let his shoulders drop a couple of inches, spread the butter, poured the syrup and carved out a section of pancakes.

Rick tore off the end of the wrapper on his straw, aimed the straw at Andrea, and blew the wrapper like a blowgun dart in her direction. It missed. She cast him a big sister's bad eye and started working on her pancakes.

Rachel gave Rick a disapproving glance.

"We got a favorable response on the Peterson Ranch," Lucky Joe said to his grandfather. "It will be our first purchase. Hopefully, the first of many."

"Good," Alfredo said. As cacique, Alfredo was advised of all tribal activity through his grandson and the war chief.

"The Quail Run Creek place is not going so well. They say it's not for sale."

"Time may change that," Alfredo said. "We should not wait. We will return to it. It is the most important piece, but there is an entire state to work on. No use worrying about one slowpoke. When the time comes, we'll get it."

"How is the council handling this?" Lucky Joe asked. "Are they behind the purchases?"

"They can be counted on, eventually," Alfredo said. "Segundo knows what he's doing. There are always different agendas. Some people oppose anything Segundo suggests. It's a problem, but it's not insurmountable. It was envisioned there would be resistance. So far, things are on track."

"As soon as we buy Peterson's, Lucky is going to visit other tribes," Rachel said.

Alfredo nodded his approval. He looked at Andrea and Rick, smiling. "You are part of a new history of the Grey Piñon," he said. "You will look back later and remember when all this started."

Lucky Joe was taking his last bite of the now-vanished pancake stack when Segundo came into the casino restaurant.

MAGIC LANCE

Greetings were exchanged. Soon Rachel gathered Andrea and Rick and made her exit. Alfredo followed shortly.

Segundo ordered a coffee for himself and a refill for Lucky Joe.

"We have Peterson's," Segundo said. His eyes expanded. "This is the first step. We have thousands more to go."

"Who handled the Peterson buy?" Lucky Joe asked.

"Initially I dealt with a guy in Ashton. An attorney named Jim Beckley. He knew what he was doing. He's handling the estate. He knows estate stuff. Fortunately, the heirs are tightwads. They didn't want to pay him to represent them in the ranch sale. We made a direct pitch. Told them no use paying attorney fees or a real estate commission. They agreed. They gave us a price. We bid it ten per cent lower than their asking, and they countered at five per cent under their original asking. If we can get everybody at a lower figure than what we expect, this is going to go like clockwork."

"Anything going, on the Quail Run Creek place?"

"Not yet, but we've just started," Segundo said. "It may turn out to be like Richmond. It's the first place we want; it may be the last place we get. But we'll get it. We can't wait around. We have to move. We're going to try to get everything lined up, and move it through as fast as we can. Speed is on our side. Every delay hurts us."

"After we make a few buys, what's going to keep the word from getting out that the Grey Piñon are buying up ranch land?" Lucky Joe said.

"Number one, we're using a different real estate agent in every county. So it's not going to look that obvious. And we're getting the agents to sign a confidentiality agreement, that they won't reveal the terms of the transactions or the parties. And to make sure they abide by it, we're holding back twenty five per cent of their commission for one year to guarantee confidentiality."

"What about the same buyer making all these purchases?" Lucky Joe asked.

"We're forming different corporations and limited liability companies, and using different tribe members as stockholders, partners, officers and directors. So anybody looking at state records is going to see different names. Less likely to attract attention. We're also using different law firms and different title insurance companies as often as we can."

Lucky raised his eyebrows. He gave Segundo credit. He was thinking ahead.

"It's close to time," Segundo said, "for you to take a bigger role." He watched for Lucky Joe's reaction. "After the Peterson deal closes you're going to be out front. I'm fading into the background on real estate. I'm the one in charge but I don't want you to even mention my name."

Lucky Joe poured Segundo and himself a refill of coffee. He watched the steam rise from the cup. He pealed off the top of a plastic creamer and dumped the cream into his cup.

"What are we going to say when people start asking about land purchases? Even with all you've said, you know the word is going to get out, one way or the other," Lucky Joe said.

"Don't be so pessimistic," Segundo countered. "After all, originally this was partly your grandfather's idea, as well as mine. You're dreaming up too many problems. Stay positive. We're going to win this. We're going to buy up all the private rural land in the state, and we're going to have a de facto Native American state, without making any announcements and without seeking any credit or recognition. It's just going to happen. Then you young guys are going to have to go out and find you some willing women, and have lots of kids so we can fill the place up. It is one thing to buy up a state; it will be another thing to hold it. To hold it, we've got to have people on it."

MAGIC LANCE

"Think of it," Segundo continued. "Thirty eight million acres of land will be ours, and we'll be under no economic pressure to work it to death. Maybe it will become a major hunting and fishing preserve. The biggest in the world, and it will generate more income than cattle ranching. And it won't require that many people to run it, and our operation will be in harmony with Mother Earth. Our people will be able to move around if they want to, from summer to winter. The buffalo herds will roam unfenced plains again; the birds will sail and soar in unpolluted air; fish will fill pure running streams and deer and antelope and bear and mountain lions will return to their old homelands. Our native culture will flourish and grow. We will have our own schools and universities, our own doctors and hospitals, our own stores and even our own radio and television stations and newspapers, and most of all our own traditions."

"Will we have our own government?" Lucky Joe said.

"We'll decide on that later. We have to stay focused on getting the land. That's not going to be easy. Don't involve too many details."

"What do I tell the BIA people, if they start asking?"

"Tell them individual tribe members are making land investments. Keep it simple. No concentrated effort. No big scheme. We're just simple Indians. Remember that. We haven't got any agenda. Just doing a few minor land purchases, as individual investments. That's all you know. There's nothing else to say."

"This is far beyond what I ever imagined we could do," Lucky Joe said.

"This is only the beginning of things that will be beyond your imagination. Do not fear. Trust the spirits. You are not to doubt what can be accomplished. You are an important part of the operation. You must have faith and courage. If you do as I tell you, all will be well."

"You are not irreplaceable," Segundo said, as an afterthought. "You are heavily entrusted, and you must perform."

"Next week," Segundo continued, "I want you to appear before the tribal council and recommend that they make some additional real estate investments. I'll introduce you as our new real estate investment advisor. We want them to approve an expenditure of two hundred and fifty million."

"Two hundred and fifty million!" Lucky Joe said. "Two hundred and fifty million!"

"We're not out there buying sandwich shops. We're buying ranches. And shortly, we're going to be buying some big ranches. You can't buy big ranches with a chicken-feed checkbook. Before we're through, two hundred and fifty hundred million is going to sound like chicken feed. You need to be ready for big deals."

Segundo shrugged his shoulders, smiled and took a long drink of coffee.

"The show," he said, "is about to begin."

CHAPTER EIGHT

At the tribal council meeting, Lucky Joe's presentation was toward the middle of the evening. The thought of appearing before the elders caused him to shift from one foot to another while standing and to squirm in his chair when seated. It was difficult to keep his voice at a normal tone and to speak at a normal rate. His mind wobbled. In one respect, he was glad Segundo was at the meeting; in another, he worried that if the presentation did not go well, he would feel the old man's condemnation.

Segundo sat in a worn wooden chair and leaned it back on two legs against the wall. When the moment arrived to speak, Lucky Joe remained seated. Council members formed a circle in the meeting hall.

Lucky Joe told the council members it was an honor to be allowed to address them. He acknowledged the distant connections of family to several members and praised Alfredo, his own grandfather, who was the cacique or community chief. He gave his grandfather credit for bringing him up in the Grey Piñon tradition. Lucky Joe quit squirming in the chair, his voice relaxed, and his hands gestured as he described recollections of some of the proud moments in Grey Piñon tradition and history.

Then he gave a thumbnail sketch of the Magic Lance Casino operation, its phenomenal financial success and its continued expansion.

As he spoke, Lucky Joe looked around at the tribal council members. He knew most were friendly, except Enrique Velasquez, Roberto Abeita and a few of their followers, who he knew were suspicious of his every word, his every move, and jealous and envious of his entire family. Their eyes narrowed when he looked at them. They shifted their positions, turning away from him. They stared at the ceiling. They scratched their legs, twisted their heads, clenched their fists, and eventually settled into a permanent frown. Lucky Joe looked at Segundo. The old man raised his eyebrows a fraction in a show of support.

Lucky Joe described the cash assets of the tribe and the danger of the tribal gaming compacts being cancelled in the coming year. Before a crisis arrived, it was wise to diversify the tribe's assets. It was prudent financial planning. The stock market was volatile. The bond market paid low rates. The Magic Lance would soon be at risk. It was time for action. It was time to diversify. It was time to return to tradition, to add to the tribe's landholding.

As soon as land holdings were mentioned, Velasquez and Abeita muttered in disapproval. They looked at other council members and raised both hands straight up, as though saying, "what else would you expect from a Cruz?"

For decades, political power within the tribe flip-flopped between the Velasquez and Abeita families and the Cruz family supported by El Segundo and his followers. For the past twenty years, Alfredo Cruz and Segundo held the upper hand. It was rarely a secure hand. The Velasquez and Abeita forces were continually picking at their power, in hopes of gathering power for themselves.

Lucky Joe ignored their gestures and gave a few more details of the tribe's financial condition. "We have over a billion dollars

MAGIC LANCE

in various banks and investment companies." It was a figure known to all council members.

"It is my recommendation that the best diversification we can make is to acquire land," Lucky Joe continued. "It is always there. Now our investments are ink-on-paper. They could disappear at any time and we would be left with some file folders full of paper. A great opportunity is ours."

Lucky Joe provided council members with numbers Segundo had given him the prior week.

There were approximately twelve thousand farms and ranches in the state. They totaled thirty-eight million acres. The average price per acre of farm and ranch land was four hundred and thirty-five dollars. The tribe could easily afford to buy a half million acres. The cost, about two hundred and twenty million.

Velasquez and Abeita threw their heads back, looking at the ceiling. They reached in the air with both hands.

"We can't even use all the land we have," Velasquez said. "What are we going to do with another half million acres?" He looked at other council members for support. They gave no indication of their position.

Sensing that most council members were giving him a hearing, Lucky Joe continued.

"If we had an appropriation of two hundred and fifty million, we could immediately begin a search for ranch and farm land that adjoins the reservation. A conservative plan is to work from the center out, from the reservation boundary out. If we meet with initial success and get adjoining land, we can try to shoestring other locations, reach out as far and as fast as we can. Obviously, just because we're buying doesn't mean that everyone who owns a ranch is selling."

"So how far do you think you're going to get? Do you think Big Bob McCoy is going to sell you his little toy ranch?" Velasquez said. "As soon as he hears the Grey Piñon Tribe is buying, he'll raise the price so high people will think this is Beverly Hills."

"Does that ranch manager lady come with the Cascade?" one of the council members asked. A hearty laugh rolled through the members.

Even Segundo laughed. Despite his age, the thought of Lightning McClain raised his blood pressure a notch.

Ignoring the remark, Lucky Joe continued. "We fully anticipate that when the word gets out, land prices will start climbing. But we think there will be a fair number of farms and ranches that are either ready to sell, or soon will be, if there is a good cash offer on the table."

"And how are you going to get the Interior to go along with it?" Velasquez asked. "You think all those bureaucrats are going to roll over, while Grey Piñons go around buying up all the land with gambling proceeds, that were supposed to be used for infrastructure?"

"We have many friends in government," Lucky Joe said. "You know as well as I do that we've been courting our congressmen for years. Besides, we're not forcing anybody. If a rancher wants to sell, is the federal government going to tell him he can't do it?"

"You're going to squander our money," Velasquez said. "You must own a new real estate company that needs some work."

Despite Segundo's warning that he should guard his temper, Lucky Joe turned red at the suggestion he would personally benefit from the dealings. He stood from his chair but Segundo was immediately at his side, his hand on Lucky Joe's arm.

"Personal insults are not what should decide this issue," Segundo said to the council members. "You form a real estate company, and we'll make some of the purchases through you," Segundo said to Velasquez.

MAGIC LANCE

"I'm not one who's looking for back-door money," Velasquez said, glaring at Segundo.

"Let him finish the proposal," Segundo said, and moved back to his wooden chair against the wall.

Lucky Joe gave a few details. They would set up corporations and LLCs, owned by tribal members, with real estate agents or commercial companies as statutory agents. Then those legal entities would transfer land titles to the Interior for the tribe when the time and procedural steps were right.

"After all, who is really going to complain?" Lucky Joe said. "The ranchers who get cash money? The real estate agents who get a big commission? We'll manage the land much better than it's been managed in the past, because we won't need to make a lot of money off of it."

"I'll tell you who's going to complain," Velasquez said. "The counties and the cities are going to scream bloody murder. You're taking away their tax base. How are you going to explain that problem away?"

"We'll offer a bigger cut on the casino revenues, to take the place of lost property taxes," Lucky Joe said. "If the county gets a bigger cut, even if they lose some property taxes, maybe they'll break even. We can work that out, maybe on a formula basis where the gambling increase will wash out the property tax loss. Ranch land isn't taxed all that high compared to city rates."

"What if the state pulls out of the gambling compacts," Velasquez said. "Legislators might give the gambling rights to someone else, even charitable organizations. The tribe's gambling income would vanish. You are recommending we kill the golden goose, to satisfy some crazy idea about buying up a lot of land. It's a seductive idea that is an illusion. The Grey Piñons are in the best condition they have ever experienced, and you're proposing we spend the money we already have, and risk all the money we may make in the future from the Magic Lance. It's insane. You are insane to propose it."

Lucky Joe became red-faced, but this time he controlled his temper and continued the debate.

"We have to act now, while the money is in hand. We don't know what's going to happen in the future. If we have the land, and it's paid for, what better thing could we leave to our children? Each generation makes its contribution and reveals its shortcomings. Events can overwhelm. Our forefathers temporarily found themselves overwhelmed by foreign cultures. Now we have a chance to turn everything to our advantage, and regain control over our own lives. It is a freedom you will pass on to your children, and your grandchildren. We have a window of opportunity. The money is only ink-on-paper. It can vanish quickly. The land will remain. It is a better investment. Which would you rather have, a few pieces of paper with ink on them, or millions of acres of land for our people?"

Velasquez argued that despite the usual Cruz silver-tongued presentation, the plan was ludicrous. It would never work. They were going to waste two hundred and fifty million dollars that was earning a good return. The land would not produce a return; it would most likely cost them money to keep the new holdings.

In the near term, Lucky Joe said they intended to keep the farms and ranches running just as they had been, worked by as many of the same people as they could hire who worked the ranches before. "That should smooth the transition," Lucky Joe said. "It won't impact the local areas that much, and from all appearances, not much will seem like it has changed. We can hold the real changes for later."

The council remained silent for a while. A majority of the members looked at Segundo. He gave them the most subtle nod.

With little further discussion, the council approved the plan to appropriate two hundred and fifty million dollars to acquire as much farm and ranch land as two hundred and fifty million would buy.

It was understood that Lucky Joe was the person who would carry out the details. Velasquez and Abeita and two other council members opposed the authorization.

Velasquez told council members who supported Lucky Joe they were crazy and their actions were going to create disaster for the tribe. When tribal members found out what the Cruz/Segundo clique was doing with their money, he doubted any council member's safety could be guaranteed.

"Is that a threat?" Lucky Joe asked.

"Not a threat," Velasquez said, turning to the council members. "But remember my warning."

CHAPTER NINE

The next week for Lucky Joe was the busiest of his life. A war room was established in one of the old homes on the plaza. Segundo arranged for underground electrical and telephone lines that fed through the old adobe walls and allowed for rows of electrical sockets and telephone jacks on the inside. Skylights were placed in the vigas and herringbone ceilings, and track lighting fixtures ran along several of the vigas. Computers, printers, fax machines, copy machines and ten telephones sat on a long table. Wall-size maps of the state hung on the walls. A complete set of topographic maps was in a case. Maps showing land ownership patterns were hung on the wall with two track lights aimed on them. A round table eight feet in diameter was in the middle of the multi-room structure. Two rooms, recently built, were on either side of the old adobe. One was a kitchen, complete with a sink, electric stove and refrigerator. The other was a restroom.

In the converted living room, an oak desk was in one corner under a skylight. A bright red telephone sat on the desk top. An executive chair was behind it. Lucky Joe liked the feel of the executive chair. He also liked the appearance of the two young female tribal members who staffed the office.

Segundo wasted no time after the council approved the two hundred and fifty million dollar appropriation to set the land acquisition plan in motion. The goal was clear—thirty-eight million acres of farm and ranch land, all the rural private land that was realistically available in the state.

If the land were to be acquired within a year, they would need to buy an average of about three million acres a month. Segundo knew that goal was ambitious. He could not gear up the purchases that fast. On the other hand, once the program gained momentum, they might be able to make up for what was lost in the first few months. Segundo told Lucky Joe that they would start on some of the state's largest ranches and give priority to those closest to the Grey Piñon Reservation. Acquisition of a few of the hundred thousand acre ranches would give them momentum. When several big ranches sold, it would give small owners confidence to sell, knowing big-money operations found the deals attractive. Tribe members would spread rumors that purchases were going so well, the tribe would reach its two hundred and fifty million dollar limit in the next thirty days. If you were a rancher and you wanted to sell, you had thirty days to make up your mind; after that, the gravy train would end.

Lucky Joe and Segundo sat at the kitchen table, talking quietly so their voices could not be heard in the adjoining room.

"I want a daily report," Segundo said. "This has got to move fast. It will take some time to build momentum. I understand that. But after a few weeks, I want results. How are you coming along on getting real estate agents lined up?"

"It's going well," Lucky Joe said. "I've got five agents in the five counties surrounding the reservation. They're hired. They know we have cash. If they find properties for sale, we're ready to make immediate deals. And they have title companies in each county ready to go. I haven't got the law firms confirmed yet. I'm working on that the next three days. We're going to have a different real estate agent, a different title company and a different law firm to represent us in each county."

Segundo nodded his approval. "I'm going to Washington on Monday. I've got appointments with all five congressmen, and the senators. I want them to know that the Grey Piñon are becoming more religious."

"More religious?" Lucky Joe said.

"Yes. We are becoming more religious. We are more dependent than ever on our ancient sacred sites. That's why the Quail Run Ranch and hot springs is so important—the Burnett place. It's crucial to our religion that these sites be preserved. That ranch is the symbol of that religious quest. Like the Holy Grail. And we want to make our contribution to the economy. All of the money we earn from our casinos, we want to make sure it stays in circulation. We want to return much of what we earn to the state. One way to do this…" Segundo's voice trailed off and he almost broke into a laugh. "One way we do this," he continued after his composure returned, "is to buy up some of the uneconomical farms and ranches that have fallen on hard times. But mostly we're concerned about our ancient sacred sites. They have been ignored too long. Now that we have the economic ability, we want to recover and preserve them. And we are going to put the environment first, just like Big Bob McCoy. He doesn't need to make money off his land, and neither will we. Breaking even is fine with us."

"But except for the Burnett place, we don't have any sacred sites that far from the reservation."

"Let's just say that we need some buffer zones between our sacred sites and the rest of the state," Segundo said.

"I want to make sure our congressmen and women have a valid defense for our position, so when the media start calling to see what they think of Indian land purchases, they will have a ready answer to quiet the concerns."

Lucky Joe scratched the back of his head.

The smell of rain came in the door of the converted adobe home. Lucky Joe glanced at the skylight, as a shadow settled over the room. A roll of thunder sounded outside. Shortly, pelting rain bounced on the skylight.

"This plan is not something you should share with anyone," Segundo said as he went to the stove and poured himself a fresh cup of coffee. "This is going to generate a hailstorm. We are playing for high stakes. There are those who will support us, but there will be people who oppose us, in the tribe and out of the tribe. Do not tell your family. Do not tell Rachel. The less they know, the safer they will be. The more they know, the more dangerous it will be for them."

"I don't see how we can keep this secret for long. Once sales get going, everyone in the county is going to know."

"They'll know there are sales, but it will take awhile for them to know who is buying," Segundo said. "By that time, hopefully we'll be on our way to the next county. Don't underestimate the power of money. Once that money starts flowing to the landowners and the real estate agents, they will do most of the work for us. We're just interested in buying our ancient sacred sites. That's all. We have no master plan, no ulterior motives. We just want to re-acquire our former sacred lands."

Lucky Joe raised his eyebrows for the first time since he and Segundo began discussing the plan.

"For yourself," Segundo said, "how old are you?"

"I'm thirty-four years old."

"That's young," Segundo said. "You need to go out and buy yourself a life insurance policy."

"Life insurance?"

"Try one million. This is going to wind up in great controversy. If you have a good policy, nothing will ever happen to you," Segundo said with a smile.

"That's reassuring."

"And while I'm in Washington next week, I want you to get hold of Charlie Otero. Tell him that Enrique Velasquez and Roberto Abeita are to be removed from the list of tribe members who are eligible for a grazing allotment. That also will make them ineligible for the per capita."

"But their families have had allotments forever," Lucky Joe said.

"Not any more. Just tell Charlie what I told you. And tell him I'm serious."

"But how are they going to support their families without a grazing allotment or the per capita?" Lucky Joe asked.

"That's their problem. They're not going to be living on the reservation much longer anyway. They're no longer friends of the Grey Piñons. It is the tribe that counts. Not a few dissidents. Velasquez and Abeita have been a thorn in our side for as long as I can remember. Since we're making changes, now is the time to get rid of them."

"Is that because of what they did at the council meeting?" Lucky Joe asked.

"For what they have always done. You bore their insults. Your silver-tongued presentation was interrupted by their insane minds. How much longer are you expected to tolerate such insults?"

"We cannot afford to take chances," Segundo continued. "If anyone is not for us, they are against us. We will act accordingly. We cannot afford to have our battle plan interrupted by cowards and weaklings. If Velasquez and Abeita are obstacles, they must be removed."

Lucky Joe's fingers shook as he lifted the coffee cup. Segundo stared straight into his eyes.

"There will be difficult decisions as we move forward with this plan," Segundo said. "There is no room for the weak-hearted. If you are weak-hearted, tell me now, so you can be replaced."

"There is no weak heart. This is all starting to move fast, that's all. I have to think."

"Think all you want. I am committed to this and nothing is going to get in my way; nothing is going to stop us from overturning five centuries of injustice to our people, of returning the land to its true servants, its true friends. This is a cause worth fighting for, a cause worth dying for. Now that we've begun, there is no turning back. You need to declare now. Are you with me, or are you against me?"

Lucky Joe's thoughts turned.

Segundo was looking straight into his eyes.

"I am with you," Lucky Joe said. "This state is going to be the first state in the United States owned by Native Americans."

CHAPTER TEN

Jan Burnett's broken ankle bones were improving. When she was ready to leave the Sierra City Medical Center, she and Lance talked again about their relationship. Lance subtly dropped the bomb. He'd been talking to Earl Wallace (he didn't mention the conversation took place at the Silver Spur). Earl told him that Jan had rented an apartment at the Desert Palms—before they went into the abandoned silver mine, before her accident. Having said that, he ceased talking.

Jan's head dropped into her hand. For a moment she could think of nothing to reply.

"I thought I could do it," Jan said after the long pause. "I am so much in love with you, Lance. I thought I could live with you anywhere. But now I know I have to be around people. I can't take the isolation. Maybe things were different a hundred years ago. Women must have felt a fulfillment being part of the West. But it's not a hundred years ago. It's today. I need people. I love teaching children. The silence out there is suffocating. For some people, it's probably a blessing. For me, I can't stand it. I need people in my life. And I think I'm entitled to a career just like you are. I want to be a teacher."

Lance shook his head. The quietness and the isolation were the things he treasured; the smell of livestock, the smell of a horse, the aroma of the forest when a light rain fell, the smell of

MAGIC LANCE

a corral, the smoke of a campfire, the smell of dry leaves and dead wood on the forest floor. He treasured the solitary life, far from the crowds.

Lance also loved his wife.

"What if we live in town for awhile, and I commute to the ranch," Lance said. "It's only about an hour. Lots of people commute from Ashton to Capital. That's about forty miles. If they can do that every day, I can commute from Sierra City to the Three V."

"Oh, you'll get plenty tired of that in a hurry."

"Maybe I can spend a few nights out there at the ranch, and be in here on Friday, Saturday and Sunday," Lance said. "This is just something we can try. And maybe on some weekends you'll come out to the ranch."

"I don't know. I really don't want to go there any more."

"What about Pepper and Nugget? They're really going to miss you."

"That's no fair," Jan said. "You know how I feel about Pepper."

"She wants to see you, I can tell you that. When I feed her, she looks all down-hearted."

"Ohhhhh...." Jan said.

"I could go out Monday morning early, stay through Friday afternoon, then be back here Friday evening. And we could try that for a while and see how it works. That'll leave you on your own through the week. What are you going to do?"

"I haven't planned that far ahead," Jan said. "I know I have to be around people more, and I'd like to have some kids to teach."

"The first thing you have to do is get well, so you're up and around. Are you willing to try it? I don't want to lose you, Jan. I love you."

"I love you too, Lance. I just don't know if it would work. We're so different. I didn't realize what I was getting into when we got married."

"Maybe we can party on the weekends," Lance said. "And during the week, you can teach. Maybe you can get your old job back with the Sierra City schools. And then we get together on the weekend, to keep our marriage together. I'm willing to try something. I don't want to lose you." Lance drew Jan next to him and kissed her. She wrapped her arms around his neck and passionately kissed him.

The couple agreed they would ask Lance's mother to assist Jan during the week, during her recovery. Lance said he would bring Pepper and Nugget to the Desert Palms apartments for a visit. They would stay in daily contact by telephone, while he sorted things out. He did not want to lose Jan.

The next day, Lance drove to the ranch, packed up Jan's clothes, some pots, pans, plates, silverware and linens. He then drove back to Sierra City and carried all the items into the Desert Palms.

The apartment had a living room with a fireplace, one bedroom, a kitchen and bath. The complex had eight other units surrounding a patio area covered with Kentucky bluegrass. Lance thought of how long that verdant, juicy grass would last with but a single Brangus from his herd.

After transferring Jan's things to the apartment, Lance made a trip to the grocery store to stock up on food. When he left the grocery checkout, his cash reserve was under a hundred dollars. He figured he could exist at the ranch on what was already there for at least two weeks. Calves would have to be sold to generate some new cash flow.

Lance spent Sunday night at the apartment. About 10 a.m. the next day, he kissed Jan goodbye and headed back to the Three V to be a rancher again.

From Sierra City, located in the Blue River Valley, Lance turned toward the foothills, past Poverty Run, a cluster of a few

MAGIC LANCE

frame houses and a one-room general store with an old gas pump out front, and headed into the Yepa National Forest. Past an old mining site, Lance drove through a two-mile-wide meadow surrounded by ponderosa pines, piñons and cedars. The paved road continued due west, but Lance turned south not far from a large stock pond. The road was gravel for fifteen miles until he reached 33 Draw. From there, he climbed over an ever-narrowing mountain road, down into cactus flats and along Quail Run Creek.

The Three V was a composite of several old homestead sites, bordered on the south by the Yepa National Forest. Quail Run Creek was one of the canyons that ran east and west. It served as a natural corridor in the days of the U.S. Cavalry–Indian encounters.

Where the cactus flats ended and a thick stand of ponderosa pine began, a two-foot-high wall of an old one-room log cabin marked the spot some early pioneer selected as a home site. A rock chimney stood at one end of the collapsed cabin ruin. Some distance beyond, when Lance was within a hundred yards of the Three V ranch house, Pepper and Nugget came racing toward him, tongues hanging out, eyes alert, saliva slinging from their mouths, jumping and yelping. Both dogs were Border Collie/Australian Shepherd mixes with tri-color markings. Lance stopped the pickup and let Nugget raise up and put his front paws on the door of the truck. He ran his hand over Nugget's head and rubbed his ears.

Lance pulled into the ranch yard and had just gotten out of the truck when he heard the sound of another vehicle coming up the ranch road.

His eyes expanded a notch when he recognized the 3/4 ton truck as belonging to the Cascade Ranch. The driver, and only person in the truck cab, was a woman.

When the truck stopped and the woman stepped out of the cab, Lance had to blink his eyes.

Pepper and Nugget raced to the truck barking. Lance reprimanded them with a loud voice. After that he didn't know what to say.

The woman was Lightning McClain.

CHAPTER ELEVEN

Lance looked Lightning over from head to toe. She smiled and approached him in a confident stride.

Lance spoke strongly to Pepper and Nugget, who were not convinced Lightning was a person who was supposed to be there. Lightning ran her fingers along the side of her head, guiding her shoulder length hair over the top of her ear. Her body radiated energy.

"Since you didn't want me to send Lupe over, I decided to come myself and see how you were doing."

"Well, I haven't been here long enough myself to see what needs to be done. But you're welcome."

"You strong, frontier types don't ever ask for help," Lightning said. "I know that. But even on the frontier, neighbors helped each other."

Lance softened.

"And there's another reason," Lightning said. "Big Bob is looking to expand. Naturally, the Three V is right next to us. He asked me to come over and see if you had any interest in selling."

Lance looked up through the ponderosa pine needles, into the cloudless blue sky. "What is this? First some religious trust. Now Big Bob. Everybody must know something I don't. What the hell is going on?"

"What do you mean?" Lightning said. "What's a religious trust got to do with anything?"

"After you walked away from me the other night at the Silver Spur, Earl Wallace came over and asked me if I wanted to sell the Three V to some religious trust, run by an Indian chief. Now here you are, wanting to buy the Three V for Big Bob."

"What do you mean I walked away from you?" Lightning said. "It wasn't like I suddenly took off of my own free will."

"You choose who you want to be with. And Scooter was acting mighty possessive."

"He may have been possessive, but you haven't asked me how I feel about that." Lightning reached down and petted Pepper. The dog was sitting on her haunches in front of Lance's leg. "Sweet baby," she said to Pepper, puckering her lips as she spoke.

"Why would Big Bob have any interest in this place?" Lance said. "You work yourself to death seven days a week, and then you can't even make the mortgage payments."

"With Big Bob, the excitement is in the chase. The way to keep his interest is to let him think he's got a chance, and keep the challenge alive."

"Is that how you deal with him?"

"That's how I try to deal with him," Lightning said with a laugh. "I do reasonably well."

"Would you like to come in for coffee?"

"No, I'm not here to intrude. I am supposed to be nice and charming to you, and see if you have any interest is selling the Three V."

"Oh, so that's why you're being nice. You're supposed to soften me up."

"Big Bob just said, do what you have to do. With Big Bob, that means I can do what I want, or do nothing at all. He trusts me."

"How much did Big Bob tell you to offer?"

Lightning shifted her eyes and tossed her head. A wide smile broke.

"We didn't get that far. I decided to come by and look the place over. Then make a recommendation."

"Have you looked the place over?"

"Just driving in. I thought, if you were interested, maybe you would show me around, so I can see what it is Big Bob would be buying. But that's only if you're interested in showing me around." She stuck her hands in the front pockets of her jeans, and looked down at her boots, then up at Lance with a smile.

Lance was struck by her freshness and beauty.

"I'm not interested in selling, but I wouldn't mind showing you the ranch. That's something I love to do."

"I can come back."

"What about right now?"

"Are you sure?"

"Sure I'm sure," Lance said. "Are you sure you're allowed to do this without Scooter being around?"

"Are you sure you're allowed to do this without Jan being around?"

Lance moved around the pickup and opened the door for her. A plastic water jug fell out of the truck when the door opened. Lance grabbed it awkwardly, nearly tripping when he did so, and tossed it into the bed of the truck.

"Margaritas," he said, as he moved around the front of the truck. "Where to?"

"You know your own place. Somewhere, if we can get an overview. Any points of interest. Maybe the boundaries."

Lance gave a whistle. Pepper and Nugget jumped up, lightly touched the rear bumper and bounded over the tailgate, right into the pickup bed. Lance never tired of watching them make that move. It was so fast and graceful; unless he focused he wouldn't see their feet touch the back bumper and it appeared they went from the ground straight into the truck bed in a single bound.

Lance drove back toward 33 Draw, up the hillside, then struck off to the right on two ruts that went into a stand of ponderosa pine.

"This place belonged to my family," Lance said. "When they moved to Sierra City, I took over. Even if I wanted to sell, they'd have to agree to it."

"I'm sure your recommendation would carry a lot of weight. Lance, I don't know how serious Big Bob is. It's part of his nature to always be on the lookout for something."

"It's nice to know people want to buy the place. Makes me appreciate it all the more."

The pickup moved up the slope to the top of the hill, then ran along the ridge in a northeast direction. Stacks of old cut trees lay about a hundred yards apart.

"What are all those?" Lightning asked.

"Slash timber. Dad thought he was going to cut down some timber, sell some wood and make room for grass up here on top. After he cut for an entire summer, he decided it was too much work. Figured he'd eventually use the wood for firewood. But about the only thing that's going to generate a fire now is lightning."

"My namesake," Lightning said.

After moving along the hill ridge for a mile, Lance dropped down on the 33 Draw side and returned to the gravel road. He headed east toward the Blue River and cruised through large elk parks, with seventy-five foot high ponderosa pine trees set widely apart, with some low brush and open grass areas.

MAGIC LANCE

"Good elk country. I've thought about giving up cattle and turning the place into a hunting preserve. They say you can make more off elk than cattle these days."

"Big Bob looked at that as well."

"What did he think about it?"

"He decided he didn't want that many strangers on the place with high powered rifles. Too many of them don't know what they're doing."

"I can agree with that," Lance said. "The thought of some of those city idiots out here with booze and bullets...it scares me to death."

Several mule deer raised their heads and tails, and watched the pickup from the far side of a grass park. Lance pointed them out.

"Is there really a hot springs here?" Lightning asked.

"Chloride Springs," Lance said. "Sure is. Used to be one of Wild Horse's favorite spots. In fact, Indians from all over the state stopped there. Some of 'em used the springs as a rest and recuperation place. So did the cavalry. We play it down. Don't want a bunch of hippie types coming in here. It's hard enough keeping the coyote population down."

"Could we see that?" Lightning looked at Lance, admiring his rugged features.

"You can even dip your feet in," Lance said. "It's supposed to cure whatever ails you. Jan and I come down here every so often. It's better in the fall when the weather gets cool."

"Ever do any skinny-dipping?" Lightning asked.

"Not usually." Lance glanced at Lightning out of the corner of his eye. She was too beautiful to be spending time on a small-time rancher, unless she had an agenda; and yet that same beauty caused him to put all such negative thoughts aside.

They drove on for another mile, then turned south on another two-rut road. They stayed on top of the hill for a half mile, then began a long descent down a slope, dropping into Quail Run Creek, far above the ranch house. In the bottom of the canyon they passed a windmill. The blades of the windmill fan turned slowly. A two-inch stream of water came out of the pipe that extended over a round metal water tank. From the windmill, they passed a log corral and resumed the trip up Quail Run Creek. A mile further along, they came to a broad clearing that was the end of the road.

"Trail head. The Yepa National Forest area starts right over there," Lance said, pointing to a fence line on the far side of the clearing.

Lance swung the pickup around a giant boulder at the top of the clearing and parked in a secluded area. When he got out of the cab, Pepper and Nugget bolted from the truck bed and began scurrying around the clearing, sniffing at an abandoned fire pit and marking several trees.

"The hot springs is up this way," Lance said, walking toward a narrow cut between two pine-covered hills. A stream, several feet wide, ran through the cut. "Come over and feel this." He walked to the stream, leaned down and stuck his hand into the water.

Lightning walked right up next to him, almost touching, and leaned down to put her hand in the water. Lance took her free hand to hold her steady. She stuck her hand in the water and looked up at Lance.

"Not hot, but warm," she said.

Lance pulled her up. Her soft warm hand was in complete contrast to his calloused palm and fingers. He inhaled a light hint of perfume as she came close to him.

After releasing her hand, they walked along the stream, farther into the cut. Lance drew in a deep breath of fresh forest smells.

MAGIC LANCE

"Did Geronimo come here?"

"Probably did," Lance said. "He was all over this country, Mexico, Arizona, New Mexico. All over."

"There's a pool up a little higher," Lance said. "A spring's in that pool somewhere. I've never been able to find it. It's in there somewhere."

"How hot is the water?"

"Oh, ninety-five to a hundred," Lance said. "It's somewhere between warm and hot. In cold weather, it feels hot. In hot weather, it feels warm."

"Can I take your arm?" Lightning asked. "I seem to be stumbling. You're seeing my uncoordinated side."

Lance cocked his elbow and extended his right arm to her. She wrapped her left arm over his.

A hundred yards up the stream, they came to a wide open area to the right, and a steep hillside on the left. The stream ran at the base of the hillside. In a flat area, encircled by shinnery oak, was a pool of water. Several big rocks lined the edge of the pool. They stopped at the pool's edge, looking into the crystal clear water.

Lightning turned loose Lance's arm and stuck her hand into the water.

"Almost hot," she said.

Lance moved upstream a few yards, looking at a Brangus cow grazing not far from the stream.

Lightning sat on one of the rocks next to the pool. She pulled off her Western boots, stripped off her socks, rolled up the legs of her blue jeans and dropped her feet into the water. A smile of satisfaction emerged, and she placed both hands behind her on the rock and leaned back, staring into the clear blue sky, allowing the sun to shine on her face.

Lance kept his eyes on her as he returned to the pool. He sat on an adjoining rock and propped one boot up.

"Why don't you join in and enjoy this," Lightning said. "Feels great."

Lance thought for a moment, then removed his boots and socks, and dropped his feet into the pool.

Lightning raked one of her feet across the surface of the pool, and splashed some water on Lance.

He reached down with his hand and threw a larger portion of water on Lightning. She half-screamed and half-laughed.

"This is a beautiful place," Lightning said. "You should turn it into a resort."

"I've thought about it," Lance said. "But then it wouldn't be like it is now. Totally natural, totally private."

Lightning smiled at him. "I guess you're right."

Lance cast a glance at Pepper and Nugget. They trotted through the trees, occasionally finding a chipmunk or squirrel, giving short chase.

"Ever run across any skinny-dipper types out here?"

"Not that many," Lance said. "There've been a few."

"I guess there's no one out here to see you really, is there?"

"Only the person you're with," Lance said.

Lightning leaned back on the rock, closed her eyes and basked in the sun. She kicked her feet several times, splashing water into the air. Her hair glistened in the sunlight.

She looked at Lance with a friendly smile and pushed her hair away from her face.

"Want to go swimming?

CHAPTER TWELVE

A quarter-mile downstream from the chloride hot springs, a four-wheel drive utility vehicle moved slowly up the road. Lucky Joe was driving and listening to Earl Wallace, riding in the front passenger seat. An older Indian, short of stature and with porcupine hair, sat in the back seat. The two Native Americans had said little since they met Earl at his real estate office in Sierra City. During the morning, they toured the newly acquired Peterson ranch in Seep Springs Canyon. Then, Lucky Joe asked that they be shown the hot springs on the Three V Ranch. Earl told them again that the ranch owner said the place was not for sale. After some discussion, however, Earl confirmed he was a friend of the owner, and thought he would not object if they drove over a portion of the ranch. Earl called the Three V ranch house. No one answered. Against his better judgment, he agreed to show his two clients the general layout of the Three V property. He intended to stay away from the ranch house in Quail Run Creek. Segundo was especially interested in seeing the hot springs. They did not mention to Earl that this hot springs was Wild Horse's summer resting area and that it was a key goal in their land acquisition plan. They sought vast tracts of land, but they especially wanted this hot springs.

When they reached the trailhead, Earl drove up the cut along the stream as far as the road ruts allowed. He told Lucky

Joe and Segundo they would have to walk the rest of the way to reach the hot springs. After discussing the general boundaries of the ranch, the trio got out of the utility vehicle and started up the cattle and game trail that ran next to the stream.

Earl was doing the talking as they approached the open area by the hot springs. While they still were in the ponderosa pine and fir trees below the clearing, two cattle dogs suddenly appeared from out of nowhere and charged directly at them. Instinctively, the three men drew back, and drew together. "Hey! Hey!" Earl shouted at Pepper and Nugget. The dogs charged to within a few feet, barking and baring their teeth. Their eyes showed red and the hair on their necks and backs bristled. There was no appeasing them.

While contending with the two cattle dogs, the men saw two human figures sprint along the tree line on the far side of the open area, away from the hot springs. It was a man and a woman. The man's shirttail flowed in the air. The woman was bare-legged and carrying a pair of blue jeans. Some item dropped from the woman's grasp as the pair disappeared into the trees on the south side of the open area.

While not certain, Earl thought the man was Lance Burnett. He could not see the woman's face well, but by the way she was running, she appeared young, and even from the distance, he saw she was beautifully formed.

After a five minute standoff, Pepper and Nugget turned and slowly moved back to the open area, moving generally in the direction taken by the man and woman.

Earl considered his options. If the man were Lance, he would be circling back to the road and would not be in any mood to see Earl Wallace, or anybody else. Earl was puzzled how the man and woman had gotten up this far in the canyon. He had seen no vehicle and it was a long way to the nearest house, which was

MAGIC LANCE

Lance Burnett's ranch house some five miles away. Earl decided his best option was to go on to the hot springs, show his clients the springs, and give Lance or whoever it was plenty of time to leave. If it were Lance, Earl thought, it was clear the woman running with him was not a woman with a broken ankle.

The men walked upstream to the hot springs. Segundo saw that two people had been in the pool. Water was splashed on the rocks, along with several wet footprints. Looking along their line of departure, Segundo spotted an object on the ground. He thought it might be a fanny pack or a purse. He walked to where the item lay and picked it up. It was a leather belt with red, white and blue Indian beadwork.

He returned to the pool, item in hand.

"If that was the owner we saw running," Segundo said, "it is not a good sign. If he can get women like the one we just saw, up here on the ranch, and they're leaving things like this behind, he's not going to sell."

When they reached the trailhead, Lance and Lightning stopped to catch their breath. Lance studied the utility vehicle. He did not recognize it or identify it with an owner. Lightning pulled her blue jeans on over her boots. Rather than tarry, the couple got into Lance's pickup parked behind the boulder and drove down Quail Run Creek toward the ranch house.

Lightning rested her head in her right hand. She laughed as they put distance between themselves and the chloride hot springs.

"If this is what privacy is, I've got to re-think it," she said.

"What burns me is they're a bunch of trespassers on my own ranch, and I can't do much about it, at least not right now. Talk about getting caught with your pants down."

He laughed as well. Lightning rubbed his upper arm with her left hand. "You can't say it wasn't exciting."

"Not exactly the ending I had in mind," Lance said.

"We'll look back on it one day and laugh," Lightning said. "I've been caught doing worse."

Lance looked in the rear view mirror, making sure Pepper and Nugget were still in the bed of the pickup. They each were standing with their front paws on the top of the pickup truck side, their heads held high.

"Good work, Nugget. Good work, Pepper," Lance hollered to his cattle dogs.

"At least they gave us some advance warning. I've never seen a guy get out of a hot springs and get his pants and boots on so fast. That was a real show stopper."

"You were moving pretty fast yourself," Lance said. He looked at Lightning's figure, noting the cleavage showing through her shirt.

Lightning perceived his glance, and nudged her shirt top together. A look of concern ran over her face. She looked in the truck seat, then on the floor, then in the narrow space between the seat and the door.

"I may have left something behind," she said.

"Oh, yeah?"

Lightning ran her fingers around her waist. "My Indian bead belt is back there somewhere."

Lance laughed. "They'll be jealous if they find it."

As he thought of it, more ominous thoughts entered his mind.

"Who were those people?" Lightning asked.

"I have not the faintest idea. I barely got a glimpse of them. If the circumstances were any different, I'd go back and charge 'em with trespassing.

"Do you think they saw us?"

"Here in the forest, I'd say those good-looking bare legs of yours would be seen from at least ten miles away. They saw us. Whether they were close enough to recognize us, I don't know."

MAGIC LANCE

When he reached the ranch house, Lance parked beside Lightning's Cascade Ranch pickup. She got out and walked to the door of the truck. He walked with her and opened the truck door.

"I'll tell Big Bob the ranch has some real attractions."

"Tell him you almost had a deal, until you were so rudely interrupted."

"I'll tell him you're not an easy mark," Lightning said. "Too many people wandering around the place."

They both laughed. Pepper and Nugget hung right at their feet.

Lightning drove back down the road. Lance watched her depart. When her truck made a left turn near the cactus flats and started up the hill, Lance saw a second beige Cascade Ranch truck pull out of a wooded area and follow Lightning out. It was not the vehicle that had been at the trailhead. Lance contemplated what was happening. Where had that second truck come from and who was in it?

Seeing two different vehicles he didn't recognize on the ranch in one day was more than he normally saw in a month. Things were going on, he concluded, and he was concerned he didn't know what they were.

The thought that he might have been set up, and that Lightning was part of it, quickly killed the sense of pleasure he had felt with her at the hot springs. His earlier thoughts must have been accurate. Lightning was too good-looking to be doing what she was doing, without higher stakes being involved, and yet the three men showing up at the hot springs didn't fit in with his conspiracy theory, unless they were supposed to have caught them together. That didn't seem likely either. Lightning had been as enthusiastic as he had been in their escape. Nothing seemed to fit, but something definitely was wrong.

After Lightning and the second Cascade pickup were gone, Lance tucked in his shirttail, ran his hand through his hair, pulled his sweat-stained cowboy hat out of the pickup and jammed it on his head."

"Come on dogs!" he shouted at Pepper and Nugget. They performed their graceful bounce into the bed of the pickup truck. Lance spun the back wheels of the truck, turned it around, and raced back up the canyon. Whoever those trespassers were, he was going to deal with them now. He relished the thought of slugging them square in the face.

Quail Run Creek was a canyon that ran east and west, parallel to 33 Draw, which was the next canyon to the north. Groves of Arizona walnut, shinnery oak and blue gramma grass grew along the streambed. The rocky streambed carried water in the spring. In wet years, water flowed from the trailhead all the way down to the cactus flats. In dry years, there were intermittent flows, with water higher up, then dry streambed, then flows and pools again lower down. This year was average. There was water in the flat areas, and dry bedrock through narrow sections of the canyon. The road criss-crossed the streambed all the way through the canyon.

The farther he drove, the madder Lance got. There was no excuse for anyone to be at the chloride springs other than himself or his family members or someone they specifically authorized. If it had been a family member, they would have called him first. What made him really mad was that he did not know who the interlopers were. Being in the mineral pool with Lightning was embarrassing to him now. It was a pleasure he had dreamed about, never expected to have, and then to have it, and be run out by some unknown strangers, caused a red blush to run over his face. The pickup flew out of a streambed, crossing into a right turn. It skidded to the left, and Lance turned the

MAGIC LANCE

wheels into the slide. He slowed a bit when he regained control. He glanced in the mirror to see how Pepper and Nugget handled the skid. They were pacing back and forth in the truck bed.

At a cross-fencing gate below the windmill he skidded to a stop. He was out of the truck, flinging the gate open and racing on through, not bothering to close it behind him. He did pause long enough to study tire tracks on the road. A truck other than his own had been there. Whether the vehicle still was there was something he would soon find out. He jumped back into the truck and sped on.

When he reached the trailhead, he parked in the same spot he parked earlier. The utility vehicle he had seen when he and Lightning left was gone. He missed them. They must have taken the back road to 33 Draw, by the windmill.

Lance slammed the truck door. Pepper and Nugget were on the ground again, racing in circles, looking back at Lance to determine what he was going to do.

Lance relaxed a notch. He took in a deep breath of mountain air and walked along the stream toward the springs. At one location next to the stream, just above a patch of moist earth, he examined the footprints. He saw his own, and assumed a small set of prints belonged to Lightning. There were numerous other footprints as well. He moved on toward the springs, looking for any signs of the people Pepper and Nugget had sniffed out and challenged.

He saw nothing. As he approached the mineral springs, he spied near the pool a tripod composed of three pine branches. On top of the tripod, neatly rolled, was Lightning's Indian bead belt.

By this time Lance's temper had eased. He plucked the belt from the tripod and stuck it in his back pocket. On his return, he tossed the belt onto the seat of his pickup, intending to return it to Lightning at some opportune time. Whoever the strangers were who came to the hot springs, they clearly saw the embarrassed couple in their escape, and they left the belt to tell Lance they had found it. If only Lightning had gotten her pants back on before they started running. Somebody knew his situation. He was uncomfortable not knowing who it was.

He wondered if there was a connection between the utility vehicle and the second Cascade pickup truck that followed Lightning. Again he asked himself, could he have been set up? The more he thought of the possibilities, the more his temper flared. If Lightning set him up, he would get her. But how would he know? If she did set him up, she would lie and deny it. At the pickup, he paused next to the truck bed and rear wheel, patting Nugget and Pepper on the head. "Man's best friends," Lance said. "At least with you two I know where I stand."

CHAPTER THIRTEEN

The next thirty days witnessed frantic activity in the Grey Piñon war room. Four staff members were added. All four were tribe members, sworn to secrecy. Two were related by some degree to Lucky Joe's family, although the relationships were distant. Juan Gutierrez had a business degree from the University of Arizona. His job was to package real estate deals that Lucky Joe approved. Lucky Joe took a leave of absence from the Magic Lance and now spent his time exclusively on the land acquisition program. Members of the tribal council came by regularly, enthused by stories they were hearing.

As Lucky Joe suspected, rumors of big land deals were flying, and not just on the reservation. His sources of information were the real estate agents. He soon learned that ranchers had their own network. Even the appearance of one of the tribe's agents on a ranch sent immediate signals throughout the area. While not every ranch was for sale, there were enough that were to get a sales fever going. The fever caused a run on the two hundred and fifty million dollars the tribal council had authorized. Segundo realized during the first two weeks that two hundred and fifty million was not going to go far. He was edgy about going back to the tribal council for more money. It was a matter he and Lucky Joe discussed numerous times. Their conclusion was that they needed to get other tribes involved in the land purchases, and much sooner than originally envisioned. Segundo said he would make informal contacts; Lucky Joe was to make more formal appearances at tribal council meetings. They would use the two hundred and fifty million authority they already had to option as many ranches as they could.

Option payments would be made at once, tying up the ranches. Their agents recommended a one-year option period. If the tribe exercised the options, they could apply the option money to the sale price. The options would lock in a price. Options were attractive to ranchers because they got their option money up front. If the tribe backed out, the ranchers would keep their ranches and the option money. If the tribe went forward with the options, the ranchers would get the price they wanted, and they would have up to a year to make arrangements for their move. To sweeten the deal, the tribe also offered to pay some of the ranchers an additional year's salary if the option were exercised, to stay on their own ranches and manage them for the tribe. For the first time, some of the ranchers would have guaranteed health, disability, worker's compensation and life insurance benefits, at least for a year from the date of purchase.

Lucky Joe knew the options were a risky strategy. If other tribes failed to join in with hard cash, the Grey Piñons would have to pour huge sums of money into the deals quickly. He wondered if tribal support would hold up, faced with such a financial drain. To meet their land acquisition goal, they could not afford a slowdown. Velazquez's warning came back to him regularly, that the whole land plan was ludicrous. If their opponents were to convince the tribal council to withhold additional funding, the plan would blow up in his face, and two hundred and fifty million of the tribe's money would be lost on the purchase options.

Lucky Joe slowly began to realize how immense the scope of the land plan was, and how little influence he personally had over unfolding developments. There were times he would get the jitters and his hands would tremble until he laid them on something solid. Other times he purposely quit thinking, unable to control the anxiety he harbored about a rising wave of land purchase problems.

Finally, he would force himself to focus on just one aspect of the plan, to keep from freezing up and ceasing to do anything at all.

One such focus was his effort to enlist other Indian tribes to join the land program. Armed with option contracts, Lucky Joe began trips to other tribes to sell them on the idea of buying ranches nearest their reservation. A Native American state was an exciting proposition. Offering a specific ranch property for a certain price made the proposition seem attainable.

His first effort was with the River Bend Tribe. While the proposal to purchase all the private ranch land in the state by Indian tribes was an initial shock to the council, it was immediately applauded. As the meeting progressed, however, a faction quickly formed that urged caution.

Lucky Joe could feel those ancient suspicions of the Grey Piñon Tribe, and feel those ancient hostilities of having another tribe in a leadership role. He told them how important it was that the basic plan be kept secret for as long as possible. Once it was known, opposition was certain, not only among the tribes themselves, but among the state's whole population. At that point, mighty political forces would oppose the effort. A Native American state would have some initial romantic appeal, but as soon as the plan was seen as a possible reality, political opposition and personal hostilities were certain.

River Bend council members assured him they would take his proposal seriously. They especially were interested in the brochures prepared by the real estate agents, showing the scenic open country of the lands Lucky Joe proposed they buy.

"We already have it," Lucky Joe said. "We have an option to buy it. All you have to do is appropriate the money, and the land is yours. I ask that you not distrust me because I am Grey Piñon, and because we are the ones who have the options. We are not going to make anything off any ranches in the River Bend purchases. We only provide the opportunity. You have the first option, since the ranches shown in the brochures are close to your reservation. You will recognize most of them."

Before leaving, Lucky Joe cautioned, "If the River Bend do not go forward with these options, we will try to sell them to others. Or the Grey Piñon may buy them. For those of you who harbor those old feelings, those old pangs of distrust, think how you will feel if we Grey Piñons suddenly become your neighbors, and we own all these beautiful ranches close to your own reservation that you could have bought. Instead, join us. Work with us. Alone, the Grey Piñons cannot acquire all the lands for a Native American state. Together, we can do it. We are providing the way for all of us to succeed. Make your decision to join us. We will visit every tribe in the state. If we succeed, we will stop there. If we cannot acquire the lands we want, we will have to go to tribes outside the state. Our preference is to keep this for the tribes in this area. We think we can do it. We can only do it if you join us. I urge you to approve this plan, and to pick up the options that are listed in this brochure. Time counts. You must move quickly. I guarantee you will never regret buying more land. It will be for your benefit, for you who are seated here tonight. It also will be for your children's benefit, and their children. It will allow all of us to return to our former life road, our former way. It will be for your ancestors. They will be proud of what you have done. You will avenge their defeats. May the

MAGIC LANCE

spirits be with you and guide you, as you decide what you are going to do."

Lucky Joe was pumped with enthusiasm when he left the meeting. With the help of other tribes, the dream of a Native American state was more attainable. But even on the way back to the Grey Piñon Reservation, he realized his speech to the River Bend Tribal Council bore great risk of letting the genie out of the bottle and launching the rumor that Indians were going to start a land grab in the state that would exceed anything anyone had ever imagined.

CHAPTER FOURTEEN

At the Grey Piñon Reservation, Lucky Joe and Segundo began daily meetings. Most often the meetings took place in the war room that adjoined the reservation plaza. For greater privacy they hired a security firm to protect the old house, now turned into an electronic base camp. During the day, an armed security guard was posted at the front door. Tribal members, and especially children, had begun to wander in and out of the house, looking at the electronic equipment, and asking questions about what they were doing, and so near the plaza. Segundo decided tribal members were getting too nosey. They needed to limit access. Several of the security guards were tribal members, but several were not. Ironic, Segundo told Lucky Joe that they needed to hire non-Indians to guard the reservation's war room. "We may have to hire them to guard our land, before long."

He laughed at the thought.

Lucky Joe hired an illustrator to create a floor-to-ceiling map of the state. As a ranch was optioned, the boundaries of that ranch were drawn on the map in red. The reservation's boundaries also were put on the map. On the right side of the map was a drawing of a giant thermometer, measuring acres rather than degrees, representing all the private land they thought they had a chance to acquire in the state. Near the bottom of the

MAGIC LANCE

thermometer, in red, they raised the measuring line up near two million acres.

"It's a beginning," Segundo said to Lucky Joe. "Not bad for a bunch of lazy guys who can't handle alcohol."

"In one year, how much money do we have to have, to exercise all these options?" Lucky Joe asked. "I'm starting to get edgy about the final number. All our money is going out there in option money. If we don't pick up the options, we could lose it all."

"My young friend, you continue to dwell on the negative. There are always chances to lose. Running that risk is what it costs to play."

Segundo called Juan over and asked him to get on the computer tell him how much land they had optioned, and if they bought it all, how much they would pay.

Juan quickly had the answer. "You have a hundred and three ranches optioned. If you got them all, you'd own almost two million acres. To pick up all the options on two million acres, you need eight hundred and ninety two million dollars."

Lucky Joe rolled his eyes. "We only have a two hundred and fifty million," he said. "Where's the other six hundred and forty two million coming from?"

"You are going to get it," Segundo said confidently. "We need commitments from our Indian brothers. The River Bends sent word they are considering a purchase of two hundred million, if we can agree on what ranches they would get. In the next thirty days, I want a full commitment, not just for six hundred and forty-two million, but for nine hundred million. So we still have two hundred and fifty million left to go out and continue our option purchases. That's the key. We have to keep this moving, and we need to be two hundred and fifty million ahead at any given time, to make sure we can continue the program for at least another thirty days."

As Lucky Joe ran his eyes over the state map, the shapely young lady who was war room office manager stepped into the room. "It's the *Ashton Times*," she said. "They want to talk to Lucky Joe." She looked him in the eye. Lucky Joe looked her over as he had a hundred times before. Her shape was never boring. He went to his desk and picked up the telephone receiver.

It was Susanne Burks, a reporter for the *Times*. She wanted to talk about the rumors of Indian land purchases.

Lucky Joe asked her what she wanted to know.

Susanne said they were told the Peterson Ranch had sold to a Grey Piñon member and that other ranches were selling to different groups that had Gray Piñon connections. She wanted to know what was going on and whom she could talk to about it. Lucky Joe told her he would make some inquiries and call her back. She told him she'd heard he was the one of the people who knew what was going on.

Lucky Joe said he knew something about it, but would need to consult with others before giving any interviews.

When could she expect to hear from him.

He didn't know, maybe in a day or two.

She said she would call back.

"*Ashton Times*," Lucky Joe said, turning to Segundo. "They want to talk to me about the Peterson Ranch sale, and others. I don't think our cover is going to last, even with all our efforts. She sounds like she already knows about some of the sales and she's trying to confirm what she's already learned.

"No problem. Stall 'em for awhile. Then tell 'em there's some economic diversification taking place. Sound financial policy. The Grey Piñons have great faith in the state. They think it's a good place to live. Keep it simple. We're already far enough along that I think we're okay, if they don't know what the final objective is. Once that genie is out of the bottle, we may have to change our game plan from secrecy to justification. Those news hounds have a better nose than I gave them credit for. That's a miscalculation we'll have to adjust to. We'll have to rely on our political support once the word is out."

"What's our average price per acre?" Lucky Joe asked.

Segundo turned to Juan. "Computer chief. How much are we paying per acre?"

"Four hundred and seventy five dollars per acre."

"So how much do we need to buy all thirty eight million acres?" Lucky Joe asked.

"At the rate we're going, " Segundo said, "that's going to be about eighteen billion dollars. I've already calculated it."

"Eighteen billion," Lucky Joe repeated in disbelief. "Eighteen billion."

"Don't worry. With our Indian brothers, we can raise it. Together we already have seven billion in the banks, our ink-on-paper. The rest we can raise during the next few years, if we can keep the gambling compacts. And we have to keep the ranchers in a good mood to sell. Both factors have to work."

"How are we going to keep the ranchers in a good mood?" Lucky Joe asked.

"Several ways. One way is to keep the carrot dangling. We keep cash offers on the table. That's the easy way. But in case that doesn't work, and it won't for everyone, we have to try other ways."

"How's that?"

"If the ranchers aren't doing too well, making a living off cattle, they're going to be more inclined to take the cash carrot," Segundo said.

"I don't understand."

"If you make your living raising cattle, you are dependent on how much money you can get when you sell your cattle. If

the price of cattle drops, or you lose some of your cattle to disease or predators, you have a problem," Segundo said.

He waited for Lucky Joe to ask another question. Lucky Joe sat stone-faced.

"What would happen to your cattle operation if the price of cattle dropped?" Segundo asked. "Or some of your cattle died."

"I'd be hurtin'."

"Right. And if you're hurtin', when somebody comes by your place and dangles a cash carrot in front of your nose, you might be more inclined to take a bite."

"That assumes beef prices are falling," Lucky Joe said. "We don't have any control over that."

"We don't," Segundo said, with a wry smile. "If we suddenly sell off the tribe's cattle, and any additional cattle we can get our option ranchers to sell, with some cash incentives, that could affect the local market.

"And then we have one more card," Segundo added.

"What card is that?"

"Ever heard of mad cow disease?"

CHAPTER FIFTEEN

A deep concern edged into Lucky Joe's mind. He personally had signed option agreements committing most of the tribe's two hundred and fifty million dollars. It was like monopoly money. If they were unable to raise additional cash, another six hundred and ninety-two million, the tribe would lose the two hundred and fifty million paid for options. And Segundo was going full steam ahead. He was demanding they not only raise another six hundred and ninety-two million, but they commit for an additional eight or nine hundred million. The confidence Lucky Joe enjoyed the past few years now was replaced by an anxiety and a life that was spinning out of control, out of harmony with his upbringing and his culture.

That evening after work, as Lucky Joe walked across the reservation plaza, heading toward his utility vehicle, a half moon floated in the sky below a canopy of stars. In the middle of the plaza, he saw several men come from between two houses at the plaza's edge and walk in his direction. He sounded a greeting. One of them responded. He recognized Sam Pichocho's voice. It was not friendly.

Four men came up to him. Lucky Joe came to a standstill in the middle of the plaza, in a glow of moonlight.

The four men formed a square around him.

"We are hearing bad things about you," Sam said.

"Who's saying that?" Lucky Joe said, sensing danger.

"Everyone is saying that," Sam said.

"What are they saying?"

"They're saying a lot of things. They say you're spending all the tribe's money."

"There's nothing to it." Lucky Joe shifted his weight to his right, and the man on his right shifted his stance.

"Nothing to it, nothing to it," Sam said. "Two hundred and fifty million dollars gone, and he says there's nothing to it. You're starting to sound like one of those Arab sheiks. Two hundred and fifty million dollars gone, and there's nothing to it."

"There's not two hundred and fifty million dollars gone," Lucky Joe said. "We have land options."

"Quit lying," Sam said. "You know what I'm talking about. That money's been pledged, and there's no assurance we'll ever get it back. How much are you getting out of it? Those real estate agents giving you and Segundo kickbacks?"

"No. I'm not getting anything. You're getting bad information from somebody."

"Am I," Sam said. "Who gave the order to cut Velasquez and Abeita's grazing allotments, and their casino share. You and Segundo must think you're pretty important people, starting to persecute members of the tribe who don't agree with you."

Lucky Joe could feel an attack coming. He glanced around the plaza, looking for any kind of help. In the moonglow, there was but one skinny dog visible, walking along the front of an adobe house.

"The money is all going for land purchases. Economic diversification," Lucky Joe said, working a stall and looking for an exit.

The men inched toward him, tightening the square. Lucky Joe faced the man on Sam's right and took a step toward him. It

MAGIC LANCE

was a feint. With all his might, he swung his right arm in a roundhouse haymaker, plunging his clenched fist right into Sam's bulging stomach. It jolted the breath right out of the man, and he crumpled to his knees. Immediately, Lucky Joe was on the run, heading to the south side of the plaza. He could feel two men right behind him, running fast.

When he reached a house on the side of the plaza, he grabbed the first thing he saw, a child's red metal wagon. With instant strength, he picked the wagon up by the handle and swung it in a circle. The two men behind him, slid to a halt to avoid the swinging wagon. In an instance, Lucky Joe released the wagon, sending it flying into the men. As they ducked, he sprinted around the side of the house, and headed across the road that ran in front of the house. On the far side of the road, he headed down a narrow way between two more adobe homes. When he cleared those, he headed across a smaller plaza in front of the Catholic church. He raced around the side of the church. Just as he passed a supporting buttress wall, he spied a wooden door. He opened it in an instant, surprised that it was not locked, and stepped inside the church, pulling the door behind him, turning a deadlock on the inside. He had perhaps thirty seconds to hide, before his pursuers would be coming through the two front doors of the church.

Hiding behind the altar at the front of the church sanctuary would be obvious. A number of votive candles were burning in the transept to the left of the altar. Lucky Joe ran to the candle stand, and blew out the candles. Then he turned back to the sanctuary. He heard men's voices outside the church, moving toward the two front doors. He had ten seconds before they came inside.

He ran to the second row of pews, dropped to the floor, and crawled under the pew, up next to the kneeler rail. To the best of his ability, he lay prone along side the folded kneeler, below the second row pew. Just as he achieved that position, he heard the two wooden doors swing open and heard the footsteps of several men walking inside. His breathing came close to ceasing.

There was only a hint of light in the church. Windows at the top of the adobe walls near the ceiling let in some defused moonlight. For a few moments, there was total silence. Then Lucky Joe heard footsteps coming up the aisle along the south wall. Those footsteps stopped. Footsteps then sounded in the aisle along the north wall. They moved slowly, irregularly.

Lucky Joe had no plan. If they found him, he would have to fight. Whether Sam still was among them, he didn't know. He would have little chance against three, much less four. After the attack on Sam, they would show him no mercy.

The footsteps along the south wall came closer. Lucky Joe held his breath. A moment later, he saw work boots in the aisle, not four feet from his hiding place. There was sound from the direction of the altar. The work boots turned toward the sound. Lucky Joe's muscles began to twitch. The man in the work boots took another step. He was within three feet of Lucky Joe's head, next to the end of the bench pew.

Lucky Joe was in a trance of fear. Just as he prepared to bolt from his hiding position, get to his feet and fight it out, a door opened at the side of the altar. Light came into the church.

"Who's there?" a voice said.

There was no answer.

"What are you doing in here?" the voice said.

There was no response.

"What are you doing in here?" the voice said again, this time stronger than before.

"We thought a friend of ours came in here," Sam said. He was in the middle aisle, only a row back from where Lucky Joe was hiding. Lucky Joe realized he was between two enemies, one standing at his head, the other standing near his feet.

"As you can see, there's no one here," the voice said.

Lucky Joe recognized the voice of Father O'Grady, the new Catholic priest at Grey Piñon.

"This is the house of God. It is not a recreation area," Father O'Grady said. "You need to leave."

For a moment, nothing happened.

Lucky Joe resumed breathing, lightly.

The work boots that were three feet from his head, in the aisle along the south wall, took a step backward.

"You are welcome to come in this house, during normal religious hours," Father O'Grady said. "Or at any time for prayer. But not for hide-and-seek."

Shortly, Lucky Joe heard the double wooden front doors squeak as they opened and closed. When the silence was absolute, he waited yet. The door at the side of the altar remained open. Lucky Joe heard no sound at all. He wondered what happened to Father O'Grady. When he was sure everyone was gone, he eased himself out from underneath the pew and rose up on his knees, peering over the back of the pew toward the front of the church.

There he saw the priest, on his knees, in front of the altar.

Slowly, Lucky Joe raised himself higher and slid back on the bench pew. Although he thought he moved in total silence, Father O'Grady turned his head and looked at him.

"Your friends are gone," Father O'Grady said.

"I'm sorry, Father, to be in God's house, at an inappropriate time."

"Were those friends of yours, those men who were looking for you?" Father O'Grady asked.

"Not tonight, Father. I feared for my life."

CHAPTER SIXTEEN

Father O'Grady rose from his knees and moved to the pew in front of where Lucky Joe was seated. He laid his arm on top of the pew back and turned his head toward Lucky Joe. The light from the open door at the side of the altar illuminated his face.

"Were you hiding?"

"Yes," Lucky Joe said without hesitation. In the ambience of the church and in the presence of the priest, Lucky Joe felt he could speak absolute truth, as he understood it.

"Why are they after you?"

"It is a complicated issue. They think I am being reckless with the tribe's money."

"Are you?"

"I believe I am a visionary. They trust ink-on-paper. I have a vision. My vision is a return to our traditional way, Father. That may not set well with you. I believe that the traditions of my people are the most satisfying explanation of life for us. They might not be satisfying to you. But they are satisfying to me. I believe in harmony with the spirits. Perhaps that is close to your God."

"Perhaps," Father O'Grady said. "Why is that vision causing people to chase you?"

"They think I am spending the tribe's money in a way that is not customary. They think somehow I am benefiting from it.

MAGIC LANCE

But they're wrong. I am not benefiting from it in any way, other than I'm being paid to do a job. It is for the good of the tribe."

"What job are you doing?"

"We are buying land with the Magic Lance profits. It is economic diversification. We are getting full value for the money we are spending. Instead of having ink-on-paper, in those bank statements we get every month, we are going to own land."

"You mean you are going to have land assets, instead of bank account assets?"

"Yes."

"And that is the reason they are chasing you?"

"Yes."

"They would rather have money in the bank than land."

"Yes."

Father O'Grady rubbed his chin with his left hand. He had focused the issue, as Lucky Joe understood it, but the focus didn't explain to him why a group of men would be after Lucky Joe.

"Was there some special reason you came in the church?"

"To get away," Lucky Joe said. "They were going to get me. I'm not sure if they were going to beat me up, or kidnap me, or kill me. They think I am squandering the tribe's money on land options, and they think we were unjust with Velasquez and Abeita."

Father O'Grady sat serene in the diffuse light of the church sanctuary.

"We cancelled their grazing allotments and their casino per capita." Lucky Joe was uncomfortable in the silence of the church. "Because they opposed us before the tribal council. We needed money to buy ranch land. They opposed us. They said we already have enough land."

Father O'Grady knew how to listen.

"They were chasing me from the plaza, and this was the first place I found to hide. And I hid under this very pew, and they were looking for me, and you happened to come in, just in time."

"Was it God's intervention?"

"I don't know."

The light in the church sanctuary dimmed. Father O'Grady looked to the door opening. Sam Pichocho entered the sanctuary, followed by three other men. The priest rose quickly and moved to the aisle of the sanctuary, standing between the four men and Lucky Joe.

"This is God's house. There will be no confrontations here," he said.

"This is not your affair," Sam said to the priest. "We will deal with this betrayer of tribal laws in our own way."

"Not in this place of worship," Father O'Grady said. The priest spoke with the confidence of enforceable authority. Every muscle in Lucky Joe's body tensed. Sam took several steps forward. When he attempted to go around Father O'Grady, the priest sidestepped, blocking his way.

"The house of God shall not be an arena for violence," Father O'Grady said. Sam was about to push the priest aside, when one of his accomplices grabbed his arm and pulled him back. "Not now. Not here," the accomplice told him. "There will be another time, another place."

Sam jerked his arm free, but the warning stopped him.

"You are not going to strut around this reservation like a tom turkey," Sam said to Lucky Joe. "There will be another time, and you will not be so lucky." Sam thrust out his chest, turned and departed through the doorway at the side of the altar. His three accomplices followed him.

Lucky Joe had involuntarily held his breath during the confrontation. When the four men departed, he first exhaled, then inhaled a deep breath and fell back onto a pew bench.

MAGIC LANCE

Father O'Grady went to the doorway and peered through, confirming the men were gone. Then he returned to the sanctuary and sat on the pew bench, several feet from Lucky Joe.

The men sat in silence for several minutes, allowing their breathing to return to normal.

"This is a serious matter," Father O'Grady said. "Do you have people who are on your side?"

"Yes, of course. My family supports me. And El Segundo. And the tribal council. And many others. What I am doing is for the good of the tribe. These people are renegades. They are shortsighted. They should be banished."

"That is a most serious punishment," Father O'Grady said. "Like excommunication in the Church."

"They deserve it. You saw how they are, for yourself."

"I believe that they meant to do you harm."

"There is no question of that. Had you not intervened, I might be dead now."

"Not my usual vespers," the priest said.

Lucky Joe considered his circumstances. He decided it was better he remain in the church for a while, in the presence of Father O'Grady. Later, he would decide how best to exit Our Lady of Sorrows.

"Are you a member of this parish?"

"Yes, Father."

"As you probably know, I'm new here, so I don't know everyone. And I'm not here to judge you, but you seem to be troubled. Does this have anything to do with your trying to reconcile Grey Piñon traditional beliefs and the beliefs of the church?"

Lucky Joe was silent. The question made no sense to him.

The two men sat in silence for a few moments.

"Our beliefs are not hostile to yours," Lucky Joe said at last. "It seems that your beliefs are hostile to ours."

"We know true salvation comes only from Jesus Christ through Grace," Father O'Grady said. "You start with faith, deny yourself and the pleasures, honors and things of this world, and abide with God and follow His will only. And He will abide in you, and you in Him. The Cross separates you from the old self and the world, and is the gateway to the new Adam and eternal life. We believe that Jesus Christ and the Holiest of All is the true salvation. Jesus is your high priest in the presence of God."

"Father, you may have saved my life tonight. For that I am grateful." Lucky Joe's thoughts flowed back through all the discussions he had heard all his life among the tribal elders, about the difficulty of accommodation between the Indian ways and traditions and the demands of the church. He himself remained ambivalent. He trusted the traditions and the ways of the elders; he also felt a kinship and security with the teachings of the church.

"I would like to save your life for eternity," Father O'Grady said. "That is the true salvation."

"If God gets me out of my difficulties, I may agree with you. And if that happens, Father, I promise that I will see that you have the biggest Catholic church in this state, right here on the Grey Piñon Reservation. This I swear."

CHAPTER SEVENTEEN

As weeks passed, Lance and Jan Burnett reached their own personal accommodation. While it was not what Lance wanted, commuting from Sierra City to the Three V Ranch was viable. Jan regained her former job at the Sierra City elementary school. Lance worked at the ranch during the week, came to the apartment on Friday afternoon, and returned to the ranch early Monday morning. On the weekend, he hired a young man to come by the place and take care of daily chores, including feeding Pepper and Nugget.

Lance was somewhat embarrassed about his new lifestyle, and he discussed the subject reluctantly with his mother and father. To his surprise, they were sympathetic with his situation, were supportive of his marriage with Jan, and did what they could to encourage their son to keep the marriage together and the ranch operating. Lance thought his parents were the last of an age, the last of a frontier mind-set who sought no outside help, who were flexible, who did what worked, abandoned what didn't work and kept things simple, without a complicated system of rules that had to be observed. He thought of that mind-set, that simple, faithful attitude, which did not focus on a violation of laws.

He wanted to maintain their confident, optimistic faith that things would work out if a person's will were properly aligned with the will of the Almighty.

HAL SIMMONS

Jan was happy with the new arrangement. She gave all indications she could live with their new life style for the long term. After four and a half days of separation, Friday and Saturday nights were passionate ones in their young marriage. On Friday nights, they usually went to the Yucca steakhouse for dinner. Lance's one regret was that he was paying a hefty fee for a porterhouse steak when he could get a better one from his own butchered cows for next to nothing.

"You pay for the atmosphere," Jan assured him. Typically, they would see half the people they knew in Sierra City. One evening, three months after the accident at the abandoned silver mine, Jan and Lance were at the steakhouse when a fashionable group of people entered. Lance's eyes expanded slightly. In the middle of the group, he saw two people he knew. Scooter Jones and Lightning McClain were talking loudly and laughing. Immediately in front of them were several big city, young businessmen, and three stylish young women. A low profile, large-stature figure, clearly the person toward whom the whole group gravitated, came in toward the end of the entourage. Although he had never seen him before, Lance knew without asking that this was the man everyone in the county talked about—Big Bob McCoy.

Jan and Lance were seated at a table in the front of the dining area, not far from the salad bar.

As the group streamed by, it was like a passenger train going through a railroad crossing. Lance and Jan were impressed by the outstanding good looks of the young business types and the fashion model appearances of the young women. Scooter Jones glanced in their direction. His eyes squinted and the sides his mouth turned down as he passed. For a split second, Lance looked straight into the eyes of Lightning McClain. Her eyes flashed from Lance, to Jan, and back to Lance, in a millisecond. There was the slightest expression of recognition, and without

MAGIC LANCE

hesitation she continued into a back room, reserved for private groups. She didn't look back. Lance felt an impassioned impulse. He couldn't take his eyes off her figure as she disappeared into the adjoining room. His eyes returned to his bread and butter plate.

"And who might that be?" Jan asked, as the party disappeared.

"Who might who be?"

"That's not your average Sierra City tourist group," Jan said. "Do you know who they are?"

"Looks to me like the Cascade Ranch group. I've never met him, but I'll bet that one guy at the end was Big Bob McCoy. He has the look."

"What about the others?" Jan said. "That looked like a bunch of people out of a Hollywood movie."

"That big guy in the cowboy hat, Scooter Jones," Lance said. "Manages the Cascade. Takes himself serious."

"What about the others though. They looked like movie stars."

"Beats me," Lance said. "I've never seen most of them before. They don't look like ranch hands, that's for sure."

Lance knew Jan suspected something had captivated his attention. He did not think she knew what it was, but he knew that she knew something was in the air.

With the presence of Lightning McClain, Lance thought, how could you not know something was in the air.

During the evening a number of couples came by Jan and Lance's table, some who knew Jan from the school system, some who knew Lance from the ranching business. In the intervals, Jan and Lance had a lot of catching up to do. Jan brought Lance up-to-date on her activities in the school system, and her visits with his parents. Lance brought Jan up-to-date on ranch operations.

Later that evening, after Lance asked for the check, the Cascade Ranch group filed out from the adjoining room. Jan's back was to the aisle, where the group was exiting. She didn't see Lightning point to Lance before exiting the restaurant. The person to whom she gave direction came to the Burnett table.

"Lance Burnett," the man said. When Lance gave a positive response, the man extended his hand. "Bob McCoy," he said. "Guess we're neighbors." He turned to Jan. "Bob McCoy, ma'am," he said.

Lance and Jan didn't know what to say. Big Bob McCoy was an international celebrity, a person whom governors, presidents and movie stars entertained.

And here he was, standing before Lance and Jan Burnett, in Sierra City, in the Yucca steakhouse, extending his hand.

An awkward silence followed.

"With your permission, I'd like to drop over for a visit," Big Bob said. "I don't get a chance to talk to my neighbors that often. You willing to visit?"

"Sure," Lance said, breaking an awestruck silence. "Drop over any time."

"Mrs. Burnett, it was a pleasure," Big Bob said, turning to Jan. In an instant, he was gone. As he reached the aisle, Lance noticed two well-built men, in sport coats, fall in behind him. Although it was the first time Lance had ever seen the two men in Sierra City, there was no doubt in his mind that they were bodyguards.

CHAPTER EIGHTEEN

Monday morning, Lance's mind was swirling. He was driving up Quail Run Creek, on the lookout for cattle, keeping an eye on Pepper and Nugget in the back of the truck, and looking for mule deer, turkey, elk and coyotes, while seeing mainly cottontail rabbits.

The weekend was a blur. He was infatuated with Jan. He could not control his passionate thoughts of Lightning. It was impossible to have two women. Of that he was certain. And yet, that is exactly what he wanted. He wanted Jan to be the mother of his children, to be his life's companion. And he knew his passion was charged by Lightning. That afternoon at Chloride Springs, if he could relive that brief time with her at the pool, he would grab it in a moment.

This morning he was checking water sources. There were isolated pools in Quail Run Creek. That meant his cows and calves could afford to spread out. At the windmill, there was a full tank. No need for cattle to bunch. Lance was aware that conservationists would love to get a picture of his cattle bunched by the stream, to lend evidence to their accusations cattle were overgrazing and ruining the stream banks. He was pleased when he saw his Brangus and Herefords spread out along the canyon. Smart cows, Lance said to himself. After all, he had told them many times not to bunch up where the environmentalists could get a picture of them. At least they were following instructions. He snickered to himself. A hundred and fifty years earlier, people living in this canyon worried about renegades stealing their cattle or attacking them at their cabin. And here he was, wondering if some citified do-gooder would sneak onto the ranch with a camera and photograph his cattle bunched at the stream.

Not exactly the Wild West, Lance thought, as he reached the trailhead.

He remembered how exciting it had been on the afternoon he brought Lightning McClain to this same location. Today, all was quiet. A light wind blew through the canyon, whispering in the pine needles. There was no human activity. Almost total silence prevailed, broken by the occasional chatter of a squirrel or the twitter of a bird.

Lance's mind was blank as he drove back down Quail Run Creek. He was a spectator in nature, neither adding nor subtracting.

When he reached the upper end of the cactus flats, he saw a Cascade pickup truck parked at the lower end; and a second pickup parked twenty-five yards behind. Without giving it a thought, he knew the first truck belonged to Big Bob McCoy, and the second truck would be occupied by Scooter Jones or a bodyguard, or both.

Lance was flattered a man of Big Bob's celebrity and reputation would seek him out. Of course, he knew what Big Bob wanted—the Three V, and not because it was a good spread but because it happened to adjoin the Cascade.

When he passed the trailing pickup, he saw it was driven by the bodyguard. No Scooter Jones. At the first pickup, he was surprised to see Big Bob was driving, and he was alone. Lance parked his pickup even with Big Bob's and walked around the front of the truck to the driver's door.

"Morning," he said.

MAGIC LANCE

"Morning," Big Bob replied. "Got time to talk?"

"Sure." Lance walked a few feet alongside his own truck bed, and put his hand on Pepper and Nugget, giving them assurance all was okay.

Big Bob slid out of his truck. At the steakhouse, Lance had not noticed Big Bob was three or four inches taller than himself, and about 18 inches rounder in the waist. Lance guessed his age in the late fifties or early sixties.

The two men shook hands. Big Bob leaned back and put both elbows on the side of his truck and the heel of one boot up on the back tire.

"Nice land you got here," Big Bob said. "I got some just like it."

"You got a lot just like it. This place is a peanut compared to your place."

"That may be, but you can do just about everything on your place that I can do on mine. And you got a mineral springs. I haven't got that."

"It's a good spot," Lance said. He immediately wondered if Lightning told Big Bob about their outing at the springs. She was sure to have given him a report about her inquiry regarding the Three V.

"Word's out that the Indians are picking up a lot of ranches around here," Big Bob said. "You heard much about that?"

"They asked me if I wanted to sell. I told 'em it wasn't for sale."

Big Bob raised his eyebrows and pushed out his lips. "Haven't made me any offers yet. Probably know better."

Big Bob had brown hair speckled with gray, a sharp nose and a lean face in spite of the fact he was carrying about fifty pounds more than he needed. He wore a Western shirt, khaki-colored jeans and alligator boots. His clothes showed no sign of ranch work.

"I'm glad your place is not for sale. I wouldn't mind buying it myself, as I'm sure my pretty young ranch manager told you.

I'd rather this land stay in private hands. If the Indians buy it, it'll be no different than government land."

"Yeah, that's about the way I see it." Lance reached back and patted Nugget on the head, to settle him.

"These Indians are making big bucks on the casinos," Big Bob said. "They got so much money now, they're starting to get a little mischievous."

"How's that?"

"Just buying up ranches. They got so much money, they're ignoring economics. Paying whatever a rancher wants. Pretty tempting for a lot of people who are hard up for money."

Lance immediately thought of his own mortgage payment. He was ninety days overdue now, and he was glad Jan wasn't at the ranch to get the telephone calls or letters from the mortgage company.

"It's a way of life out here," Lance said. "Hard to put a figure on that."

"That's exactly the way I see it. And I fully admit I'm not out here enjoying it the way you are. I wish I were. But then, if I was working out here, I wouldn't have been able to buy the ranch in the first place."

Lance smiled, and looked off up the road.

"Lightning says you're a man I ought to hire, if you have any interest."

The statement took Lance off guard. He anticipated Big Bob might make him an offer on the ranch. He did not anticipate Big Bob might offer him a job.

"I'm in the market for some new properties. If I pick some up, I might need a new person to run 'em."

"What are you interested in," Lance asked.

"If you mean what properties, yours was my first choice, but if that's not for sale, I'm going to be looking first for adjoining

MAGIC LANCE

properties to the Cascade. If I get some of those, I might continue the expansion."

"Sounds like you may be running the Indians some competition," Lance said.

"You got that right. Before it's over, this Indian land grab thing is going to be a big issue. It isn't going to be long before the county commissioners realize that all the ranches the Indians are buying are going to go off the tax rolls. And if they get enough ranches, county government is going to be out of business. I don't think that's what Congress intended when it gave 'em all these gambling rights. And I don't think the state had that in mind when they signed those gambling compacts twenty-five years ago. 'Course, all that's coming up for reconsideration pretty soon up in Capital. A lot of people are starting to get concerned about it. But in the meantime, the tribes are buying up a lot of land. They're trying to cover their tracks, but the word's leaking out. And once they get the land, if they do, we'll have a hell of a time getting it back. They'll suddenly discover they have a lot of sacred mountains on it. Or sacred rock drawings. Stuff like that. Hell, they may even try to condemn your place, to get their sacred hot springs."

"I've never heard anybody claim that springs was sacred," Lance said.

"Don't hold your breath. These aren't the same Indians we were dealing with before. Now they got lawyers and politicians and all kinds of people working for 'em. It's a different ball game out there, you can bet on that."

"It doesn't matter to me, 'cause I'm not selling."

"Man, am I glad to hear that. There are a lot of people saying yes to offers that don't make economic sense. I can't say I really blame 'em."

"Maybe you ought to see what they'd pay for the Cascade," Lance said.

"I'm with you. The Cascade is not for sale. I'm buying... not selling."

"I'm not buying or selling," Lance said.

"If you ever get to the point where you do want to sell, give me a call. I'll meet any offer those Indians are making and I'll add ten per cent to their offer. Fortunately, I can afford to be as uneconomical as they are."

"I don't know what I'd do, if I weren't ranching," Lance said. "Ranching is all I know."

"I'd be interested in having you work for me," Big Bob said. He laughed. "Hell, if you sold me your ranch, you could be the foreman of it."

"I'm not following that."

"If I expand with some new ranches, I'll need someone to run 'em. You might end up being the manager of this place, along with some others."

"What about Scooter? I thought he's your manager."

"Scooter. He's got his hands full running the Cascade. He'll stay with that. This expansion I'm thinking of will be a totally new operation. If you sold the Three V, that would be the first piece of a bigger pie. As soon as I got it, I'd need someone to run it. And not Scooter Jones."

"You know, I'm not living out here full time right now. I live in town on the weekends. My wife got hurt in a mine accident, and I'm staying in town to be with her several days a week."

"That doesn't sound like a problem," Big Bob said. "If there are several ranches, you might be better off being in a central location."

"If I ever get to that point, I'll give you a call."

MAGIC LANCE

"Even if you don't sell the Three V, if you want to talk about coming to work for me, drop on over. You can get me through the Cascade office, any time."

Lance and Big Bob talked about the chances for rain, the price of cattle, and the problem with range weeds.

When Big Bob took his leave, Pepper and Nugget gave him a barking send off. Lance watched him drive past the second pickup, which promptly turned around and followed him up the road.

Lance wondered what it would be like working for Big Bob. Stories abounded that he would fight you for a nickel. He also had the money and the power to do whatever he wanted, when he wanted. Working for that kind of organization would be 180 degrees off what Lance did.

He knew the idea of working for the Cascade organization would be attractive to Jan. A regular job with salary and benefits. In any case, he didn't own the Three V; his parents did. And even if he eventually inherited it, he would own only a third, with his brother and sister. He was glad he didn't tell Big Bob that. If he had, Big Bob no doubt would contact his mother and father, and make them an offer.

As he leaned against the truck, pondering the situation, he decided he didn't like the idea of selling the Three V, and he didn't like the idea of working for someone else. This place was his, just like the Cascade belonged to Scooter and Lightning.

There was no way he was going to give it up, and there was no way the Religious Land Trust, or Big Bob McCoy, or anyone else was going to make him.

CHAPTER NINETEEN

Earl Wallace called before he came out to the Three V Ranch. Lance suspected Earl had some new purchase proposal to make, but he thought there was no harm in hearing what people were offering. Even if he were three mortgage payments in arrears, it made him feel better to hear that the ranch was worth more than the mortgage balance.

When Earl arrived, the two men sat in the kitchen and drank coffee. Earl talked about their former football days at Sierra City High School. Earl had played left tackle and Lance was a running back. "Remember Coach Simms," Earl reminisced. "He wasn't that big, but he was a hell of a fighter. When he got mad, even McCormick was afraid of him." McCormick was the Wildcat's center, and he outweighed Simms by seventy-five pounds. Earl and Lance had to laugh when they remembered Simms, who recently had retired.

Earl asked Lance if he would take him to the hot springs. The Religious Land Trust still was interested in the property even though Earl had told them it wasn't for sale. They had asked him to inspect the hot springs, which held special significance for them. Earl said he needed to see the springs so he could tell his client he had inspected it and what its condition was. He wasn't going to go there without getting Lance's advance permission. Lance obliged and the two men drove to

MAGIC LANCE

the trailhead in Earl's four wheel drive SUV. Nugget and Pepper rode inside by the tailgate. On the way to the site, Earl told Lance the Land Trust was willing to pay above the going market rate for the ranch.

"I think if you hit them with a high figure, maybe like five hundred thousand dollars, they just might pay that."

"How much is that an acre?"

"Six hundred and twenty-five."

"What did they pay for Peterson's place?"

"Four hundred and seventy-five."

Lance made no reply and changed the subject. When they reached the trailhead, they parked the SUV and released Pepper and Nugget. They took only a few steps from the vehicle when Lance spotted his top bull, Igor, grazing about twenty-five yards upstream. Igor stood close to the ground and weighed almost two thousand pounds. For several years he had served the ranch's breeding operation in fine style. When he saw Lance and Earl start in his direction, he snorted and flexed his thick neck muscles, raising his head.

"That bull all that friendly?" Earl asked, halting in his tracks.

"He bears watching," Lance said. "I haven't had any trouble with him lately, but he can be ornery."

Igor stroked his front hoof on the ground and flicked his ears forward. His tail swished to and fro.

"I don't like the looks of that," Earl said, starting to move off to his right. "Maybe we better go back to the truck."

"If you want to see the springs, we've got to go around him," Lance said. "Come on, let's see what he does."

Earl fell back several more feet and let Lance take the lead, walking parallel to the path but several yards off of it. He moved close to Lance as they walked, keeping Lance between himself and the massive animal.

Igor took a couple of steps in their direction, his head erect. His heavy horns went out a distance from his skull and then curved upward before reaching a point. When Igor advanced, Earl instinctively jumped back from Lance, and shouted "Hey."

That quick movement and sound was all Igor needed. It was like a bugler had sounded: Charge!

Igor picked up speed, moving straight at them. Lance held his position and bent his knees, ready to bolt. Earl had no such hesitation. The instance he saw Igor coming, he started a run-for-your-life toward the SUV. At that instant, Nugget and Pepper came from out of the bushes and went straight for Igor, barking and snapping at the bull's rear legs. Igor was momentarily distracted by the dogs, but quickly re-focused on the fleeing Earl. The bull literally shook the ground when he took off in pursuit. Lance saw the danger Earl was in and started yelling and ran after Igor, thinking he could cause him to swerve. Without thinking, Lance grabbed hold of Igor's tail and dug in his boot heels, trying to slow the animal down. Instead, Igor drug Lance off his feet, and a dozen yards through the trail head meadow before Lance let go. Earl got to the SUV and reached for the door handle, with Igor close upon him. When he realized how close Igor was, Earl abandoned the door and circled the vehicle, thinking he could corner faster than Igor. The bull made one pass but missed his target by several feet. Earl ran to the far side of the vehicle.

With the charging bull, Earl's panic running and Lance's being drug along the meadow holding onto Igor's tail, Pepper and Nugget were confused as to what they should do. At one point when Earl circled the SUV and appeared to head back to where Lance was picking himself up, they decided Lance was in need of protection. Thereupon, both dogs attacked Earl. Snarling and growling, Nugget bit Earl on the back of his right thigh, and

Pepper bit him near the ankle. He screamed at both of them and flailed his arms, keeping one eye on Igor as he did so.

Dust was flying in the melee. Lance jumped up and ran to Earl's rescue, calling off Nugget and Pepper. By the time he got the dogs under control, Igor had taken a standing position on the far side of the SUV and was a spectator to the action. He scraped his front hoof on the ground, and then turned and trotted back down the road.

Earl brushed himself off, and rubbed the back of his thigh and ankle where Nugget and Pepper had made their mark. There were teeth marks, but no blood.

"Do these dogs have rabies shots?" Earl asked.

"Yeah, they're good," Lance answered. "If you hadn't started running, I think we would have been all right. Are you okay?"

"I think so," Earl said. "That's a mean-ass bull. And these dogs aren't any better."

"Igor gets that way every so often. I'm not sure what ticks him off. Most of the time you can walk right up to him, and he's okay. Obviously, he wasn't in a good mood today."

Lance and Earl resumed their walk to the hot springs. After they looked around at the hot pool, Earl brought up some additional options for a sale of the ranch. He suggested Lance might be able to sell part of the ranch. Lance said it barely was economical to operate with eight hundred acres and the U.S. Forest Service grazing leases. Earl asked Lance how much he owed on the ranch. Lance told him he didn't want that information out on the street. Having made no headway on a sale proposal, Earl then suggested that maybe they could work out some kind of land trade, where the Religious Land Trust would buy another ranch, better than the Three V, and then trade that ranch to Lance in a tax free-exchange. That way, Earl said, Lance could have a better ranch and the Religious Land Trust could get the land they wanted.

"Who is the Religious Land Trust," Lance asked finally. "We both know it's the Indians, and they're just using a name cover. Isn't that what it is?"

Earl confessed that was the arrangement. He said the Grey Piñons were particularly interested in the hot springs, because it held some traditional or religious significance for them. That's why they were putting so much pressure on him to get a sale price.

"Surely, there's some price tag you can put on it," Earl said. "At some dollar figure, you got to change your mind. Think it over, and come up with something. I don't care what it is. Just so I can tell them I got an offer."

"What do you get out of it," Lance asked.

"Real estate commission—and the Indians will pay all of it. You don't have to pay any commission out of your part."

"How much do you get?"

"Usual, ten per cent. I won't net that. I got some pay backs to give. Probably closer to six per cent."

"You mean some kickbacks?"

"That's about it. Nothing I can discuss."

Lance shook his head.

In the open area by the hot springs, Earl went over and stood by the three fallen pine branches that had composed the tri-pod, on top of which Segundo had placed Lightning McClain's belt. He pushed the branches around with his boot, and looked around the area.

As the two men walked back to the SUV, Lance reached down and patted Nugget and Pepper. The two dogs had a dislike for Earl Wallace.

"That hot pool is pretty secluded," Earl said. "Ever get any skinny-dippers up here?"

"Occasionally," Lance replied.

He wondered if that question was the real reason Earl Wallace wanted to come up and see the hot spring, to see if Lance would admit or even brag he was the man running with the young lady with the bare legs. If that were his purpose, then Earl Wallace must have been one of the three men that he and Lightning saw through the trees. And if that were his purpose, then Earl lied to him about the Indians wanting Earl to come up and inspect the hot springs. If Earl was one of those three men, it also might explain why Nugget and Pepper disliked him; they had come upon him before at about the same place. Lance routinely was suspicious of anyone Nugget and Pepper did not like.

His next thought was whether Earl was going to say that blackmail was part of the purchase price for the ranch.

CHAPTER TWENTY

On Friday evening, Lance and Jan went to a restaurant owned and run by a local woman and her daughter, located in a near-ghost town in a wide canyon several miles from Sierra City. The place had been a stage stop in the 1880s and a retail hub for ranchers and miners. Now, only a general store and the restaurant remained, along with an art gallery and curio shop. The restaurant dining room was rectangular and about the size of a single car garage. A kitchen doglegged off the dining room. Six square tables filled the dining room and were covered with red and white checkered table clothes. Red fabric curtains covered three windows and the glass center in the entry door. Tourists always were surprised to see the newspaper restaurant reviews that were framed and hung on the dining room walls. Despite its postage stamp size, total absence of five-star decor and rustic surroundings, the Carreta Café was a favorite among journalists.

Jan and Lance each ordered cheese enchiladas on blue corn tortillas, with red and green chile, a combination favored over in New Mexico. Lance knew Mrs. Lucero had come from New Mexico many years earlier and apparently had family roots in the Sierra City area.

While awaiting their meal, Lance casually mentioned that Big Bob McCoy made him a couple of offers: one to buy the Three V, and another to hire him as a ranch manager.

MAGIC LANCE

As expected, Jan's eyes expanded.

"Oh, that's wonderful, Lance," she said, raising her right hand. Almost immediately, she dropped her hand back to the table top.

Both waited to see what the other was going to say.

"Tell me about it," Jan said.

"That's about it. You know how he came by the table the other night at the steakhouse. He followed up on it. When I came back to the house the other day, he was parked there at cactus flats. Along with his bodyguard."

"Bodyguard," Jan said. "Isn't that a bit melodramatic out here?"

"He's big bucks. I guess they have to be careful."

"How much did he offer for the ranch?"

"Didn't get there. He said he's heard the Indians are buying up a lot of ranches. Said he was in the market for more land himself. And since the Three V adjoins the Cascade, he'd like to get the first shot at it, if it's for sale."

The café owner's daughter brought two hot plates, each generating a wisp of steam off the enchiladas, pinto beans and fried rice. A red plastic basket full of crispy, puffed-up sopapillas and a pitcher of honey were placed in the center of the table.

"Isn't that exciting," Jan said, resuming the conversation.

"Interesting," Lance said. "'Course, it's not our ranch. It belongs to mother and dad."

"Yes, but they at least ought to know about it. Have you told them?"

"Told them what?"

"That there's an offer on the ranch." Jan flashed a frown.

"It's only an offer," Lance said. "It doesn't mean we're interested in selling."

Jan cut hard into the enchilada and stiffened her spine.

"Do you want to sell?" Lance asked.

"Yes," Jan said, without hesitation.

Lance's shoulders drooped. He looked right into his plate.

"Lance, I'm sorry. It's not my ranch to sell. If you want to keep the Three V, that's fine with me."

Lance revived a half smile.

"You didn't mention the other part. He talked about making me a ranch manager, but he didn't make any formal offer on that."

"You mean manager of the Cascade Ranch?"

"No, not that. Jones would still be the manager of the Cascade. Big Bob was talking about managing some new ranches he wants to buy, including the Three V. He even said I might be able to live in Sierra City, and work the ranches out of a central location."

"That would be wonderful." Jan took a bite of enchilada, and a swallow of coffee.

"You aren't going to do it, are you?"

Lance looked deep into his wife's eyes. The sides of his mouth turned up on each side, and his eyes glistened.

They looked directly in each other's eyes for a moment.

Lance made no verbal answer. Jan did not push the question.

On the drive back to Sierra City, Lance thought of the letter he received earlier in the day from the mortgage company. It did not say the company was filing a foreclosure action but it demanded he call the office at once to discuss the account. Lance had gotten a similar letter on two previous occasions. When he called the mortgage office on the two earlier letters, they wanted to know why he was late on the payments, and what his plans were to get things caught up. He told them he would try to get some calves to market in the next thirty days, and try like blazes to get the payments caught up. That type of conversation bought him thirty days. On the two previous occa-

MAGIC LANCE

sions, he made good. Tonight, he was not so sure. He would make the same call Monday morning, and ask for thirty days, but if the price of cattle dropped much lower, he would be in deep trouble with his financial obligations. With his mind focused on his financial problems, Lance had little to say to Jan.

When they entered their apartment at the Desert Palms, Jan went to the telephone and pushed the "play" button on the answering machine. A strong country voice asked for Lance Burnett. The man gave his name, which Jan did not recognize.

The state Cattle Growers Association needed a witness in Capital on Tuesday, the voice said, to tell legislators what's happening to small ranchers who are getting whipsawed by low cattle prices and rising costs—and especially what all this is doing to their personal lives and why so many are having to sell to the Indian tribes that are buying up all the ranches with their federal- and state-sanctioned gambling money.

"We've heard you've been having a tough time of it, and you're getting offers to sell," the voice said. "And you've had some tough personal matters to deal with. I hope we can count on you. Give me a call as soon as you can." The speaker left his name and number.

"What do you make of that?" Jan asked.

"I don't know," Lance said. "Why would they be calling me?"

Jan pressed the play button and listened to the message a second time.

"What is he talking about, 'tough personal matters'?" Jan asked.

"Beats me," Lance said.

A wave of anxiety surged through his mind. Could this have anything to do with the mortgage company? Or worse, his relationship with Jan, or his outing at the springs with Lightning McClain?

CHAPTER TWENTY-ONE

On Tuesday morning, Lance threw his suitcase containing a clean set of clothes and shaving kit into the pickup and headed to Capital. It was a four-hour drive up the Interstate. Lance's agricultural eye watched every change in the grass the State Highway Department people had planted along the roadway shoulder. Each time he saw a bush or tree or new grass, he tried to identify it. The closer he got to Capital, the more wildflowers appeared along the road shoulders. Lance knew the increased water flow off the pavement when it rained or snowed gave added moisture to the first twenty feet off the shoulder. Beyond the right-of-way fences on either side of the Interstate, the natural landscape prevailed, and it was dry.

As he pulled into the capital city, he thought of the history of the state. No doubt several centuries before, Spaniards all the way from Mexico City were driving their wheel-squeaking carreta wagons along this same roadway. And the local Indian tribes no doubt cringed at the loud, eerie squeaking of those wheels. They knew that raucous noise meant the coming of more outsiders.

Lance drove directly to the government complex, found a parking place only two blocks from the Capitol Building, and headed directly to the legislative hearing rooms. Notwithstanding his love of open spaces, Lance found excitement in appearing before an audience. For most people, public appearances and public speaking were a dread. For Lance, they were exciting. While at State University, he participated on a debate team for one semester and on occasion made class presentations on agricultural subjects. The thought of appearing before a legislative committee gave him some anxiety pangs, but not enough to suppress his enthusiasm.

In Western attire, including dress cowboy hat and clean boots, Lance bore a wholesome image. He noted how many overweight people plied the halls of the state's legislative building. Lance's lean, muscular body testified to hard, physical work done on a daily basis.

Lance wandered up and down the hallways to locate some of the ranchers who were interested in his appearance as a witness. Shortly, he teamed up with Charles Pharris, the country voice who called him at the apartment. Executive Director of the state Cattle Growers Association, Charles knew his way around the labyrinth of political pathways and state agencies. Almost everyone who passed them in the hall extended a hand or bid Charles a greeting.

After expressing his appreciation for Lance coming up for the hearing, Charles suggested they go to a restaurant next to the legislative building and discuss their strategy. The bill they were opposing, Charles said, had been introduced by about two dozen legislators to extend the present Indian gaming compacts for another ten-year period. If that bill passed, it was clear the small-time ranchers in the state would be history. Even the biggest ranches were starting to sell.

"What's generated all the buying all of a sudden?" Lance asked, as they wove through the lunch crowd at the Olla Restaurant. "I've heard of more ranches selling in the last few months than I've heard of in my entire life."

"We're not sure what's behind it," Charles said. "We know it's happening. Whether its just one tribe, or all of them, or just some rich Indians, we're not sure. They're trying to keep it quiet. But you can't buy millions of acres and keep it too quiet."

"Is that what they're buying. Millions of acres."

"That's it. And they seem to be picking up momentum. They're leveraging money. Buying purchase options, for one year. So they got a year to raise the cash. We have no idea what their ultimate game plan is. The only thing I can figure is they want to get as much land as they can, as fast as they can, at a locked-in price. They must need some time to raise the cash. They're also trying to keep it secret, using different legal entities to make the buys. That worked for a couple of months, but there were so many ranches selling, the title company people kind of figured out what was going on, what the pattern was. Mainly, the buyers' checks were coming from just two banks, even though there were all these different buyer's names. When they started checking with the Secretary of State's office to see who the qualifying parties were, they all turned out to be Indian names, and all the ones they could determine were Grey Piñons. Now we hear about it any time there's a ranch sale and there's an Indian name anywhere in the paperwork."

Lance and Charles took a round table in the corner of the bar area, next to a narrow window that ran from one foot off the floor, to within one foot of the ceiling. The room had a Southwestern motif, red-brick floors, white-washed adobe walls, turquoise blue window curtains and a latilla ceiling between aspen vigas.

Within a quarter hour, a half dozen ranchers joined them, none of whom Lance knew. The talk was about Indian land purchases, the gambling renewal bill, and finally, the light counter punch of Big Bob McCoy.

MAGIC LANCE

"Big Bob is buying, but nothing on the scale of the Indians," Kendall Schlenker reported. Kendall owned a fifty thousand acre ranch next to the Peterson's former place at Seep Springs, and had been contacted by the Grey Piñons. "Those rich guys know how to make it. He's probably buying before the price gets out of hand; then he'll sell and make a few more hundred million."

"What's he buying?" Lance asked.

"Don't know for sure," Kendall said, "but it seems like he's staying in the area around the Cascade. George Stevens, my neighbor, told me he thinks Big Bob is the buyer of the Double Bar over near Copperton. "That's two hundred thousand acres. Paid about a hundred million for it, what I've heard. Five hundred an acre."

"Who's leading this Indian thing?" another rancher asked. "They gotta have somebody telling 'em what to do."

"Advisors," Charles said. "After all these years of gambling money, they got advisors like a cow chip's got flies."

"So what are the odds of these gambling compacts getting renewed?"

"Up for grabs," Charles said. "They're lining up allies. Casino suppliers. They're the big contributors, and they got high-priced lobbyists. They got two dozen representatives to sponsor their bill. Those are political chips they're calling. "

"What about the federal level?" Lance asked. "I heard Senator Walton's starting to talk about what's gone wrong with the Indian Gaming Regulatory Act. It was supposed to provide money for the reservations, like roads and sewer systems... not give 'em so much money they wind up buying up the whole West."

"We've got to work the federal level as hard as the state level," Charles said.

A waitress circled the table, taking lunch orders.

Several state legislators came by, shaking hands and talking to people they knew from their home districts. All the legislators agreed to do what they could to get a fair result on the gambling bill.

"Ain't it great being an elected representative," one of the ranchers said, after the legislators moved on. "Some of their friends are for the bill; some of their friends are against the bill; and they're going to vote with their friends."

A roll of laughter went round the table.

"It's laughable, but it's also serious," Charles said. "If all the ranches in the state go over to the Indians, there isn't going to be any tax base, and these legislators may not have anybody to pay their fat pensions."

"Then they'll sell 'em the state's public land to pay for their retirement," a rancher said.

"What should we do?"

"We have some ideas," Charles said. "The simplest thing to do is not sell your ranch. Easy said, tough to do, when somebody stands there offering you twice what the place is worth."

Lance felt a camaraderie with the Western accents and uncomplicated way of approaching things. Despite the lighthearted analysis, they all knew the situation was getting more serious by the day.

"We have another approach," Charles said. "But keep this quiet," he added in a whisper. Everybody leaned in toward the table.

"We're going to introduce a new bill that would open up gambling all over the state, and the winning proceeds will go to local charities instead of the Indians. We're getting some good initial response. Everybody in town would like to get hold of their own casino, even if they have to give a share to charities. They figure they'll get rich doing it. That approach also may undermine some of the tribe's support, if the suppliers and the

MAGIC LANCE

legislators think there may be a bigger pie they can sink their teeth into. It might not be that good overall, but at least it'll shut off the spigot that's pouring money into private land purchases."

"My read is a lot of city folks and rural too are starting to question how good a deal this gambling really is for the state," Kendall said. "Too many stories about people getting wiped out, losing their families, houses, savings, everything."

"We need to do something," Charles said. "For starters, I need people to go with me next week up to Washington, to make the rounds of the congressmen and senators. We need to give them a first-hand report of what is happening to the ranchers down here. Indian gambling wasn't supposed to support a land grab. Do I have any takers?"

"Who's going to run the ranch?" a rancher asked. "Hell, that's the whole problem. Those Indians got money to burn. We got to work for a living."

"How about you, Lance?" Charles asked. He knew a young rancher in a cowboy hat and boots would make a good impression on Capitol Hill. Lance also had a relaxed presence that would play well in the frantic pace that was standard fare in the world's most powerful city.

"I'd like to go," Lance said, "but I've got the same problem. Who's going to run the ranch and pay the bills while I'm gone?"

Charles waited an appropriate minute.

"There might be some way through that," he said. "If you had financial backing, would you be willing to go?"

"Sure," Lance said, without thinking.

"We'll take a look at it," Charles said.

More legislators came by the table. Several ranchers took their leave, several lobbyists joined the group, and the discussion drifted in a more general direction.

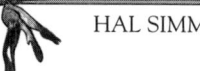

After lunch, when Charles and Lance returned to the legislative building, it sank into Lance's mind what he had agreed to do. A trip to Washington, D. C. was a major change in his routine. Who was going to take care of the Three V? What would Jan say about it, and who would be paying him to do all this?

CHAPTER TWENTY-TWO

Lucky Joe observed how Segundo dealt with Grey Piñon lobbyists in Capital. Generally, Segundo listened when he was in a group. His style was to work behind the scenes. Rarely did he express an opinion in the group setting. It was when he was alone with someone he chose to talk to, that he announced what he wanted done. If what he wanted done was not done, the person responsible was disciplined or dismissed. Segundo rarely showed his displeasure outwardly. When he was displeased, only he knew, until the axe fell.

In the legislative halls and meeting rooms, Lucky Joe was caught up in the excitement of political maneuvering. An atmosphere of self-importance was part of the legislative process; after all, what lawmakers were doing would affect the lives of everyone in the state. How could they not feel important? They considered a budget that ran over ten billion dollars. They set policy for state government. They had plenty of money to run the day-to-day operations of the legislative session. They were treated as wise and important persons by the lobbyists and citizens of the state who came before their committees. They were featured on television and in newspapers on occasion, although not always in a favorable light. Dozens of attractive and energetic young people scurried from office to office, onto the legislative floor and along the halls, doing the tasks their political employers suggested.

Groups from all walks of life mingled in the legislative building during breaks: civil rights advocates, pro- and anti-abortion advocates, spokespersons representing the medical profession, car dealers, ranchers and farmers, lawyers, educators, bankers, city and county government officials, advocates for the disabled and homeless, the news media, police, firemen, transportation lobbyists, oil and gas industry figures, the insurance industry, the tobacco industry, pharmaceuticals, liquor, utilities, and an occasional celebrity artist, movie star, writer or singer. This year, there were numerous representatives of the Indian tribes, including the Grey Piñons and every other tribe in the state that had a gaming compact.

Halfway through the three-month session, renewal of the Indian gambling compacts with the state remained undecided.

Segundo and Lucky Joe correctly predicted a major public backlash against the immense wealth the Indian tribes had built up over the past several decades. Gone was the romantic aura of the past, when there had been a consensus that something had to be done to bring the Indian tribes out of poverty—and to alleviate the guilt feelings of many people who still wrung their hands over the way Indian lands had been ceded to the U.S. government in treaties, and then sold to individuals for homesteading and ranching and farming, or left in government ownership as national forests or state or federal land under the authority of the U.S. Bureau of Land Management.

Most of that guilt complex now was gone. Indians in the state had become so rich that even the guilt-laden advocates realized they had lost their cause. It was hard to be an advocate for poor Indians when those same Indians had a hundred times more wealth than the average guilt advocate.

A feeling of change was in the air. The mixture of forces at work remained complex and the political and social pressures off-setting. Casino suppliers, including the slot machine industry, food and beverage suppliers, maintenance firms, security firms, insurance agents and even utility companies all supported their cash-laden casino customers, but also kept an eye on the possibility that wide-open gambling in the state might provide an even bigger pie for the same services.

Legislators, who stuffed their pockets with campaign contributions, at a minimum, were moving the debate, wanting to show support for their present benefactors but wary of being caught off-guard should the gaming climate change quickly.

And there were outside interests. Although out-manned and outspent, there was the ever-present anti-gaming coalition. There was a hard-to-ignore history of the thousands of people whom gambling had ruined financially. The problem with gambling, anti-gambling coalition advocates told legislators, is that it takes money from a large number of people, often those who can't afford to lose it, and funnels that money into the pockets of a few. And now the chosen few at the bottom of the funnel were so rich, they lived like country club members—no, better than country club members. And a lot of people were destitute because the money from their now-empty pockets had been funneled into the pockets of that wealthy few.

It sounded like an attack on capitalism. The anti-gaming arguments were logical but hardly persuaded people who benefited from the same gambling profits.

Other opponents of gambling joined the morally motivated. Among them now appeared the small ranchers in the state, concerned that their way of life was about to be eliminated—notwithstanding the fact those doing the selling were getting a hefty price for their land.

Then there were pro-gambling interests who opposed a situation that allowed the Indians to get all the gravy. This group included private interests who wanted their own casinos, or at least slot machines in their bars, lounges and tourist resorts. And finally, there were groups who opposed gambling but thought they lacked the political clout to stop it. They proposed to change the rules: either eliminate Indian gambling rights or expand the rights to allow charitable groups to run competing casinos and channel the profits to their causes, such as helping people who had lost everything gambling.

The passion of the contending groups produced a flammable social and political atmosphere.

It was in this atmosphere that Segundo summoned the half-dozen lobbyists in the employ of the Grey Piñons to consider their strategy for the second half of the legislative session. Since the existing Indian gaming compacts in the state were going to expire six months after the end of the session, everyone knew something political had to happen.

Segundo asked their media relations lobbyist, Whitney Fay, for an update.

"There are pros and cons, as always," she said. "We have some favorable comment about the prospect of leaving Indian gaming in place, even if a considerable amount of new gambling is allowed. That may be your best position."

"Can you pass the word that the Indians are going to file a lawsuit against the state if it tries to take their source of income away?" Segundo said.

"Who should they contact?" Whitney asked.

"Lucky Joe Cruz, Grey Piñon," Segundo said.

Whitney looked at Lucky Joe. As best he could, he suppressed his shock at Segundo's statement. "Sue the state," Lucky Joe thought. "Not again. The last lawsuit like that lasted ten years." The Grey Piñons were recognized as the lead tribe on land purchases. Lucky Joe was becoming known as the state's Indian land czar.

MAGIC LANCE

Segundo got an earful from the other lobbyists about the angst and anger over Indian land purchases. Of all the issues involved in the gambling debate, this one galvanized the opposition groups. Even the environmentalists were involved. If Indian tribes got the land, environmentalists would become irrelevant, having no entry rights or legal rights over Indian lands or land uses.

Like a lightning strike, ranchers and environmentalists formed an alliance to oppose Indian land purchases. They knew the money for those purchases was coming from casino profits. With the ranch owners and environmentalists united, they might form a strong coalition with other casino forces, and even the anti-casino forces, to torpedo the Indian gaming compacts. What would happen to gambling in the state if the Indian gaming compacts were not renewed was an open question.

"If you are suggesting that we back off from land purchases, that is not an option," Lucky Joe said. "Not only are we not backing off, we are going to increase our purchase activity. And we need environmentalists to stay with their campaign to cancel ranchers' grazing leases. Just for your information, we are starting to put sizeable amounts of cash into two environmental groups to support them in their grazing lease strategy. You will see the effects of that during the next few months."

"Can't you at least put a hold on new land purchases for the next thirty days, until this gambling pact thing is resolved?" Whitney asked. "One more media story about a big ranch being bought by Indians, and it may kill us on this bill."

Lucky Joe looked subtly in Segundo's direction. Segundo showed no change of expression or gave any indication of his position.

"We will continue to support the environmentalists," Lucky Joe said, "and reassure them that ranch land we acquire is not going to be subject to land development for starter castles and

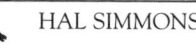

trophy homes. We also are negotiable on the gambling tax split with the state to balance the loss of local taxes on land that is transferred to Indian tribes and taken off the tax rolls. But having said that, I wish to emphasize that the land purchase program still has top priority. You'll have to do the best you can. We'll try to keep any new land purchases quiet, but if we get a chance to pick up a ranch, we're going to pick it up."

Segundo gave the hint of a smile.

CHAPTER TWENTY-THREE

After the meeting with lobbyists, Lucky Joe and Segundo returned to their hotel. In Segundo's room, Lucky Joe sat back in a chair near the window and sighed. He was exhausted. The conflicts involved in the land acquisition plan and the state gaming compact controversy, swirled in his mind. He found no rest, no peace, no confidence, no answer to the mushrooming problems. Most of all, he was concerned so much tribal money now was committed, and the Grey Piñons might not be able to raise the additional sums required. If the state gaming compact was not renewed, and income from the Magic Lance casino stopped, the tribe could be financially obliterated. His fears were not something he wished to express to Segundo.

"We are picking up momentum on ranch purchases," Segundo said. "It is going better than I ever expected."

Lucky Joe nodded.

"You would think that with all this success, we would be getting enthusiastic support from our brothers," Segundo said.

"Some of our brothers are not acting like brothers," Lucky Joe said. "Maybe we shouldn't have gone after Velasquez and Abeita for their opposition. It opened a second front."

"We had no choice," Segundo said. "If you do not cow the opposition early, they will be emboldened. Besides, they got exactly what they deserved. How far do you think we would be if we had to please those two jackasses?" Segundo assumed a formal standing position as though he were about to deliver a majestic speech. "Oh, pardon me, your most royal highness Velasquez, but we're trying to form a Native American state, and we humbly need to seek Your Excellency's permission for the first two hundred and fifty million."

Lucky Joe laughed at Segundo's improvisation. "I'm signing you up at the comedy club."

"We're getting tired," Segundo said, "but we can't afford to take a break. This whole thing is moving too fast now. It will be coming to a head shortly. First the gaming compact matter will be resolved. Then we'll accelerate ranch purchases as fast as we can, without worrying about what anyone else is saying or doing. Once the legislative session ends, there is nothing the state can do to us for awhile, unless they call a special session."

"You were right about that Burnett place," Lucky Joe said. "The Three V was one of the first places we started going after, and we haven't made any progress on it. Do you think we'll ever get it?"

"I had kind of forgotten about it, but now that you mention it, it reminds me that we ought to do something. I may be losing focus. That is not the biggest piece of land we need, but it's the most important and that fact keeps eluding me. Sitting around doing nothing is not going to get it for us."

"What can we do?" Lucky Joe asked.

"I don't know for sure. Let's start with a title search. See who owns the place, see if they owe anything on it. I assume that young couple owns it, but you never know. Let's see if there are any mortgages or liens against it, anything we could use for leverage."

MAGIC LANCE

Lucky Joe took out a spiral paper pad and made a couple of notes on what he was to do. So many orders were getting into his schedule, he found he needed to write himself notes. One of the young ladies at the war room tried to get him to use an electronic note pad. Lucky Joe didn't trust it. There was something about writing on paper that appealed to him more than electronic letters on a palm screen.

"And one more thing," Segundo said, raising his arm and poking his finger into the air. "Remember that afternoon at the hot springs, when those two dogs charged us, and then we saw that half-naked woman running—with that man? What if that guy was the landowner? And what if that woman wasn't his wife? Would that story be worth something to him? Too bad we didn't get a video of it."

"But how do we know whether it was him or not, and who the woman was?"

"Call that real estate agent, Wallace. One way or the other, tell him to find out who the guy was and who the woman was. Tell him it'll be worth a good bonus for him to get that information—a double commission."

Lucky Joe wrote the project down, as he had the others.

"And while we're getting aggressive, write this down. Round up several ranchers who've sold us ranches. Get them up here as witnesses, and say what a good deal we made them, how fair we were, how that extra money they got was put to good use. We want to show these legislators what a good deal these land purchases are for the citizens of this state.

"That's item one. The second thing is to get some environmentalists up here, to testify what good land stewards we Indians are. How it's part of our beliefs to respect Mother Earth. That always plays. And have them say the tribes are environmentally oriented, not dollar-driven."

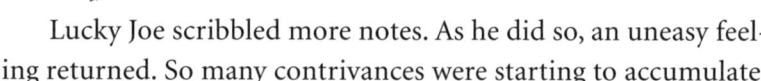

Lucky Joe scribbled more notes. As he did so, an uneasy feeling returned. So many contrivances were starting to accumulate.

Segundo's orders were directions he felt obligated to carry out. But in the deep feelings of his heart, they also were orders that seemed contrary to the will of the spirits that resided within him.

CHAPTER TWENTY-FOUR

On the weekend, Lucky Joe returned to the Grey Piñon Reservation. He wanted to be with his wife Rachel and two children. In Capital, there was an excitement in the legislative atmosphere, a feeling of power, a feeling of control, a feeling of self-importance. It was exhilarating during the day. It was when he lay in bed at night, just before sleep, that Lucky Joe's thoughts were uneasy. There was danger in all this activity, the land purchases, the fate of the gambling compact, the hostility of people who opposed the grand plan. Lucky Joe wondered why any of this was important, why he was involved in it.

He wanted to be with his family, he wanted to enjoy the communal life of the tribe's traditions—the dances, the tribal meetings, the hunts, the camaraderie of his friends of youth. Instead, he was engaged in a foray into the white man's world—the world of power, of acquisitions, of adversarial combat on a wide variety of issues. He acknowledged he was not prepared to give up his position and possessions without a fight. Nobody was going to take his utility vehicle, or his job with the Magic Lance or various positions in the tribe. He knew he should get back to the basics. Perhaps that was the cause of his uneasiness; he was straying from the basics. If he spent more time with his wife and children, with his grandfather and grandmother, with tribal activities, he would re-orient and re-stabilize his spiritual existence. While abstract, he knew innately that he ultimately was not in control of things, that he was subject to forces that were far beyond his comprehension and that were not physically based and not perceived by his physical senses.

On Sunday morning, Lucky Joe went to his grandfather and grandmother's home. Alfredo was sitting in a wooden rocking chair, slowly rocking. His grandmother was in the kitchen, making apple empanadas.

Lucky Joe turned a kitchen chair backwards, and sat down in front of Alfredo.

"How is it?" Alfredo asked.

Lucky Joe shook his head slowly. "It is complicated. There are so many things happening in the Legislature, on the land purchases. It makes my head swim."

Alfredo had a benign smile. "It is well you are young. These things draw much energy from the heart. It is well you are young."

Lucky Joe's grandmother, Maria, came into the room with two hot empanadas on a tray. She offered them to Alfredo and to Lucky Joe. Her smile and eyes told Lucky Joe his presence was her deepest wish.

"You have prepared me well," he said to both grandfather and grandmother. "I will do the best I can. I hope to make you proud of me. If my father and mother had survived, I would wish to make them proud as well."

"You need not do anything to make us proud of you," Maria said. "You are our grandson."

Alfredo strummed his fingers on the arm of the chair.

"You are doing the right thing," Alfredo said. "Few people are able to look at the long term. It is for visionaries and the true leaders to do that. You are one of the true leaders. You must persist. Do not be dismayed. Do not be discouraged. Persevere."

MAGIC LANCE

Lucky Joe licked his lips after munching the empanada. "Any more of those?" he asked Maria. She returned to the kitchen and shortly reappeared with a plate of four empanadas. She offered Alfredo a second helping, and then Lucky Joe.

From his grandparents' house Lucky Joe returned home. Rachel was working on a turquoise necklace in the living room.

"You need better light," Lucky Joe said, looking at the tiny turquoise beads Rachel was stringing. He glanced at the ceiling, imagining how much better the light would be if there were a skylight above Rachel's work bench.

"It's all right," Rachel said. "I can see them."

"Where are Rick and Andrea?"

"Over at the plaza," Rachel said. "They're practicing the corn dance at Olinka's place."

Lucky Joe nodded and smiled.

He sat on the couch against the wall, picked up a magazine and flipped through the pages, without reading anything, and barely looking at the pictures.

"That Velasquez guy was by to see you yesterday," Rachel said. "I don't like him."

"What did he want?"

"He didn't say anything. It was his look, you know. I don't like him."

"He's against our land purchase program. Segundo took away his grazing allotment and casino share. He's out to get me."

Rachel lowered her head closer to the turquoise beadwork, and focused all her energy in her fingers.

"I've been thinking," Lucky Joe said. "I think it might be a good idea if you and the kids went out to California for awhile, to visit your sister. This could get unpleasant around the reservation for a while, especially for us. I can feel bad vibes building. And not just with Enrique Velasquez."

"I've heard some bad things," Rachel said. "They say we're driving fancy trucks, wearing expensive jewelry and all new clothes. And they also say we're putting those ranches in our own names."

"Who's saying that?" Lucky Joe said, tossing the magazine to the other end of the couch.

"Just rumors. But they're mean-spirited. Everybody's saying them."

"That's why I think it's a good idea for you and Andrea and Rick to visit your sister. I've been hearing a few things like that myself."

Rachel moved to the couch and sat next to her husband. "So who do you have something going with, that you want to get me out of the state? I've seen the kind of clothes that Martinez girl is wearing in your office over there. She's saying come-and-get-me, if anybody ever did."

"What Martinez girl?" Lucky Joe asked, pleased his wife had a touch of jealously.

"What Martinez girl? Oh, come on, Lucky. How many Martinez girls are there in your office?"

"You mean Anita?" Lucky Joe asked, with feigned surprise.

"Yes, Anita. As if you didn't know." Rachel snuggled up to Lucky Joe, and kissed him. "You're such a handsome man. You have all these young women running after you."

"Yes, you're right. And you better watch out. I am really in demand, all over the tribe. If you weren't so observant, I'd probably have a lot of romances going on right now."

"Yes, and there would be a lot of frightened young women out there, when I found out about them."

"In that case, I am calling off all of my affairs," Lucky Joe said. And, after a pause… "so that you will go to California."

"There, you see. You said it. You'll do anything to get me out of town, with our children, so you can play around."

"Does that mean you're not going?"

"The reason I'm not going is because what you are doing is important for the tribe, and my duty as your wife is to love and support you in everything you do. So yes, I am not going to California. And neither are Rick or Andrea. For better or for worse, we are going to be here with you and support you. And you will win. How can you fail with backing like us?"

Lucky Joe wrapped his arms around Rachel and rolled over with her on the couch, kissing her as he turned.

CHAPTER TWENTY-FIVE

It was not easy for Jan to convince her school principal that she needed two days off to go with her husband to Washington, D.C. That city was a vacation destination, as far as the principal was concerned, and visiting with congressmen and senators is something they all could do when the politicians came to Sierra City during political campaigns.

Nevertheless, Jan prevailed, convincing the principal that family unity was important, even a Christian duty. Her soft eyes and good looks were part of her persuasion.

When the jet plane lowered its flaps and altered power on the final glide into the airport, Jan peered through the window and focused on the Washington Monument, then the Jefferson Memorial, the U.S. Capitol Building and the White House. It was like a postcard. All the patterns on the ground were neat and clean, no rough edges.

From the airport, Lance and Jan took a shuttle to the hotel chosen by the state Cattle Growers Association. It was the Hay Adams.

"Kind of old timey, isn't it," Lance commented as they walked into the lobby.

From their colonial-decorated room on the fifth floor, Lance looked out the window, over Lafayette Park, and right into the windows of the White House.

MAGIC LANCE

"Long way from Quail Run Creek, isn't it?" Lance said, turning to unpack his suitcase.

"It's wonderful," Jan said. "Let's move here."

Lance laughed. While he suppressed a reply, he knew this was the last place in the world he would want to live.

In the late afternoon, Jan and Lance walked across Lafayette Park. A half-dozen street people solicited handouts. Their presence and entreaties caused Jan to inch closer to Lance and place her arm over his.

From Lafayette Park the couple walked completely around the White House, then toward the basin and the Vietnam Veteran's Memorial. At the memorial, Jan gazed at the endless rows of names, each representing a body and soul who perished in the East Asian conflict. She ran her fingers over the carvings. The names looked so familiar, like boys she knew in her neighborhood back home, and at high school and college.

By the time they returned to the hotel, Jan and Lance were ready for a rest. At 6:30 that evening, they were to attend the state Cattle Growers Association dinner, complete with two congressmen and Senator Walton. Hours before the dinner, Jan began to fret about what she was going to wear for the evening. Formal clothes in Sierra City were a rarity, close to nonexistent. She had brought one floor-length black dress, with straps and bare shoulders. She was having second thoughts about wearing it. She asked Lance about it. He told her to wear what she wanted. He reassured her she had good taste. Jan knew well that the black wool crepe dress was the only option, the only formal attire she had.

Lance had a dark Western coat and Western pants, boots and a cowboy hat. He didn't give his attire any thought; he knew he needed to wear a coat, but beyond that, he wanted something comfortable.

Jan spent over an hour before the mirror, working on makeup and hairstyle. Lance flopped down in a sitting chair and watched a television sports channel. Occasionally he got up, walked to the window, pushed back the veil and curtain and looked at the White House.

"Wonder what the president is doing over there?" he said. "Probably getting a hot dog for dinner."

"When you're president of the United States, you have your own chef, and you get more than a hot dog," Jan said. "And you have people wait on you, and they wear stylish clothes."

"Everything you've always wanted," Lance said, leaning over Jan who was seated before the mirror. He kissed her bare shoulders.

"It would be nice for a while," Jan said.

The high ceilings, velvet-covered walls and curtains and paneled columns provided an elegant atmosphere for the hotel dining room. The maitre d' and staff wore tuxedos. Once in the restaurant Jan relaxed, feeling the admiring glances of other diners. Her youthful and svelte figure, the wool crepe dress that clung to it and Lance's tall, lean physique and Western look were enough to draw the attention of people accustomed to wealth and European influences.

In a private room off the main dining area, Lance and Jan found some local folks, all the way from the Blue River Valley. Jan recognized Senator John Walton and his wife from newspaper and television coverage. She wasn't sure, but she thought an older man on one side of the room was the same person who had stopped at their table at the Yucca Steakhouse in Sierra City—Big Bob McCoy.

Charles Pharris came up to them as they walked into the room, greeted them, and after some conversation exchange, suggested they meet one of their congressmen. He told them some of his group had met with most of their representatives and sen-

MAGIC LANCE

ators earlier that day and explained the land situation. Tonight he asked that Lance and Jan bring up the subject again as they visited and thank all their political representatives and their staffs for their consideration of the land issues.

Lance understood the purpose of the trip was to influence the senator and congressional representatives and their staffs about the plight of the small rancher. He and Jan did their best to encourage all the congressional representatives and Senator Walton to support reining in the Indian land purchases. Jan was an ideal social mixer—attractive, informed, good conversationalist, bearer of a strong spirit and an engaging smile.

About sixty people were at the gathering. Lance knew only two of them, Charles Pharris and Big Bob McCoy. He recognized the congressmen and Senator Walton, having seen them on television newscasts and in newspaper photos. Jan and Lance sat at a round table for eight. Two of the couples were ranchers, like themselves, but from other areas of the state. The husband of the third couple was a lobbyist; his wife was an employee at the Library of Congress.

Jan was surprised to see fresh lobster as one of the entrees offered. She pointed it out on the menu to Lance and looked into his eyes. Could she order it?

Lance shrugged. He knew he wasn't paying for dinner at the Hay Adams. Jan ordered lobster. Lance ordered a porterhouse steak, medium rare.

Following dinner, Charles Pharris moved to the speaker's podium and told some light-hearted stories and jokes and then introduced the senator, the congressmen, and many more persons in the audience. Lance and Jan were not among those introduced. Big Bob was. When the spotlight turned to Big Bob, he subtly raised his right hand to acknowledge his introduction. He needed no buildup. He sought no recognition, although he would have noticed its omission. What Big Bob wanted, he got during private audiences in the congressmen' and senators' offices.

As Big Bob lowered his hand to the table, Lance saw a young woman to Big Bob's left. How could he possibly have missed her. He could not take his eyes off her. Finally, she looked in his direction. It was a brief look. Her eyes passed over Lance as though he were a stranger.

How could she do that, Lance thought. Had she forgotten that afternoon at the springs? Lance realized he was staring. He quickly turned to Jan.

"Good lobster?" he asked.

"Yes, it is." Jan rubbed her hand on Lance's leg. "Isn't that Big Bob McCoy over there?"

"Yes, that's him."

Jan dipped a succulent piece of lobster in a cup of melted butter. "Who's that young woman next to him? Certainly not his wife."

"Who's that?"

"The one you were staring at."

"Oh, that one...Judy McClain. She manages the Cascade headquarters buildings."

"She looks like she might manage more than that."

"I wouldn't be surprised."

After dinner the crowd mixed for a while, then broke up and drifted out of the dining area into the hotel lobby. Lance and Jan, after the long flight, the walk around the capitol area and lobster and wine, were ready to go to their room.

Big Bob was still in the dining room when Jan and Lance left. He talked on for a half hour with Senator Walton and the two congressmen.

As he strolled through the lobby he summoned Lightning to his side and raised the subject of the Three V Ranch. It was a

MAGIC LANCE

matter that kept coming to mind and when he saw the young couple in the cowboy hat and the black dress, it reminded him of some things he wanted done.

His list of instructions to Lightning were as follows:

1. Check on the Three V's grazing leases with the U.S. Forest Service and see when they come up for renewal, and check to see if there is any overlapping of leases with the Cascade Ranch that might generate a conflict, anything at all.

2. Run a land title search on the Three V and see who the legal owners are, and whether there are any liens, mortgages, mineral rights or water rights owned by anyone else. If there are, contact the people who hold them and buy them out.

3. Find out how much the Indians are offering for the Three V, assuming an offer has been made.

Lightning was free to work with the Denver office staff and its attorneys to help her get this information. If she had any problems, get back with him.

CHAPTER TWENTY-SIX

From the Hay Adams Hotel in Washington, D.C., Lance and Jan returned to Sierra City. Early Monday morning, Lance returned to the Three V. During those few days in Washington calling on congressmen and senators, Lance blanked out his credit card woes, the late mortgage payments, the cash shortages. Soon the credit card companies would call the house. They are the dregs, Lance thought. They charge you twenty percent interest, and if you're a day late on the payment they self-righteously charge an outrageous penalty. And then they hire some young person who needs a job to call you up and insult you over the fact you're a few days late on a payment, all the while hoping you'll be late every month by a few days, so they can fatten their income on the penalty.

As he neared the ranch, Lance's attention focused on the grazing conditions. If they got some rain and snow, the whole area would be ready to burst forth in new growth the following spring. Looking at the rooster tail of dust that flew up behind his pickup, he knew there were no guarantees.

When he reached the turnoff to the ranch, he glanced to his left up Quail Run Creek in the direction of Chloride Springs. He could still picture Lightning running along with him, carrying her pants. He ran his tongue over his lips.

He also thought of Jan, how beautiful she looked in Washington, D.C. in that long black dress. He knew she drew

MAGIC LANCE

looks from every man at the party. He savored the passionate night after the cattle grower's reception and dinner. It was time to get Lightning out of his mind. If only he could do it.

As expected, Pepper and Nugget came running to the truck as he neared the ranch house. Pepper seemed happiest to see him. She jumped and yelped next to the truck door as she ran alongside the last few yards to the house.

Lance petted both dogs and rubbed their ears before going into the house. Once inside, for the first time he realized how quiet and lifeless the place was without Jan's presence.

He put coffee on and sat at the kitchen table, waiting for it to brew. He flipped on the computer and brought up his cattle inventory. By electronic count on the screen, he had 258 cows, fifty-seven heifers, ten bulls and 193 calves. What he actually had in the field should be reasonably close to that. To make one mortgage payment, he needed to sell four calves, maybe five. Then there was the property tax that was two years past due, and insurance on the pickup truck and Jan's car payment and the credit cards and utility payments. And insurance on the ranch house.

After drinking half a cup of hot coffee, Lance called Mike Wilson, his primary cattle trader. He asked what he could expect per pound for yearlings. Mike told him to hold on to his hat. He had never seen so many cattle being offered for sale in the region. Auctions around the state were reporting the same thing. What was everybody doing, selling cattle at the same time?

"What's behind that?" Lance asked, somewhat shocked to hear cattle prices were sinking. "Only thing we can figure out," Mike said, "is that a lot of these people are selling their ranches and culling their herds. Maybe the Indians are going to switch to buffalo, or they want the price of cattle to drop."

"How long do you think that's going to affect the market?" Lance asked.

"I have no idea," Mike said. "I quit trying to call the cattle market twenty-five years ago. All you do is see what it is. What it was, or what it might be tomorrow, don't mean a thing."

"I thought I only needed to sell about a dozen calves," Lance said, resting his elbow on the kitchen table, and resting his forehead in his hand. "Looks like it's going to be twice that many, for the same money."

"I hear you," Mike said. "It's happening to everybody who's selling right now. Can you afford to wait? But I can't guarantee the market won't keep going down. There're even some totally unfounded rumors that a mad cow turned up somewhere along the border. Vague and unfounded, but it spooks the market. Prices go down."

Silence.

"I'm going to think about it," Lance said finally. "I'll call you in a day or two."

Lance walked around the kitchen, wringing his hands. If he didn't raise money to pay those three past-due mortgage payments, he was going to be in deep trouble. He would have to let his father know he was in financial trouble. His ability to maintain his ranching life was suddenly at risk. If he couldn't make the mortgage payments on the ranch, he was out of business. The thought of some city job scared him. On the Three V, he had no boss. He was the boss. He determined how he spent his time, when he did things, where he went. He made the decisions and was responsible for those decisions. He got up when he wanted, went to bed when he wanted. He answered to no one. In a city job, it would be eight to five, and some boss telling him what to do from the time he got to work until the time he left. The thought made his stomach turn.

MAGIC LANCE

Lance knew he had no influence on the cattle market. If he had to sell his herd down, it was the beginning of the end. He wouldn't have enough calves to keep the operation afloat, and once the calves were sold, he would have to start selling cows and prepare to shut down.

Suddenly his whole life's foundation was shaking. Why had he wasted three days going to Washington, D.C., acting like some big-time politico, on somebody else's money. He was a small time rancher, and he was busted.

On a lark and in desperation, Lance went to his pickup, called to Pepper and Nugget to jump on, and headed east from the Three V, straight to the Cascade Ranch.

When he drove into the large ranch yard, he marveled at the size of Big Bob's ranch house. It looked like one of the big mansions he had seen in Dallas once, on Swiss Avenue, and in Kansas City near the old section. When he walked up on the porch that ran in front of the ranch house, he made a weak knock on the front door, almost hoping no one was home.

A young Hispanic woman greeted him at the door.

"I've come to see Mr. McCoy, if he's here," Lance said.

"He's not here," she said politely.

Lance thanked her and started back to his truck. He reached the first step off the porch when he heard another voice call his name.

"Lance, what are you doing here?"

Lance's spirit returned in an instant. It was Lightning.

"I came by to see Big Bob, or get in touch with him. Thought I might talk to him about that job he talked to me about, a while back."

"Oh, you're interested in a job are you," Lightning said, walking slowly until she was within a few inches of him. There was magic in her eyes.

Lance had an overwhelming impulse to grab her and kiss her. He couldn't quite muster the courage to do it.

"I thought I'd talk about it, if he were around, or I could call him somewhere." He stared straight into Lightning's blue-green eyes.

"Why don't you talk to me about it." Lightning raised her hand and rubbed his right upper arm. Lance was about to reciprocate, when Scooter Jones came out the front door. Lance had assumed the big ape must follow her around. Every time he saw her, Scooter was there.

"Big Bob here?" Lance asked.

"Hardly. He's rarely here. I run this place," Scooter said. He pushed right up next to Lightning, forcing her to move to the side.

"What's your business?"

"Something Big Bob and I talked about. It'll wait."

"You call before you come over here," Scooter said. "Seeing Big Bob is something a lot of people want to do. You don't just drop by to see him."

"I'll do that," Lance said. While he had been wary of Scooter Jones in the past, due to the man's size and unfriendly demeanor, Lance was not in the mood today to give him any perceived respect. Lance nodded to Lightning and walked back to his pickup truck. When he was within a few feet of the driver's side door, he realized Scooter Jones was not far behind him. He turned, in a defensive mode.

"You ought to sell out to us," Scooter said. "That little ole pissant place you got won't keep you off the streets much longer. Better get out while you can."

Lance took the tone of voice as a threat.

"I'll decide that," Lance said. He kept a close eye on Scooter as the man moved to the bed of the truck. Pepper came over and sniffed at Scooter's thick hand.

MAGIC LANCE

"Good thing these mongrels didn't get out of your truck. Our dogs would tear 'em up."

Lance tensed. He said nothing further, but got into the truck and started to back out of the ranch yard. Suddenly, Pepper gave a yelp of pain. The dog frantically rubbed her eye with her paw. Lance started his backing, passing within a few inches of Scooter Jones. Red-faced, Scooter laughed as the truck backed away. He folded a pocket knife and slipped it in his pocket. Lance slammed on his brakes, then pulled up right next to Scooter. "You hurt that dog and you'll answer for it," he said, looking at Scooter, eye to eye.

"You come by any time," Scooter said. "I'll be waiting." He laughed heartily.

On an impulse, Lance reached over and picked up Lightning's Indian bead belt. "Here," Lance said, as he tossed the belt at Scooter, "this is something I need to return to Lightning."

Then it was Lance's turn to laugh, as he drove out of the Cascade yard.

Once he was off the Cascade property, he stopped the pickup and went back to examine Pepper. The dog's left eye oozed blood. The eye was cut.

CHAPTER TWENTY-SEVEN

The mortgage company was too quiet. While it was a pleasant lull, Lance knew he was three mortgage payments behind. He should have heard from them by now. For reasons unknown, he had not. Late in the afternoon, his curiosity and anxiety caused him to call the woman he had talked to numerous times about late payments. In early conversations, she had been accusative and demanding. After she harangued him for almost a year, her mood softened and eventually she became his friend. Her name was Susan. He did not know where she was located. He never asked. She never volunteered. He dialed her telephone number. She took the call.

Some good-natured chit-chat ensued. He told her he was several payments behind (he didn't say how many) and wondered what could be worked out.

A pause followed as she brought up his account on the computer screen.

To her surprise and his, she reported his mortgage had been sold.

"Sold," Lance said. "What do you mean sold? I thought I had a mortgage with Continental Mortgage."

"You did," Susan said. "But a few days ago, it was sold to another company called..."

A pause followed.

MAGIC LANCE

"Hold on, I'll find it," she said.

Lance rubbed his hand along his upper right leg. Maybe his account was lost. That's why he was not hearing anything. That was good news. At least it bought him some time.

"The RM Mortgage Company," Susan said. "It was sold to The RM Mortgage Company."

"Where the hell are they from?" Lance asked.

"Let's see," Susan said. Another pause followed.

"Denver," she said. "Want an address?"

"No, I'll be hearing from 'em soon enough. Does that mean I'm no longer dealing with you? I'm going to miss you, Susan," Lance said, half in jest.

"Yeah, I'll miss you too. This job sucks. People like you make it more bearable."

"Thanks for all your help in the past. Maybe our paths will cross again."

"I hope so," Susan said.

As he lay the telephone receiver back on the phone, Lance considered his financial situation. He had to raise money. He would call Mike Wilson first thing tomorrow, find out what the cattle market was doing, and determine how many calves he had to sell. Whatever the market, he had to sell. Whether it would be with a trader, at the auction, or on the Internet, he had to sell.

During the remainder of the afternoon, Lance drove out to see how many head he could locate. He wanted to know where they were. When the cattle truck arrived, he needed to have a good idea where his sales were.

After putting ointment on Pepper's severely injured left eye, Lance left both dogs at the ranch house and drove slowly along the unimproved ranch road that ran up Quail Run Creek. Stands of ponderosa pine glistened fresh and green, reflecting sunlight off the pine needles. In flat meadow areas gambel oak,

Arizona walnut trees and a few piñons formed walls of green along the creek banks. Blue gramma, sideoats gramma, three awn and wheat grass provided ground cover Lance coveted for his stock. Rock cliffs rose along either side of the narrow canyon, starting a half mile beyond the cactus flats.

Normally, when Lance saw the creek, trees, bushes, grass and rock cliffs as one panorama, there was perfect balance, indescribable harmony. Lance had sensed that balance and felt that harmony many times. Today he could not find it. A feeling of uneasiness turned his stomach. Jan was not at the ranch. The price of cattle was dropping. People were trying to get the Three V. He could not suppress an animal desire for Lightning McClain. What Scooter Jones did to Pepper's eye was criminal. It demanded a payback. He should have given that payback the instant Pepper yelped. He should have gotten out of the pickup and slugged Scooter Jones square in the face and beat him into the ground. In truth, he had been afraid to try it. Scooter was a big, tough man. Lance would not be able to handle him, and he knew it. He wondered if Scooter's possessive actions toward Lightning were the real reason Lance wanted to get even. Hurting Pepper was cause enough. Trying to intimidate Lance in front of Lightning McClain was premeditated incitement.

During the drive up the canyon, Lance's thoughts vacillated between revenge and financial disaster; the farther he went, the less he perceived the canyon landscape. He reached the cross fence below the windmill when he saw his first stock. There were two cows and a calf in a grassy patch to the right of the road gate.

Further along, beyond the windmill, Lance stiffened. At the base line of a pine covered hill, he saw two cows on the ground. He parked his truck on the road and walked to them. Flies cruised around their eyes, ears and mouth. Lance felt the carcasses. Stiff and cold. He saw no signs of injury. He got hold of the front legs of one of the cows and pulled them to the opposite side, causing the carcass to roll over on its back and then flip to the other side. No signs of injury were evident on the newly exposed side. He did the same with the second carcass. No noticeable sign of injury on the second carcass.

Lance's concern about the cause of death soon shifted to a more immediate reality; he had just lost a thousand dollars. He had to determine what caused the deaths. Two previously healthy cows, dead of unknown causes. He had no money to call out a veterinarian. He wondered if he could get Mike Wilson to come out and take a look. He examined the cows more closely, looking for any details that might have been overlooked on the first review. He saw nothing.

Where had the rest of his stock gone? Two cows and a calf at the fence gate. Two cows dead near the windmill. He should have seen at least a dozen head by now. A new layer of concern settled over him as he continued up Quail Run Creek. At the trailhead, his breathing shortened. On the far end of the meadow he spotted another carcass. He knew before he reached it, the cow was dead. Again, he found no sign of injury. Another five hundred dollars lost. Lance felt a tinge of panic creep into his chest. What if all his cows were dead? He was wiped out. The ranch was lost. His means of livelihood was gone. He had nothing. The mortgage would be foreclosed. He would be an abject failure in the eyes of his family, of Jan, of everyone he knew. He thought of Scooter Jones sneering at his loss. He imagined the disdain Lightning would feel for someone who couldn't even manage his own small ranch.

Lance looked around the trailhead clearing, undecided what to do. He could move out on foot into the National Forest grazing lease area, or he could drive to other areas of the ranch and continue the search. At least he had seen two live cows and a calf. That was some relief. Not all his cattle were gone. If just these three were dead, he might survive. Had a vandal come in and shot 'em? He went back to the carcass at the trailhead and made a more detailed inspection. Perhaps there was a .22 bullet hole in the ear, or behind the head at the neck. There was no blood. He found no bullet hole.

Lance looked at the cow's tongue. It was swollen and dark grey. Natural causes—or could it be poison? It had been several days since Lance had been up this way. He could not tell how long the cows had been dead. His best guess was one or two days.

For the rest of the day until sundown, Lance drove his ranch roads, looking for cattle. He counted over a hundred cows and calves, about what he expected to see for the area he covered. On his way back to the ranch, Lance mulled over his options. He needed to find out who or what killed these three cows. And he needed to find out where the rest of the stock was. That was a job for the next morning. Tonight he would get on the Internet and check sources. Given the unremarkable condition of the cows, he needed to get some advice on what to look for to determine cause of death. Looking for the rest of his stock was going to take time, using his truck, a horse, and Pepper and Nugget. He speculated how easy it would be if he had a helicopter to fly over the ranch; he could spot all his cattle in an hour. On foot, on horseback and in a truck, it might take a couple of days. In the old days, Lance thought, when bandits or renegades ran off a rancher's stock, the rancher was in deep trouble. Usually he got a bunch of friends together and gave chase. But at least that early rancher didn't have to worry about some mortgage company coming in and taking away the land.

When Lance pulled into the ranch house yard, it was strangely silent. He expected Pepper and Nugget to run out on the road a hundred yards away. They were nowhere to be seen. An intuitive feeling caused Lance to lock his teeth and squint his eyes. He reached under the seat and pulled out a .357 revolver. His eyes flicked to and fro as he stepped down from the truck and walked toward the front steps of the ranch house. He looked in all directions.

As he started to climb the two steps up to the wooden porch by the front door of the ranch house, he saw something through the wooden slats. He moved to the side of the porch, stooped down, and looked beneath the porch. There, lying together, head to head, were Pepper and Nugget. They were as dead as the cows the flies were buzzing around near the windmill in Quail Run Creek.

CHAPTER TWENTY-EIGHT

For Lance, the loss of some livestock was part of his business. Cattle were raised to sell and go to slaughter. A few calves, usually ones he identified with when they were a few weeks old, did generate some personal feeling. Was it right to raise these critters only to ship them to slaughter, to wind up as hamburger meat at a fast food restaurant? Lance was philosophical about it. An animal was an animal. It was an economic unit. It was a number stamped in its ear. And yet there were certain calves, those spry, energetic, playful and mischievous animals that were able to establish some kind of attachment with him, an attachment that remained as the calf grew older. Lance was reticent and sad when those few, special animals were herded into the cattle trucks.

With Pepper and Nugget, it was different. They were his workers, his associates. They were loyal, ready to sacrifice themselves for him. Lance remembered one early morning encounter with a black bear, not far from the trailhead. The bear was coming downstream, and Lance was walking upstream. The meeting was a chance encounter. Nugget and Pepper had not hesitated. As soon as the bear appeared, they attacked. Lance felt fortunate he was able to get them back before the bear made mincemeat of them. Nonetheless, he knew his two dogs were protecting him, attacking anything and anybody they sensed were hostile.

MAGIC LANCE

He remembered how they had gone after the intruders who approached when he and Lightning were at the mineral springs.

And now Pepper and Nugget were gone.

He could buy other dogs, younger and not that dissimilar to Pepper and Nugget. They were animals. He reasoned all that out. And yet on his way to Sierra City, he pulled the pickup off the road and placed his face in his hands, and cried.

Later that day, in Sierra City, Lance described to his father and mother all that happened at the ranch. His father was suspicious that dirty work was being done by persons unknown. They talked of the possibilities. Vandals were one possibility. Did Lance have any enemies, anyone he had fought with, insulted, betrayed, fired, owed money to, gambling debts, drugs, other women, anyone who verbally threatened him—all those things that Lance didn't want to think about and which his father hoped were not a possibility.

His father thought poison was the most likely explanation for the cattle deaths, and probably for Pepper and Nugget. He said the dogs should be replaced immediately. Too easy for someone to sneak up at night, he said. You need some backup out there. Dogs are your first line of defense.

After discussing the incidents, Lance's mother told him it was getting too dangerous for him to continue the ranch operation. She and his father were on the verge of moving to Ashton to be near doctors and medical facilities. Sierra City's facilities were fine for minor medical problems, but their concerns involved things more serious, especially his father's heart condition and lower back problems. Perhaps he should move to Ashton as well.

And Earl Wallace, the real estate agent, said the Grey Piñon tribe was anxious to get the ranch because of its religious sites and historical values, his mother said. She and his father had no idea there were any Indian religious sites on the ranch. The Grey Piñons must have used the hot springs as a rest and recreation area before the Spanish and the Americans moved into the area. Now, Earl Wallace said they wanted to return the springs to the tribe's ownership. They were willing to pay a premium to get the ranch, far above the fair market value.

"When did Earl Wallace get hold of you?" Lance asked, surprised and irked that his former high school classmate would go directly to this father and mother when he knew Lance ran the ranch.

"Yesterday," his mother said. "And we talked to Marc and Peggy about it, and they said we should sell. They said if you want to buy it, we should give you first option, but since the Indians might offer about twice what it's worth, we should just go ahead and sell. We'll use some of that money as a down payment and help you get a better place somewhere else."

Lance sunk back into his chair. His personal commitment to keep the Three V now was against the wishes of his own family, the people who were part and parcel of the tradition he was trying to preserve.

"What about the time and sweat we've all put in the Three V," Lance asked. "Does that have a price on it?"

"Times are changing," his father said. "Western ranching is a dying art, a dying way of life. People are coming out here from the cities and buying up the land. It's no longer economical to ranch, to live out in the country. These are trophy places. Look at Colorado. Used to, when you drove along those river valleys, you'd see green pasture and cattle grazing. Now you see trophy homes, two stories with big glass windows, on thirty five-acre tracts, looking into the mountains. And most of the time nobody's even living there. A caretaker is the main owner of the place. Everybody wants those big trophy homes, and the ranch-

MAGIC LANCE

ing life is dying. Just some holdouts now, who like the old lifestyle. It's not economical any more. And the economic disease is coming here. There's no way anybody can buy a ranch and run cattle and make it pay. If you inherit the ranch and don't have a mortgage, you can run a coyote operation and barely get by. But a person can't buy the property anymore and make it pay. It's over, Lance. The Western ranching life is over. The only people who can make a go of it are those who have an independent income and can operate without worrying about the economics of raising cattle. And a few big operators who inherit big operations from the previous generation, and can keep them going."

Lance listened to his father. He knew that much of what his father said was true. He also knew that was not what he wanted to see happen to the Three V. He wanted to be a small-time rancher, run his own operation, protect the land, make a living raising cattle and be his own boss, free and independent.

Lance made no mention of the fact the mortgage obligation was three payments behind. He made no mention of the fact a new mortgage company had purchased the mortgage. He made no mention of the fact Big Bob McCoy said he would pay ten per cent more than what the Indians would pay. He made no mention of the fact his own chance of buying the ranch for the price the Grey Piñons would offer was zero.

Lance left his parents' house in a somber mood. He did extract a promise from them they would not sell the ranch or sign any papers until they talked to him first. From his parents' house he went to the old soda fountain at the Rexall Drug store on Main Street. He ordered a cup of coffee. Jan would not be home from school for an hour.

He sat on a red plastic chair with chrome legs and a padded back at one of the tables with a grey plastic top and chrome legs.

He was reading the Sierra City *Sentinel* when the newspaper editor came by his table.

"Good to see you have such good taste in newspapers," the young man said. Lance recognized him at once—Jim Sorenson. Jim started the *Sentinel* weekly from scratch and now was a crusading newspaper editor.

"Hey," Lance said, "good to see a person who still talks to small ranchers. This is a good newspaper. Local news. And you aren't afraid to take on the federal government, about water and grazing rights and ranching. Sit down."

Jim waved to the waitress and ordered a cup of coffee.

"You one of those instant millionaires?" he asked. "Everybody who owns a ranch around here is hitting it big."

"Word's out," Lance said. "What the hell is going on? This land sat here for a hundred years and you darn near couldn't give it away. Now they got people lined up to buy it for more than it's worth. What the hell is going on?"

"It's all that gambling money. Grey Piñons are either plenty dumb, or plenty smart. Converting all those gambling winnings to land. Is that smart, or is it dumb? The jury's still out."

"What the hell has happened? I got all kinds of people trying to buy a ranch that's uneconomical. It doesn't make sense. But it's sure ruining my way of life."

"Maybe we ought to do a story on you. Plight of the small rancher in a red-hot real estate market."

"I can't stay up with it," Lance said. "You can't begin to make enough money off cattle operations to keep up with the value of land around here. It's almost as if they're forcing you to sell. How can you justify not selling if they offer you twice what the land is worth? And how can you justify not selling to your partners, if you're offered twice what you'll ever make off the cattle operation?"

MAGIC LANCE

"Gambling money seems to be driving it," Jim said. "The Grey Piñons want their old lands back, and they got money flowing in that boggles your mind. Can you blame 'em?"

"I may not be able to blame 'em, but they're sure screwing up my way of life."

"That's where the story is," Jim said. "Passing of a way of life. New owners of land and what they intend to do with it."

"You better watch your back," Lance said, suddenly defensive at the young newspaper man's acknowledgment that changes in land ownership were a foregone conclusion. "Think about it. I sell my ranch and move. And my family moves with me. No rancher out at the old Three V. We don't come in to buy gasoline any more. We don't buy insurance, we don't use utilities, we don't pay property taxes, we don't buy food, or clothes, or cars or eat at restaurants, or hire maintenance people or use a dentist or a doctor; we don't get our car repaired, or buy flowers or cards or belong to the local church, or send our kids here to school, or buy books or CD's or appliances or furniture, or anything like that. We don't subscribe to your newspaper. How many subscriptions have you got out there on the reservation? What's the Grey Piñon tribe going to buy? Not much. So what's going to happen to all your valuable advertisers and all your readers? You're going to go out of business. And I'll be living in Ashton on my fat land check from the Grey Piñons. Maybe that's the story."

"Actually, I've been thinking about that," Jim said. "If the Grey Piñons buy up all the land, it'll be off the tax rolls. It'll be de-populated. All the ranches will be part of the tribal lands. And what economic benefit does the town get from tribal lands? Not much."

"Somebody better publicize that," Lance said. "'Cause I'll have my Indian money, cash, and I'll be living the life of leisure in Ashton. And people like you will see the town go, and your newspaper right along with it, and you won't have any of that easy gambling money. You'll be out of business and broke. Just like the old mining towns when the mines shut down."

"Maybe there's a story in that angle," Jim said. "The ranchers wind up making a windfall profit, and the end result is the local land goes to the Grey Piñons. It'll create a stranglehold on the town. The economic basis of the town collapses. You'll be gone with your winnings and Sierra City will be surrounded by tribal lands. That does sound like the old days when the mines shut down and the silver belt towns became ghost towns, or close to it."

"All this talk about sacred lands and holy places is a bunch of crap," Lance said. "This is a political power play if there ever was one, and if it isn't stopped your newspaper and this town are gonna be history."

CHAPTER TWENTY-NINE

When Jim Sorenson left, Lance called Earl Wallace and said he wanted to discuss the sale of the Three V Ranch if Earl could meet him at the Rexall Drug. As expected, Lance recognized an immediate air of excitement in Earl's voice. "I'll be there in ten minutes," Earl said.

Lance smiled to himself as he thought of Earl skidding to a stop in front of the drug store in that fancy Japanese sports vehicle, with four-wheel drive. For Earl to contact his parents behind his back caused Lance's anger to maintain a slow burn. Earl should have known better. The greedy-gut, Lance thought. On his way over here he'll be sloshing the taste of that anticipated ten percent real estate commission around in his mouth, like a spoonful of lard. What he's actually going to get is a butt-chewing. Sure enough, while Earl's vehicle didn't skid to a stop, it came to a fast stop by the curb outside the Rexall front door. Earl was almost floating when he came to the soda fountain area where Lance sat at the grey plastic top table with chrome legs.

"Lance, good to see you, old buddy. Sounds like you're moving in the right direction finally."

"Oh," Lance said. "And what direction is that?"

"Well, you said you wanted to talk about selling the Three V."

"Yeah, I want to talk about that, 'cause you've been sneaking around behind my back and talking to my parents. Who the hell do you think is running that ranch out there, some lackey?"

"No, no, of course you're running it." Earl's hands started to tremble. "There's never been any doubt about that. But you have to admit, Lance, their names are the ones on the deed. In most people's book, that makes them the owners, no matter who's running the operation."

"Thanks a lot, Earl. We've known each other since high school, and when there's money involved, suddenly you start sneaking around behind my back." As he spoke, his temper toughened, and he debated whether he should slug Earl right in the mouth.

Earl raised both hands in the air in front of him, as though someone had told him to stick 'em up. "If that's the way it is, I'll do everything through you. If you're running the deal, I'd just as soon deal with you in all particulars. I just assumed your father and mother were the ones who would have to sign the deed, so I needed to talk to them."

"You make too many assumptions. I told you once before, the Three V is not for sale. Now I'm telling you again. If you push this thing, I'll make sure if it ever sells, you'll be the last real estate agent in the county who'll ever get a commission on it."

"Okay, okay. I read you, Lance. I read you."

Lance's temper slowly dissipated. Saying the Three V was not for sale reinforced his position. It took Earl Wallace's sneaking to his parents to solidify his stand. There was not going to be any retreat, no backing down, no selling the Three V. Lance made a commitment to himself at that moment, that he was going to lead the ranching life, and he was going to lead it on the Three V Ranch, no matter who stayed and who left, no matter

MAGIC LANCE

who supported him and who opposed him. Whatever it took, he was going to save the Three V.

Earl's anxiety dropped as he felt Lance's change in demeanor.

"Notwithstanding all that, there're some things you ought to know," Earl said.

"Like what?"

"Like your federal grazing leases. There's an environmental group that's going to try to pick them up when they come due. And they got plenty of money behind them to do it, from what I hear."

Lance shook his head. He had heard of the tactics of the environmental hardballers, using their citified money to bid against little ranchers who were poorly financed. They used the carrot and the stick. Threaten to bid for the federal and state grazing leases when they came due, then offer to pay more than what the land was worth if the small rancher would agree to sell out. Get the cattle off federal and state lands in the West. That was their one objective. They had no sense of history or love of the ranching life in their zeal to do away with the Western rancher.

"To hell with the environmentalists," Lance said. "I'll call Senator Walton. I met him in Washington. He said I could call on him if I needed any help. I'll get him to talk to the Forest Service. He's on some kind of Interior committee that has a funding role. They listen to guys like that."

"I'll support you on that," Earl said. "I'm all for private land ownership. I'm all for that."

"You're all for making a buck," Lance said, his ire rising again as Earl Wallace weaseled and waffled, hoping he still would get the listing and the real estate commission on the Three V.

"There isn't going to be any sale of the Three V," Lance said. "And even if all of the grazing leases are lost, I'll turn it into a guerilla training camp. A bed and breakfast for Army Special Forces."

"Don't kill the messenger," Earl said. "You're better off knowing what those yo-yo's are up to. I didn't say I supported 'em. I just told you what I've heard."

"Yeah, well I thank you for that. You're right. I'm better off knowing. I'll tell you one thing. If I catch one of those goofballs coming onto my ranch, they're going to regret they ever heard of the Three V."

"'Nough said," Earl said. "I'll even pass the word they're persona non grata, so they won't make the mistake of thinking they can waltz on the place and look it over."

As Lance and Earl talked about the local real estate market and what the Grey Piñons were buying, Lance saw a Cascade pickup truck pass slowly by, in front of the drug store. The truck was almost past the big glass window when he spotted it.

Several moments later, to Lance's delight, Lightning McClain came into the drug store. She looked around the cosmetic counter for a moment, then came over as soon as she spotted Lance and Earl sitting at the table.

Lance stood up.

"Nice to see this place has such attractive clientele," Lance said, as Lightning arrived.

"Thank you," she said, smiling and shifting her eyes toward Lance.

"I'm Earl Wallace," Earl said when it appeared he might not get introduced.

"Oh, sorry," Lance said. "I assumed you two probably knew each other."

"I'm sorry I haven't had the pleasure," Earl said.

Lightning ignored the remark, as she seated herself and focused her attention on Lance. She had some ranch matters she needed to discuss with him, she said. It was about some cows that had strayed off the Cascade and might be on the Three V.

The tone of voice communicated the desire for one-on-one conversation.

Although disappointed, Earl told them he had another appointment and took his leave.

As he rose to leave, Lightning also stood up, to shift her seating next to Lance. When she did so, Earl spied the Indian bead belt she was wearing.

"Nice belt with those Indian beads," he said, as he walked away.

CHAPTER THIRTY

A low-level excitement filled Lance's chest when Lightning was present. He wondered if it was a feeling all men experienced in her company. She had natural beauty. Lance knew that was the initial attraction. He also knew physical qualities were not the whole story in an attraction. It took you a way, Lance thought. Was this attraction for Lightning so strong he had to go forward? Was a sense of daring part of it? Did he feel a resentment toward Jan for leaving him at the ranch? For desertion. Was Lightning a payback?

Today, Lightning's usual casual, confident demeanor was missing. She looked over her shoulder, turned her head and looked when the front door opened, shifted her hands on top of the table, squirmed on the red plastic chair.

"Lance, things are starting to happen around here that I've never seen before."

The waitress arrived and asked for an order.

"Something to eat?" Lance asked, turning to Lightning.

"Sure."

Lance raised his head, looking in the waitress's direction. She shifted her weight, raised her order book and placed her ballpoint pen on the tablet.

Lightning squirmed again.

"Oh, pie and coffee," she said finally.

MAGIC LANCE

"We got cherry and apple."

"Cherry."

The waitress turned to Lance.

"Cherry with some vanilla ice cream and a refill on the coffee."

The waitress was impressed with his brevity.

Lance gave her a look that said adios.

"Lance, a lot of what I do is acting," Lightning said. "Like in Washington, D.C. at the cattlemen's meeting. I barely looked at you. I never spoke. But you were the only person on my mind."

Lance sat back slightly in his chair. His face blushed.

"You saw who else was there. I didn't have any choice. But I want you to know how I really felt. This whole life I'm leading seems like it's out of control. I thought what I wanted was social status, money, things. Big Bob's operation with Scooter gives me that. And they're good to me. Big Bob doesn't put any pressure on me. He let's me do exactly what I want. Only I know the situation. I'm a pretty face; I'm Scooter's girl."

"You're Scooter's girl?"

"He treats me well," Lightning said, "most of the time. He also does what I tell him most of the time. And hey, it gets lonely on a ranch. You know that."

Lightning cut her eyes, looking directly at Lance.

"Scooter's temporary," Lightning said. "Basically, he's not very smart. He is very strong. In fact, you darn near got us both killed the other day. Why did you give Scooter my belt? Didn't you realize how he would interpret that? You know how possessive he is."

"I did it on an impulse. He stabbed Pepper in the eye; blinded her in that eye, I think. What did he say about it?"

"He wanted to know how you got hold of my belt. And by the tone of his voice, he was guessing how you did it. I had to do some quick thinking."

"What'd you say?"

"Would I lie? I told him I bought a silver concho belt at the flea market that I couldn't live without. When I put it on, I took my Indian bead belt off and left it on the seat of the pickup. Then, when Big Bob sent me over to see the Three V and talk to you, it must have fallen out of the truck, and you must have found it. That's why you had it."

Concluding her explanation, Lightning took a deep breath and flashed her wide smile at Lance.

Lance shook his head. He also became uneasy. Despite an attraction for Lightning, he wasn't sure at what level he wanted to get involved. There would be Scooter Jones to deal with and he had his marriage to consider. How would his own relationships change, within his own family, if he became involved with Lightning?

"When I drove by just now, out front, and saw your pickup, something compelled me to come in. And it wasn't because of what I just said. Or maybe it was because of what I just said. What I'm trying to say," she said, looking again over her shoulder, and around the lunch area of the drug store, "is that there are some troubling things developing, and they all affect you."

Lance leaned in on the table, drawing close to Lightning.

"What troubling things?

"I don't know all the pieces. I know the Cascade Ranch part. But there's something bigger going on. I can feel it. What I can tell you is that Big Bob McCoy is going to get your ranch."

"Oh," Lance said, with some surprise. "He's already offered to buy it. That I know. Along with the Grey Piñons. But I've told 'em it's not for sale."

"You're not seeing the whole picture." Lightning put her hand on top of Lance's hand.

A wave of heat surged through his body.

"These men you're dealing with are ruthless. They're rich and powerful. They have friends at all levels. They have you totally surrounded, Lance. And I don't think you're aware of it."

Lance pulled back, and pulled his hand off the table. "You must think I'm some kind of amateur. I assure you I am not. People who work like me aren't made of cotton candy. I admit these rich guys can do things I can't. But I'm no pushover. You must think I'm naive."

"No, no Lance. I don't think you're any of that. Most of all I've never thought you were naive. That's not the problem. These forces against you are just so strong."

"Give me some details then." A tinge of suspicion ran through Lance's mind.

"Don't take this personally," she said. "I'm on your side, Lance. But you need to know."

The waitress returned to the table with Lance's cherry a la mode in one hand and Lightning's pie in the other. She cast them on the table with the grace of a professional card dealer.

The waitress looked at each of them, awaiting any other requests, then flitted to the next table. Lance mixed a portion of ice cream and sweet cherry pie. He had not forgotten Lightning's last sentence.

"So what is it I need to know?"

"For starters, who do you have your ranch mortgage with?"

"Continental Mortgage," Lance responded, remembering his many telephone conversations with Susan.

Lightning looked at him for a moment, awaiting any change in his answer.

When Lance said nothing, she asked if he had ever heard of RM Mortgage.

Lance thought for a moment, then remembered his recent telephone conversation with Susan. "Oh yeah," he said. "I think they told me that's the company that bought my mortgage from Continental. Before that, I didn't even know you could buy mortgages. I thought my deal was with Continental."

"That's what I'm telling you," Lightning said, with some sense of satisfaction. "Your mortgage is now owned by RM Mortgage. And I happen to know you're three mortgage payments behind."

Lanced sat up straight.

"How do you know that?"

"Who do you think RM Mortgage is?"

"I have no idea," Lance replied, while at the same time, starting to assemble obvious facts.

"Robert McCoy. RM Mortgage," Lightning said.

Lance's body rose an inch off the chair.

"See what I mean," Lightning said. "You're dealing with ruthless people. They're working you into a difficult position, and you're not even aware of it."

"I know I'm in a dangerous position on my mortgage, but I didn't know who the other side was. That's worse than I thought."

"Exactly," Lightning said. "And that's just the start."

"Just the start. How's that?"

"How're your cattle doing?"

"What do you mean?"

"How're your cattle doing?" Lightning asked again.

"About the same."

"About the same?" Lightning said. "Found any dead ones around the ranch lately?"

Lance slammed his fist on the table, bouncing the silverware. "How do you know about that?"

Lightning ran the long strands of her blonde hair over her left ear and took a bite of cherry pie and a sip of coffee.

MAGIC LANCE

"What killed those cows?"

"I don't know what killed 'em," Lance said, "'cause I haven't got enough money to hire somebody to tell me. Is that what Big Bob paid you to do, come over here and find out everything I know?"

Lightning propped her chin on the palm of her hand, her elbow on the table, and stared into Lance's eyes. She held the gaze.

Lance took a deep swallow of coffee.

"Well," Lance said.

Lightning held her position. She made no comment.

"Forget I asked that."

Lightning smiled and placed her hand on his.

"Lance, this whole scenario is way beyond anything I can imagine. I know you have a valuable ranch. The Grey Piñons want it. Big Bob wants it. The environmentalists are after your grazing leases. You don't want to sell. Do you see the difficulty that puts you in."

"It's worse than I thought."

"You're dealing with incredibly high stakes. Your ranch is the pivot point in some kind of high-stakes competition that I don't even understand. It's between the Grey Piñons and Big Bob. And it's caught up in the gambling issues and the environmental issues. You have to be careful. You're a target."

"So who's done what to my cattle, and to Pepper and Nugget. They were more important than the cattle."

"Big Bob heard you lost your dogs and some cattle. He wondered if someone in his organization was involved. He said if he'd thought of it, he might have done it; but he didn't think of it. I don't know who did it. It must be somebody giving you a combination of warning and intimidation. You either sell, or you're going to be cut off."

"What do you mean cut off?"

"You're dealing with an Indian tribe that has so much money they don't even count it and an individual who has unlimited resources and strong political connections."

"So where does that leave me?" Lance asked.

"You're a target, that's all. For the Indians, and for Big Bob."

"Where do you stand?"

"Lance, you could be a millionaire. All you have to do is play these two parties against each other. All you have to do is tell Big Bob you'll sell. He'll pay whatever you want. It's not you. It's not even the Three V. At some point, Big Bob gets caught up in the battle. He wants to beat the Grey Piñons. And he wants them to know he's beat them. That's what drives him. You're superfluous. He doesn't care about you. He doesn't even care about the Three V. He's in a battle with the Grey Piñons. What matters to him is beating the Grey Piñons."

"So, what should I do?"

Lightning tilted her head and smiled. "Your call," she said. "You have a beautiful wife. I saw Jan in Washington. And so did Senator Walton. Did you see how he was attracted to her?"

Lightning shifted her eyes and turned her head.

"Senator Walton. Attracted to Jan?" Lance said. "Get serious."

"It was obvious, wasn't it? You didn't notice?"

"Senator Walton said he would help me any way he could."

"Oh," Lightning said. "Isn't that interesting."

"You seem to see things I don't."

"Women specialize in relationships. They're important to us."

Lance raised his eyebrows and looked away. The thought of someone showing interest in Jan caused him to grit his teeth.

"So who poisoned my cows, since you seem to know everything."

"I have no idea," Lightning said.

She turned her coffee cup. She looked at Lance. She raised her head, keeping her eyes fixed on his.

"It's probably someone who wants your ranch, or it could be somebody who doesn't like you. Take your pick. Round up the usual suspects."

Lance ran through the possibilities: the Cascade Ranch, the Grey Piñons, or somebody working for them. He could think of no one else.

It clearly was someone who sought to do him harm. Would they get him before he figured out who they were?

And did this woman at the table have an agenda, and was she all that interested in him?

CHAPTER THIRTY-ONE

Lucky Joe watched Anita Martinez walk through the doorway and into the adjoining office. His wife was right. This woman is saying, "Come and get me." Lucky Joe leaned back in his swivel chair, fingers interlocked and resting on top of his chest. He thought of the similarity of his conducting the land purchase operation and the Magic Lance operation. In both cases, he had people working for him. Except for his close administrative staff, they were not Grey Piñon tribe members. They were white eyes. In land purchases, it was white eyes helping him buy land from other white eyes, re-distributing money white eyes put in the slot machines. It had a good feel to it. Bottom line, white eyes were doing most of the work, white eyes' money was being put in the slot machines, transferred to the banks, paid to ranchers and other landowners, and the Grey Piñons were becoming the biggest land owners in the state. "It's full circle," Lucky Joe thought. In reverse, from the way it was when the Spanish, then the Mexicans and finally the Americans came to the state. The tribes originally roamed the land, and belonged to it in their own sense, not in the land owning sense of the Europeans. And after four centuries, the land was returning to the Indians. He felt a mystical union with a spiritual power far beyond himself.

For a few seconds, he perceived himself as really nothing. The Lucky Joe ego, that entity he thought was himself, was actu-

MAGIC LANCE

ally nothing. In his body there was another soul, separate from the self, separate from the ego, separate from the world. This other soul was the entity that blended with the spirits. He was a steward for the spirits. It was not Lucky Joe Cruz who mattered. It was this soul that belonged to the spirits in Lucky Joe Cruz's body that mattered. The ego of Lucky Joe and the cares for the world were gone, like a train engine and cars that detached and moved on down the track, leaving the true life spirit in the caboose. Lucky Joe's true spirit was in the caboose. He was no longer in the world. He was no longer in his flesh. He was suspended. He was somewhere else. He was merged with the spirits. He answered to no one. He sought no possessions, longed for no honors, dreamed of no pleasures. He sought no approval of other people. He was totally contained, totally filled by the spirits. No one could reach him. His will was in harmony with the will of the spirits. They were One.

The dugout, as Segundo and Lucky Joe called their headquarters in the low adobe building adjacent to the plaza, was a busy place. Computer screens flashed e-mail messages by the dozens. Telephones rang. Faxes poured in. People dropped by. Tribal members sent messages by family members. Food caterers came and went regularly. Tribal police, tribal council members, gaming commission members, politicians, real estate agents and appraisers, title company executives, utility workmen, occasional journalists, family members—it was a social zoo. Yet in an atmosphere that otherwise resembled a war room, it was not unusual to see a spider run across the adobe wall, or a stream of dust fall from herring bone aspen branches that ran from viga to viga. In all this chaos, Lucky Joe was entranced, in another place, detached from the world, detached from his own body. It was only when Segundo sauntered into his office area that Lucky Joe returned to the world.

"The pot is starting to boil," Segundo said, as he walked into the room. "The Legislature is going to call a special session after the main session ends, to consider renewal of the gaming compact. We have a fifty-fifty chance of keeping gaming rights for the tribes."

Lucky Joe rose from his chair, but not in the same cadence or with the same intensity he had when Segundo came into the casino several months prior. His reverence for Segundo had waned. There still was respect. A more cautious attitude had been grafted into his psyche.

"Have you heard?" Segundo asked.

Lucky Joe said nothing but communicated with his eyes and facial expression that he had no idea what Segundo was addressing.

"Our good friend, Sen. John Walton, has introduced a bill in the U.S. Senate to repeal the Indian Gaming Regulatory Act. Our land purchases are starting to get national attention."

"Repeal the federal gaming act?" Lucky Joe exclaimed with shock.

"Repeal the federal gaming act," Segundo said. "The distinguished senator has forgotten all the political advances we have made to his campaigns. He has decided he is the champion of the small Western rancher. The very ones we are taking advantage of, by offering them twice what their ranches are worth, and only if they want to sell. What a crusader. What a Robin Hood. Protector of the poor. Nemesis of the rich. What a hypocrite."

"I thought he was a political anchor we could count on," Lucky Joe said.

"The political sands shift quickly," Segundo said. "All the more reason we have to go full speed ahead on our land acquisitions. In fact, we have to double our effort. The money spout could be cut off. The people have gotten soft. They are accustomed to easy money flowing in so fast, they don't know what to do with it. If the money stops, before they wind up spending all of it on fancy cars, Ivy League schools and retirement funds, we have to get these land purchases wrapped up. When the largess is over, we have to have the land in possession. If we don't get it in the next six months, our window of opportunity will close. We have to quadruple our efforts. There is no room for the weak-hearted now. Our enemies must be crushed quickly. Our objectives must be achieved faster than I ever dreamed. We have but a precious moment to act. We can tolerate no opposition. We have to strike like lightning."

CHAPTER THIRTY-TWO

"There are too many bases to cover," Segundo said. "The issues exceed our ability to cover them all. The environmental groups are whores. They accepted our money, and guaranteed the small rancher would become extinct in the West. Now they are backing off. They're afraid if we Indians buy up private land, they won't have any control over it. I have to admit they're right," Segundo chuckled. "Only they figured it out sooner than I anticipated. I have to give them credit for that."

"Are the environmental groups turning against our land acquisition goals?" Lucky Joe asked, knowing full well they had.

"Whores," Segundo said. "They take your money, then kick you out as soon as anyone offers them a better deal."

"The bigger danger," Segundo added, "is the Las Vegas crowd, if gambling goes open and they come in with their hundred-million dollar casinos. They would make us look like small town operators in a couple of years."

"Those are the big issues," Segundo continued. "We have to keep a focus on the details as well. We have to keep these land purchases going. No matter what happens in the Legislature, we can probably keep gambling issues and jurisdiction issues tied up in the courts for several years at least. During that time,

we need to finish off our land purchases. We are high rolling, are we not?"

"How's that," Lucky Joe said.

"Our land options. We've leveraged two hundred and fifty million dollars to pick up two million acres of land, and we have to complete the purchases in a year. If we don't pick them up, the two hundred and fifty million will be lost, and the ranchers we have optioned will have so much money they'll never sell."

"We better have a second place to go," Lucky Joe said. "If we lose two hundred and fifty million of the Grey Piñons' money, they may kill us."

"That is one problem you have," Segundo said. "You've had it from the day we began this crusade. You are always worrying, always looking at the pessimistic side. I am the leader of this tribe. I set the program. I call the shots. I am the one everyone comes to for a decision. If I were as pessimistic as you, nothing would ever get done."

Lucky Joe turned in his chair.

"We have to accelerate," Segundo said. "No holding back. No more pessimism. Follow my direction. I will tell you what to do."

Lucky Joe squinted his eyes as he looked at Segundo. The old man had lost the aura. Lucky Joe did not intend to be treated as an underling.

"We need to clear up several hangnails," Segundo said. "The biggest step we need to take at once is to get the Tribal Council to appropriate an additional nine hundred million dollars to purchase the top options. They have the money. It's in the bank. All they have to do is appropriate it."

"The bankers are starting to work against us," Lucky Joe said. "They visited with me last week. They say we're paying way above market value on the land, and it will cost even more to manage it. They claim we're making bad investments. And they're telling the same thing to the council members."

"Of course they are," Segundo said. "We're taking money out of their banks and paying it to ranchers. They're stuck pigs. Why would they support that? That's our money, not their money."

"The tribal council members are listening," Lucky Joe said. "And Velasquez and Abeita are supporting the bank. They claim the bankers are right."

"That's one of the major hangnails," Segundo said. "Velasquez and Abeita are one of the major hangnails I was talking about. We need to take care of them. Buy 'em out. Whatever it takes, buy 'em out. Tell 'em we'll re-instate their allotments and even go back and make all back payments. Shut 'em up. And if that doesn't work, we're going to have to take stronger measures."

"What kind of stronger measures?" Lucky Joe asked.

"Look, Lucky Joke," Segundo said derisively. "This is a life and death affair. If this land purchase plan doesn't work and we lose two hundred and fifty million, do you think you're going to walk away from this thing? Your body is going to be found at the bottom of a steep cliff, and they'll say you jumped off to avoid the shame and financial embarrassment. Only you didn't jump off, you were thrown off."

Segundo stared straight at Lucky Joe. Those dark eyes and porcupine hair worked their intimidation.

"Get it together," Segundo said. "Buy Velasquez and Abeita off. If they won't sell, take care of 'em."

Lucky Joe thought of syndicate meetings he'd seen on TV. Their conversation was as blunt and direct as what Segundo was saying.

MAGIC LANCE

"And that's hangnail number one," Segundo said. "Hangnail number two is that rancher guy. Do the same thing to him. Buy him out, or take care of him. We've got a double danger there. I found out Big Bob McCoy bought the mortgage on the Three V Ranch. That means he's going to try and foreclose it. If Big Bob gets that ranch, it's going to cost us ten times what Burnett will sell it for, and we might not be able to buy it at any price. We have to move fast on that. If Big Bob gets it on a foreclosure, we're in trouble. Whatever it takes, buy him out."

"And by the way," Segundo continued, "I also found out that Lance Burnett guy doesn't even own the Three V. His parents own it. They live in Sierra City. Bad health. Talk to them and buy 'em out. I heard the old man has a heart condition. Tell him we'll put him and his wife in our reservation health system, same as the Grey Piñon tribe, for life, at no charge. That ought to get their attention."

"Why is the Three V so important?" Lucky Joe asked. "We've got two million acres optioned already. What difference is another eight hundred acres going to make."

"It's part of Wild Horse's territory. That hot springs was a resting area for our people for hundreds of years. Even if that is the only piece of land we get out of this whole thing, it would be worth it. It has traditional value. It inspires the tribe to think we can recover Wild Horse's hunting grounds, and his spirit as well. It's clear spirits inhabit certain places on this earth, and for the Grey Piñon the spirits that count can be found at the hot springs. I should have tightened the focus on that place from the beginning. The spirits may resent my neglect."

"What if the Burnett guy still won't sell?"

"By God, I'm telling you to go out there and buy it," Segundo said, his voice spiking to a high pitch. "If you can't understand that, I'll get somebody who can understand."

Anita Martinez came into the room, bringing a written message to Lucky Joe. His face flushed red, as he realized Anita heard Segundo berating him.

Segundo held further words until the young lady left. His eyes followed Anita's sensual figure.

"That reminds me of something," Segundo said. "You young bucks can't keep your eyes and hands off the young maidens. That's fine when it comes to family and marriage and all that, but when you're involved in a major campaign, you have to put that aside. It gets you in trouble. Move that young lady's desk over next to my desk, where I can keep an eye on her. And speaking of that, we have one more card to play in this Burnett ranch deal. Get back with our real estate agent. What's his name?"

"You mean Wallace?"

"Yeah, Earl Wallace. Get back with him. Tell him to find out who that guy was at Chloride Springs, and who the woman was. If it turns out it was Burnett, and he had some chick up there who was other than his wife, we need to find that out, and let Burnett know we know who he was with and what he was doing. And if he agrees to sell, that'll all be history. But if he doesn't agree to sell, his wife is going to get all the details. See how he responds to that."

CHAPTER THIRTY-THREE

In the days and nights that followed, Lucky Joe found it more difficult to sleep, more difficult to eat, more difficult to concentrate, more difficult to communicate with his wife Rachel and with Rick and Andrea, more difficult to avoid a tenseness in his stomach. His fingers developed a tremble when he held a coffee cup.

Rachel asked him what was wrong. Was it Segundo? Was it Velasquez and Abeita? Was it the pressure of running the land acquisitions? Was it other people in the tribe who were criticizing them? Was it the danger the tribe would lose its two hundred and fifty million? Was it the growing public opposition to Indian gambling? Was it the environmentalists and the gambling figures who no longer were friendly to the Grey Piñons' position? She asked all those questions. Lucky Joe said it was all of those things and none of those things. Maybe he was not the man for this job. He had persevered until now. He wondered if too many problems coming from too many directions had gotten to him.

"Maybe we should consider that move to California," Rachel said one evening.

"You mean you and the kids?"

"Yes, me and the kids, and you too."

"I can't do that," Lucky Joe said. "I'd be running away."

"You wouldn't be running away. You need a temporary leave of absence. You've been under intense pressure for a long time. You need a break. Maybe after a month or two, things will look different."

"They will look a lot different," Lucky Joe said. "And they won't look good. Look what happened to Velasquez and Abeita. They just voiced a different opinion and their allotments were cut off."

"But you said Segundo told you to re-instate them."

"Yes, but only because we have so many other problems we can't deal with all of them. We're trying to eliminate as many problems as we can, so we can get things back under control."

"Do you really believe you can get things under control?"

"I've barely got myself under control," Lucky Joe said, "and I'm not sure I can hold that, the way things are going."

"Think about it. I'd rather be married to a healthy, inactive Grey Piñon than a stressed-out, nervous breakdown, active member."

"It's not that simple," Lucky Joe said. "If I pull out now, I'd be considered a quitter. Segundo would blackball me on everything, including my job at the Magic Lance, our per capitas, everything."

"Oh, that's not true. Not even Segundo would go that far."

"It's going way beyond anything I ever imagined. But for right now, I have to ride it out. My security and your security and Rick and Andrea's security all depend on it."

Rachel stroked Lucky Joe's back with her hand. She felt the tenseness of his back muscles. It caused her to rub all the harder and faster. Her intensity, massaging his, caused Lucky Joe to pull away and head for the front door.

"Where are you going?" Rachel called.

"Not sure. I've got to walk around a while and think all this through."

MAGIC LANCE

From the house on a low mesa overlooking the old village and the plaza, Lucky Joe drove to the Cottonwood River, which ran through the reservation. He parked in a sandy area and walked to a tall cottonwood tree at the river's edge. He sat by the bank and stared at the water flow. The smell of cottonwood trees and the river mixed in a natural aroma. Lucky Joe picked up some pebbles and cast them into the water.

He thought of his earlier ambition of being the leader of the Grey Piñons. It was easy, sitting in an air conditioned office in the Magic Lance, with money pouring in and staff members following his orders. Now that adversarial forces were loose, his courage was wavering.

Things were out of control. His life was miserable. He and his whole family might be in immediate danger. People who benefited from the present arrangement of gambling were not going to let things change without a fight. They would target the key people. He was one of those people.

It seemed strange that this way of life, which seemed so simple and peaceful for so many years, now was center stage for momentous events. Had it not been for Segundo's grandiose plan to buy all the farm and ranch land for a Native American state, perhaps nothing would have happened. The gaming compacts would have been renewed, the status quo maintained.

And yet there was vision and courage in the plan. The idea of an all-Indian state appealed to him. Perhaps the plan still could be accomplished, at least to a substantial degree, and the gaming compacts maintained. Segundo might be right. Correct a number of hangnails, and balance and harmony would be restored.

Re-instate Velasquez and Abeita—that should help correct some problems with tribe members. There was no question Segundo's heavy-handed move against them had backfired. The sooner he got that problem corrected, the better. He remembered the night Segundo said he was going to dis-enroll Velasquez and Abeita. Lucky Joe felt in his bones it was a mistake. He should have asserted his opinion then, before the fester became an all out sickness.

He remembered the night in the church, when Velasquez's men just about had him, and the entry of Father O'Grady. Now that was courage, Lucky Joe thought. Father O'Grady ordered them out of the church. There were four of them. They could have overpowered the priest and himself. But Father O'Grady's courage prevailed.

Lucky Joe threw a few more pebbles in the stream. Across the river, he saw the church bell tower in the old village. "The church saved me once before," Lucky Joe thought. "That's where I'll go again."

Lucky Joe drove to the church and went inside. It was a traditional church like others on Indian reservations of the Southwest, made of adobe with thick lower walls, high windows, heavy wooden vigas across the top with aspen branches in herringbone design between the beams. Double wooden doors led through a foyer. In the interior, the altar was raised on a low platform with a cross hanging on the wall behind the altar. Wooden pews with kneelers stretched out on either side of the middle aisle. A once maroon-colored rug that now was the color of the earth outside ran down the center aisle.

Instinctively, Lucky Joe crossed himself as he walked up the aisle. He stopped before the altar, then turned and looked at the pew under which he had hidden the night Velasquez's men chased him into the building. Maybe Velasquez was God's cattle prod, Lucky Joe thought. He got me into the church.

After a long silent spell, Lucky Joe left through the two double doors at the front, walked around the side of the church and

MAGIC LANCE

entered an arched gateway that led to a garden area in front of the church residence. He was hesitant, but eventually knocked on the door. Shortly, Father O'Grady came to the door.

Lucky Joe immediately observed Father O'Grady did not recognize him.

"Father, I was hoping to talk to you. I am the person you rescued some time ago, when my friends were about to beat me up."

"Oh, yes," Father O'Grady said. "The friends who were not that friendly. Let's talk in the church."

He and Lucky Joe went through the side door that Father O'Grady used the night of his rescue. He flicked on the lights that illuminated the altar, highlighting the cross. The two men sat on a pew, one in a black shirt and pants and a white collar, the other in blue jeans, a western shirt, rodeo buckle and low heel boots.

"I am deeply troubled, Father."

Father O'Grady meshed his fingers together and perched his hands across his lower stomach. He listened.

"My enemies are starting to surround me and I do not know what to do."

"Who are your enemies?"

"Everybody," Lucky Joe said, with some conviction. "Tribal members. Those same guys who chased me into this church. And I want to thank you for saving me that night. It was your courage that prevented them from beating me, or killing me."

"Anyone else?"

Lucky Joe studied the priest. He had a smooth complexion, glasses with gold-plated rims, hair turning grey and blue eyes. Lucky Joe thought the man was probably ten or fifteen years older than himself. In that black uniform and white collar, Lucky Joe did not think of Father O'Grady so much as a man, but as a religious figure who would understand Lucky Joe's situation, and be motivated to take action on his behalf.

"Legislators, other Indians, gamblers, religious fanatics who don't like gambling. They're all lined up. That's just for starters. Anybody who is benefiting from Indian gambling is turning against me. Some old ranchers, environmentalists. Everybody. They don't even have to have an interest in gambling to be against me now."

"You sound like a one-man community scapegoat. Maybe you should charge for playing that role."

Lucky Joe smiled. His wide mouth showed a row of straight teeth, and his eyes showed a touch of humor for the first time in weeks.

"Maybe I should volunteer to be like old man Zozobra; that big statute they set on fire over in Santa Fe every September, Zozobra, Old Man Gloom."

"That would end your worries. But the side effects are terminal. Do you know what it is you're doing to cause all this animosity?"

"It's the land acquisition plan," Lucky Joe said. "I'm sure you've heard about our visionary plan to acquire as many ranches as we can, to return land to the Grey Piñons and other tribes. The land should come back to its rightful owners. That is just. Time has passed since all those land grabs occurred, but my people have not forgotten. We have a brief time to set things straight. We have the ability if we can sustain our will. And we're doing it the fair way. We're buying the land instead of taking it."

Even with the priest, Lucky Joe was guarded, not expressing his ultimate vision of a Native American state.

"I've heard of the activity for sure," Father O'Grady said. "I don't have a position on whether all this land buying is a good idea or not. I know some tribe members are worried all their

MAGIC LANCE

gambling profits are being spent, and they're not convinced the money is being spent wisely. Maybe the land purchases will provide a base for economic development, so the tribe will not have to rely on gambling. That would be preferable."

"The money is being spent wisely. Only the plan is generating lots of opposition. Anyway, I'm not sure we can accomplish our original vision. Even the U.S. Senate is getting involved."

"How is that?"

"Senator Walton has introduced a bill to eliminate Indian gambling. That will have a devastating effect if it passes."

"You are Lucky Joe Cruz, are you not?"

"Yes."

"You have become something of a minor celebrity around the tribe. Obviously, that is not particularly comforting."

"I'm miserable with all this," Lucky Joe said.

"There often are spiritual solutions to human problems, even when those human problems do not appear to be spiritually based."

Lucky Joe placed his chin in his hand and propped his elbow on his knee.

Father O'Grady had a listener.

"It all begins with faith in God," Father O'Grady said. "Once you have established that, Lucky Joe Cruz, the self of Lucky Joe Cruz, the ego of Lucky Joe Cruz, must be surrendered, crucified, given up. Pride is eliminated. Trust in your own abilities is abandoned. Trust in your own wisdom, your own courage, your own discipline, your own luck, is abandoned. And in its place is humility. God's will becomes your will, through obedience. You put your trust in God, you enter into fellowship with him, and God is revealed to you through his son, Jesus Christ, and the sustaining power of the Holy Spirit."

"What's all this got to do with my enemies?" Lucky Joe asked.

"You are set free from them, and yourself. You are directed by God's will through the Holy Spirit. It's no longer Lucky Joe Cruz doing all this. It is the Spirit of God working within you, through you. You become an instrument of God, day by day, minute by minute. You will be motivated by God's love, the desire to do what's best for every person with whom you come in contact, good and bad alike."

"Like love your neighbor as yourself?" Lucky Joe said.

"Do you normally do what you think is in your own best interest?" Father O'Grady asked.

"Sure."

"Then do the same for all with whom you come in contact. Do what you think is in their best interests. And come back in awhile and tell me how you're doing."

Lucky Joe smiled. "Thank you Father. I'll do my best."

Lucky Joe took a deep breath of fresh air as he walked out on the plaza. The instruction from Father O'Grady was reassuring. It was similar to what Lucky Joe thought of his own relationship with the spirits. One had to be in harmony with the One.

A deep relief from worry and strain caused his body to relax.

The spiritual instruction was timely, for tomorrow would be one of the darkest days of his life.

CHAPTER THIRTY-FOUR

The word of Alfredo's death came suddenly. It came the day after Lucky Joe had talked with Father O'Grady, and the word came through the priest. Lucky Joe was in the dugout that morning, talking on the telephone to real estate agents, surveyors, bankers, lawyers and others who worked with the land acquisition program. Among the people who often visited the dugout, there were no church representatives. Perhaps for that reason, Father O'Grady's appearance created some excitement in the office. Anita Martinez straightened her dress and brushed her hair back. Lucky Joe tucked in his shirt on the sides. Two visiting tribal members stepped back, giving the priest a clear path.

Father O'Grady had no smile today. There were no friendly greetings. He asked to talk to Lucky Joe in private. Everyone cleared out.

"I have some difficult news," Father O'Grady began.

Lucky Joe focused his attention immediately on the priest's eyes.

"It's about your grandfather. He had some kind of medical emergency. We're not sure if it was his heart or a stroke. I'm very sorry to report that whatever it was, it was fatal."

Lucky Joe's eyes widened, and his lower jaw dropped.

"What?"

"Within the last half hour. Word came through your grandmother. She was anxious that you be told at once."

"I must go to her."

"She is at home," Father O'Grady said. The two men left the dugout together without saying another word. Those remaining sensed the solemn air that accompanies the passing of the spirit of a loved one.

Lucky Joe remained in a state of shock for several days. Customary burial ceremonies were conducted by tribal leaders and by Father O'Grady. The grief Lucky Joe felt was partly the realization that his grandfather was a person who strived for Lucky Joe's best interests in all aspects of life. How many people could he say had that love in their heart for him? Other people might like him, might work with him on projects or goals, might do favors in hope of reward or personal gain, but who else in his life had only one objective, to do whatever was in Lucky Joe's best interests? It was in that sense, Lucky Joe felt Alfredo's love. And it was that love he knew was gone, and would not be replaced in another human being. For a week after Alfredo's death, Lucky Joe was inconsolable. With some respect for his grieving, friends and foes alike left him alone. Lucky Joe wished to be only with his own family, particularly Rachel, and to some degree with his grandmother, to empathize with her loss and her sadness, and with her joy at having been Alfredo's wife.

A week later, Lucky Joe returned to the dugout. He was without spirit. He was not sure he could do anything. He had no motivation. He knew he had to get back with the program. The land acquisition program could not wait. It was a concern to him when Segundo came into the dugout office on his first day back, and shut the door.

During the ceremonies of the past week, Segundo had dutifully expressed his condolences.

MAGIC LANCE

Now, in the dugout, Lucky Joe watched Segundo's nostrils flare as he began to speak. The subject was the power vacuum that appeared suddenly, and without warning. Alfredo had appeared to be in good health. His death was a shock to the entire tribe. It unleashed deadly forces, Segundo said. "As I am sure you are aware, you and your immediate family have been protected by your grandfather's leadership position in the tribe. That is now history. You all are in great jeopardy."

"Jeopardy? Jeopardy from what?" Lucky Joe said.

"From people who oppose not only this land acquisition plan, but you personally and your position with the casino that has made you rich. They believe you personally are benefiting from this land program. There are some who resented your grandfather's leadership. Now that he is gone, they may try to get even for real or imagined inequities."

"Who are you taking about? Velasquez and Abeita I already know about. Who else?"

"Unfortunately, there appear to be many," Segundo said. "Without formal proof, it is not wise for me to start giving names. Some of them would surprise you."

Lucky Joe rubbed his hands together. "Do you think Rachel and Rick and Andrea are in danger?"

"Immediate danger," Segundo said. "I think you have no choice but to leave at once, and find a place of safety far away, until the situation is sorted out."

"Where could I go?"

"Doesn't your wife have some relatives in California?"

Lucky Joe ran his fingers back and forth on the edge of his desk, as though he were playing a piano.

"I know this comes at an awkward time," Segundo said. "You know we need you here. But personal safety cannot be ignored. Alfredo's passing has created a crisis situation in the leadership of the tribe. Until it settles down, your opponents are going to consider you and your family fair game."

"What have you heard?"

"I have heard rumors only," Segundo said, "second-and third-hand. I think there is a group that intends to eliminate you and your family, for past grievances against Alfredo, and since he is gone, now against you. While he was tribal leader, and alive, they were cowards, afraid to act. Now they are emboldened. They intend to strike quickly, at night. You must leave at once."

"Why haven't I heard these rumors? I haven't heard anything."

"The rumors have just started. I myself only heard them this morning. The former cacique has been dead a week. It has taken the wolves that amount of time to sharpen their teeth."

Lucky Joe paced the room. He clasped his hands. "This is totally unexpected. I have to act."

"Yes. At once," Segundo said. "We can stay in touch by telephone, and e-mail. I will keep you advised of all developments. I don't think the crisis will last that long. In a month or so, I think it will be safe enough for you to return."

Segundo stood next to Lucky Joe and put his hand on the younger man's shoulder. "I will explain to the tribe that you are overcome with grief, and that you have taken a brief leave of absence, and that you are expected to return."

Segundo walked to the window, hands joined behind his back, and looked out on the plaza.

"Alfredo's passing has been a shock to the whole tribe," Segundo said pensively. "It is likely I will be appointed the next cacique. If that happens, I will send for you and your family at once. I will be able to guarantee your safety, just as your grandfather did before me."

"That settles it then. Rachel and Rick and Andrea and I will leave this afternoon. I'm not sure where we'll go, maybe to her sister's in California. Wherever it is, I will call you. I may not tell you where I am. But I will call you and see what's happening. As soon as things settle down, I'll be back."

"You are wise," Segundo said. "I will wait a day before I announce you have gone. By that time, you hopefully will be far away, and those who seek revenge on you and your family will be too late to carry out their monstrous schemes."

Lucky Joe rushed to his home. He was relieved to see Rachel in the living room. He quickly explained the situation as he understood it, and told her to find Rick and Andrea. They needed to leave in haste. Their lives depended on it. They would talk about the details of their exit and decide exactly where they were going as they drove.

CHAPTER THIRTY-FIVE

Rachel left at once to find Rick and Andrea. Lucky Joe began gathering personal items to take on their trip. He pulled the SUV near the front door of the house to load items they would need. As he got out of the vehicle, he saw Rachel running along the dirt road that led from the plaza. She was shouting his name. He immediately ran to meet her.

"Lucky, Lucky," she said breathlessly. "Rick and Andrea are missing. They were supposed to go to the store to get some snacks. And they got to the store, but they left there. And then Rita Jaramillo said she saw them going down toward the river, and after that, she saw Sam Pichocho going behind them."

"Where toward the river?" Lucky Joe asked.

"I don't know. She just said they were going toward the river."

"Come on," Lucky Joe said. "Let's get down there."

The couple ran down the road that led to the village area, then off to their right. They looked in all directions.

"Where did Rita see them?" Lucky Joe asked.

"I don't know. Oh, here she comes now," Rachel said, pointing in the direction of the plaza. Rita Jaramillo soon joined them.

"We've lost Rick and Andrea," Lucky Joe said. "Rachel said you saw them going toward the river."

MAGIC LANCE

Rita lived two houses down the road from the Cruzes and had been a trusted neighbor for years. She was known to have a keen eye when observing what was going on in the environs of her home. Lucky Joe asked her exactly when and where she had seen Rick and Andrea and in which direction they were going. She reported they were walking together with Rick carrying a paper sack. They turned off the road just beyond where they were standing and headed toward the riverbank. Moments later, Sam Pichocho walked by, carrying some metal fence posts and wearing a tool belt. Further along, he caught up with the kids, and they walked together toward the river.

"Show us where they were the last time you saw them," Lucky Joe said. Rita pointed to a spot a hundred yards up the road near the river.

Lucky Joe asked Rita to call the tribal police and tell them Rick and Andrea were missing on their way home from the store, and ask that they start looking for them and tell them the kids were last seen with Sam Pichocho.

Lucky Joe and Rachel half walked and half ran in the direction Rita had pointed. They reached the riverbank and looked in all directions. There was no one in sight.

"Do you think Sam Pichocho could have done anything with them?" Rachel asked. Lucky Joe said he had no idea, but he would put nothing past him. To himself, Lucky Joe wondered if Segundo's warning had come too late.

While walking along the riverbank, Rachael spotted a brown paper bag. She looked inside it and discovered a packet of Twinkies and an orange soda, Rick's favorite snacks. She showed them to Lucky Joe. They searched the bank area thoroughly, observing only some footprints of what appeared to be two children and one adult. The adult's prints showed a thick heel and wide soles, most likely from a work boot.

Lucky Joe and Rachel felt a rivulet of fear run through their veins. Why would Rick leave his favorite snacks on the riverbank. And what were they doing down here in the first place?

Lucky Joe pondered the situation momentarily. "Let's go upstream and downstream for a distance, and see if we can see any more tracks," he said. "It looks like they must have been standing right here, with someone else, probably Sam Pichocho. But what did they do next?"

"There're a bunch of tracks right here, but I don't see them going anywhere," Rachel said. "Oh, wait. Look there. The boot tracks head down river, and then angle off back toward the village. But where are the kids' tracks?"

"You go up and I'll go down," Lucky Joe said. "Not very far. Let's see if we can find anything."

They separated. Lucky Joe moved quickly along the riverbank, looking for any signs that might indicate Rick and Andrea had been there. Rachel did the same in the opposite direction. Lucky Joe went a hundred yards before he came upon a spot on the riverbank where a Russian olive tree grew, holding the soil together and creating a diversion so a limited pool of water formed on the upstream side of the roots. Some green grasses grew along the river's edge, and a bunch of white and brown-colored foam coated the top of the pool.

There Lucky Joe spotted a green and white baseball cap. As he plucked it from the pool, his heart trembled. It was Rick's hat. He quickly looked out across the river, upstream and down. Then he ran downstream, looking for any further signs. Seventy five yards further he stopped, at a spot where he could look down river for another hundred yards. There was no sign of the children.

Grasping the hat in this hand, he went quickly back to find Rachel. She had found nothing. He showed her the hat and told

MAGIC LANCE

her where he found it, and that he had run downstream and seen nothing.

"We need to get help," Rachel said. "Lucky, I'm scared. Do you think they could have fallen in the river?"

"Or been pushed," Lucky Joe said. "I don't know."

"Or worse," Rachel said.

"Don't say that," Lucky Joe said. "Why did they come down to the river, if all they were doing was buying some snacks? And why would Rick leave his snacks by the riverbank? And why was his baseball hat in the water?"

"Let's go back and call the police," Rachel said. "Hurry!"

Lucky Joe said that he was going to go downstream further and then would return to their house. Then, thinking again of Sam Pichocho and Segundo's warning, he decided to accompany Rachel to their home and get police help to resume the search.

As the couple walked up the slope away from the riverbank, they saw Rita Jaramillo running toward them along the top of the ridge. She was waving her hand and shouting.

"They found them! They found them!" Rita called as Lucky Joe and Rachel drew closer.

"How are they?" Lucky Joe shouted back.

"They're okay," Rita yelled. "They're okay. They got on an old log raft and floated down the river for a ways, until Andrea got wet. Then they got off and walked home. The police found them a hundred yards from your house. They were on their way home."

Lucky Joe and Rachel clutched each other. Rachel was crying. "Oh, thank God, thank God," she kept repeating.

"What did Sam Pichocho have to do with all this?" Lucky Joe asked Rita.

"I don't know," Rita said. "I think he was just going over to his father-in-law's field to do some fence-mending."

Lucky Joe felt a rush of guilt, knowing he had vowed to himself that if Sam Pichocho had done anything, anything at all, to Rick and Andrea, his soul would depart this world as soon as Lucky Joe caught up with him. With that thought in mind, Lucky Joe was more convinced than ever that it was time to put some distance between his own family and the Grey Piñon Reservation.

CHAPTER THIRTY-SIX

It was traditional in Grey Piñon culture. There always was a backup location. It went back to early days. It was reinforced during the days of conflict with the U.S. Cavalry after 1848. You had a plan. You had an encampment. If the enemy were waiting at the planned encampment, there was a second location designated. Everyone might scatter, everyone might be chased, but each one knew where the second rendezvous location was and they headed for it. Lucky Joe had that feeling today, even though the enemy was not the U.S. Cavalry. The enemy was his own tribesmen. He was fortunate Segundo warned him before he was attacked. Never had he thought of an actual second location. The Grey Piñon Reservation had been secure during his lifetime. The reservation was both the primary location and the secondary location. Now, for the first time, he experienced the need for a location off the reservation. California was his first thought. Rachel's sister was there. She would welcome them. It was not as if they were poor relatives showing up. Lucky Joe was well prepared to pay his room and board. California was far away. That was what he thought he needed.

As hours passed, Lucky Joe became more reluctant to leave his home country. He loved the mountains, the desert floor, the river banks, the foothills. Realistically, he had no identification with large cities, heavy traffic, pollution, endless streams of people. Even the best big cities were not his ideal.

As he packed his four-wheel-drive vehicle and small trailer, he thought of options. When nothing seemed right, he imagined what his ancestors would have done. To them, such a tactical move must have been second nature. Water was a prime consideration. They would have to be close to sources of drinking water. Isolation. They needed to be in a place where their enemies would not find them. Supplies. He needed supplies, although with a vehicle, he could make a trip to places to get supplies. He would only have to watch his back trail.

Lucky Joe discussed his thoughts with Rachel. They needed a second place. They needed to get away from the Grey Piñon Reservation for a time. But where? It was during the discussion of the second place, that Rachel began to probe more deeply into what convinced Lucky Joe he needed to leave. Lucky Joe repeated Segundo's warning. There were those who feared Alfredo and opposed his leadership of the Grey Piñons. Now that Alfredo was gone, they would seize the opportunity to get even. The land acquisition program was brilliant and visionary, but it generated passionate enemies. Velasquez and Abeita were two. Segundo said there were many more. Rachel was mildly skeptical but not skeptical enough to oppose Lucky Joe's plans for a temporary move, especially after her scare over Rick and Andrea's brief disappearance.

In a compromise, it was decided they would leave immediately and find a temporary campsite outdoors and away from the reservation to rejuvenate and revitalize their spirits. Then, Rachael, Rick and Andrea would fly directly to California to stay with Rachel's sister. Lucky Joe would return to the reservation to follow the tribe's deliberations over who would follow his grandfather as the tribe's cacique.

"What about your Taos tepee?" Rachel asked. "We're not tepee Indians, but for living outdoors for a few days, it makes a good camp."

Lucky Joe purchased the tepee in Taos, New Mexico, several years earlier, thinking he would use it on hunting trips. He set it up in their back yard and left it up for several weeks but had not used it since. He wondered if he could remember how to set it up.

Lucky Joe imagined himself riding with Wild Horse a century and a half earlier. Wild Horse's meager supplies would be hauled on pack horses or travois. He clearly would not have had a tepee. Where would Wild Horse have gone in similar circumstances?

Then it popped into Lucky Joe's mind. His second location was obvious. It was Chloride Springs, the rest and recreation area of the Grey Piñons when Wild Horse was chief. It was an isolated area. With luck, the young rancher would not visit the site for a while. And if he did, Lucky Joe would negotiate a temporary deal to allow him and his family to stay for a few days. Lucky Joe also heard Lance Burnett was spending the weekends in Sierra City to be with his wife. Lucky Joe thought this made it less likely he and Rachael would be disturbed. When they left, they would leave no trace.

A primordial excitement filled Lucky Joe Cruz. He was going to the traditional resting site of Wild Horse. Perhaps there he would encounter the chief's spirit and learn what his instructions were for the Grey Piñons. That very thought reversed years of negative thinking, reluctance to take action, fear and anxiety that life was out of control, that others had the upper hand, that he was without the ability or the spirit to lead the Grey Piñons. At Chloride Springs, Lucky Joe knew his spirit would be rejuvenated, that he would be prepared and equipped

to lead the Grey Piñons to their destiny in the land of their forefathers and in the way of their tradition. What started as a retreat now was a redemption. He would merge his soul with his ancestors and the Kachinas and the Cloud People, and the land that was the flowing fountain of their spirit.

CHAPTER THIRTY-SEVEN

There was an air of excitement in Lucky Joe's chest as he drove the last quarter mile to Chloride Springs. He was conscious of every tree, of every branch on every tree and of every leaf or pine needle on every branch. He was conscious of the shinnery oak, the blue gramma, the three awn grass, the piñon trees and the alligator junipers. He saw the dark-eyed junco, the white wing doves, the pinyon jay, raven and canyon towhee. He saw details in the rock ledges that ran along the canyon and in the thick ponderosa pines that reached for the sky.

The country had changed little since the days of Wild Horse. Lucky Joe imagined himself riding along the canyon floor, at the side of Wild Horse and other Indian braves. If only it could be that way again.

At the trailhead, Lucky Joe pressed his large four-wheel-drive utility vehicle through some bushes that overgrew an old roadbed. The abandoned road ran for another two hundred yards, then ended at a clearing near the springs. Lucky Joe thought the situation near perfect; his utility vehicle was beyond the trailhead, and would only be seen by someone coming toward the springs on foot. He hoped it would be some time before any such person appeared. Until then, he was living in the past, living in tradition, living in fellowship with his ancestors and the spirits.

For the first few hours after their arrival, the Cruz family spent their time unloading the utility vehicle and attached trailer. Lucky Joe laid the long wooden beams for the tepee out in the grass and the canvas next to them.

Since it had been several years since he'd set one up, he had to experiment with methods of connecting the tepee poles and raising them. He finally got it. He used a spare pole to push the tepee canvas to the pole tops, and then wrap it around the slanted supports.

Rachel got the food organized and the cooking utensils arranged.

"How did they ever travel without utility vehicles and trailers," Rachel said to herself.

Rick could not have been less interested in camp arrangements, but was fascinated with a long-handled axe. He took it up and went right to the nearest ponderosa pine tree and started whacking at the trunk.

Andrea hollered at him to stop and ran to Lucky Joe for backup support.

"Whoa," Lucky Joe said, going over to Rick. "What happens when you get into that thing and it falls over?"

Rick shrugged his shoulders. Lucky Joe surveyed the area and suggested Rick go to an area of fallen trees on the far side of the clearing. "Go over there and chop some firewood for the fire," he told his son.

As hours passed, the tepee was erected and bedding moved inside. A cooking fire was made by digging a depression in the ground and placing a ring of stones around the depression. Lucky Joe took a half-inch iron stake and drove it in the ground at the rock ring and slipped the curlicue end of another iron rod over the stake. On the opposite end of the curlicue rod was a loop, suitable to hold a coffee pot handle.

MAGIC LANCE

"That's one thing we learned from the U.S. Cavalry," Lucky Joe said to Rick. "How to make coffee and how to use this iron stake deal. That's about the only thing, now that I think of it," he muttered to himself.

For dinner, Rachel prepared a pot of mutton stew. It was cooked in a cast iron pot hung on the stake handle over the wood fire. Rachel kept a close eye on Rick as he continued to chop firewood.

The activity consumed him. Rachel saw only the sharp edge of the axe slamming into the fallen tree limbs. One missed swing, and that same sharp edge could go right into her young son's foot.

Lucky Joe spent a half-hour gathering pine needles scattered under the ponderosa pines. He arranged stacks of the needles inside the tepee, then put a ground cloth over the needles. Sleeping bags and a pillow were put on top of the ground cloth.

In less time than he anticipated, the camp was arranged. The family joined forces to drag a pine tree trunk up near the fire, and outside the opening of the tepee. Rachel stacked food items and utensils along the trunk, leaving room at one end for several people to sit.

When the fire subsided to glowing coals, Rachel took out a flat skillet and placed it over the fire, balancing it on three rocks. She spread corn tortillas on the skillet and let them cook until they were showing brown spots.

Before long, the stew was ready and the tortillas were hot. Rachel flicked a tad of butter on the tortillas, sprinkled on salt, and handed to each of her family a bowl of steaming mutton stew and a buttered and salted corn tortilla. She was rewarded by appetites that told her she had a winner.

Following dinner, Rick and Andrea went out to explore, although hardly out of sight. Lucky Joe and Rachel pulled their camp chairs near the ring of stones at the fire. Lucky Joe took a deep breath, and laid his head back, staring into the fading light of the sky and watching the slow swaying of the pine needles at the top of the trees.

"Maybe we should have done this before," Rachel said, "instead of waiting until we were forced into it."

"This is so peaceful," Lucky Joe said. "No cars and trucks, no music blaring, no doors slamming, no people shouting, no dogs barking. It's almost scary."

As shadows crept up the walls of the canyon, a quiet settled over the area. Light faded. The noise of birds and squirrels ceased. The forest prepared for darkness, awaiting the animals of the day to change shifts with the animals of the night.

Before complete darkness arrived, Rick and Andrea returned to camp, pulled up two additional chairs, and sat with their parents around the camp fire. Rick needed no encouragement to throw additional wood on the fire. Left to his own, he might have built a bonfire that would have been seen as far away as Sierra City. As it was, Lucky Joe and Rachel kept him on a short leash.

While there still was some light in the sky, Lucky Joe led his family to the warm springs pool. Next to the pool, he laid down a packet he had carried under his arm. He laid out the soft leather and displayed four prayer sticks, pieces of wood decorated with painted figures and hawk and duck feathers. The family discussed the significance of Chloride Springs in the history of their tribe.

Lucky Joe directed Rick to assist him in piling up some mud from the edge of the pool. With his fingers, Lucky Joe flattened the mud like a pancake and drew a border around it. Then he drew circular symbols and connecting lines in the soaked earth. Lucky Joe directed Rachel and Andrea to jab their prayer sticks

MAGIC LANCE

into the circular symbols. He and Rick placed their prayer sticks so that all four geographical directions were marked.

"Tomorrow night we'll see if the prayer sticks remain upright. If they do, that is positive. If they fall or lean, we will have to beware," Lucky Joe said.

When the family returned to the tepee, Lucky Joe used a flashlight to usher everyone inside and let them crawl into their sleeping bags. He pulled the flap closed and tied the cotton straps. The temperature of the mountains was dropping now and the family appreciated the warm down of the sleeping bags.

Within a few moments, Rick said there were too many people in the tepee. He would be the sentry for danger and would sleep outside, as he imagined the young braves would have done in an earlier era. Ignoring Rachel's protest, and with Lucky Joe's acquiescence, Rick untied the cotton straps and dragged his sleeping bag out the canvas doorway. He placed the bag a few feet way, between the tepee and the utility vehicle, then returned to the tepee and tied the cotton straps.

For a time, Lucky Joe lay on his back, staring into the darkness of the tepee. He knew this experience was not far removed from what his ancestors experienced. He was aware of the modern advantages he had that his ancestors did not, especially the backup systems in place in modern society—hospitals, police, highways, telephones, gas, electricity, a secure food supply and known water sources.

Lucky Joe had visions of Wild Horse riding up to the spring on a spirited Indian horse, bedecked in fine fighting attire, the chief's magnificent lance carried in his hand. It was like a dream. The glory of it was more than anything Lucky Joe had experienced. In that mood and with those dreams, consciousness faded and he was asleep.

Later that night, he did not know how much later, Lucky Joe was awakened by Rachel's anxious whisper.

"Lucky! Lucky!"

"What is it," Lucky Joe stammered, barely aware of where he was and what was happening.

"There's something out there."

"It's probably Rick."

"No, I don't think so. But Rick is out there."

"I don't hear anything," Lucky Joe said, irritated.

They lay in total silence, hardly breathing.

Then there was a deep grunt, almost like the bark of a giant dog.

"There! See! What is it?"

"I don't know," Lucky Joe said, his senses suddenly alert. He sat straight up in his bed roll.

For several moments there was total quiet. Then the sound of some object falling.

"See," Rachel said. "There's something there. Rick's out there."

Lucky Joe fumbled for his flashlight. He had placed it under his pillow, he thought, but when he reached for it, he couldn't find it. A line of curse words followed.

A scurrying noise sounded outside the tepee doorway. Lucky Joe feverishly ran his hands all over his pillow and sleeping bag. Finally, he came upon the flashlight. He jumped up, sprang to the doorway, and tried to untie the cotton straps that held the canvas door closed.

A piercing yell came from outside. It was Rick.

"I'm coming," Lucky Joe yelled back. He got the top strap undone, but fumbled with the lower strap. It was caught in some kind of knot. Cursing again, Lucky Joe ripped open the top of the tepee door, and lunged through. In doing so, his right

MAGIC LANCE

foot caught on the bottom cotton strap and he fell face first out the tepee doorway, twisting as he did so and landed flat on his back. The flashlight fell to the ground inside the tepee.

At almost the same instance, while lying on his back on the ground at the tepee doorway, Lucky Joe partly felt and partly saw a large object pass right over his chest and face. Rick was yelling at the top of his voice.

Lucky Joe was on his feet about the time Rachel got the doorway flap open and shined the flashlight outside.

"What's happening?" she screamed.

Lucky Joe looked in all directions.

"It's a bear!" Rick hollered. Lucky Joe finally spotted his son. He was on top of the utility vehicle roof.

Lucky Joe grabbed the flashlight out of Rachel's hand and shined it in all directions. He saw nothing. "Which way did he go?"

"Over there," Rick said, pointing toward Chloride Springs. Lucky Joe shined the light all around the area, looking for any movement.

"He was right over here," Rick said, shaking as he shifted his feet to maintain his balance on the roof. "He ran right over you, Dad. I thought you were a goner."

Andrea stuck her head out of the tepee. Her eyes were wide and she clutched the canvas of the tepee doorway. "Is he gone?"

"He seems to be gone," Lucky Joe said. "You're right. I think he ran right over me when I fell down."

"We better get out of here," Rachel said. "This is more dangerous than the reservation."

"What was he doing?" Lucky Joe asked.

"I don't know," Rick said. "I heard him snorting around. He woke me up. He was over there by the campfire. When I saw what it was, I got the heck up here on the roof."

229

"You did exactly the right thing," Lucky Joe said. "You're one smart Indian."

"What if he comes back?" Rick asked.

"If he comes back, I think if I were you, I'd be in the tepee," Lucky Joe said.

"Do you think this canvas is going to stop a bear?" Rachel said. "He could come right inside the tepee, then what?"

"I've got a gun," Lucky Joe said. "A nine millimeter. That'll stop him."

"Oh, sure, and you'll probably blow one of us away in the dark," Rachel said. "We need to get out of here."

"He's probably more scared of us than we are of him," Lucky Joe said.

"Fat chance," Rachel said. "If I were any more scared, I'd be dead. And he isn't dead."

"We have to decide what to do," Lucky Joe said. "I'll put my gun right under my pillow, and we'll all get inside the tepee. We'll hear him if he comes back, and we'll all get together, and I'll shoot right through the canvas to scare him away."

"You sleep in the tepee if you want to," Rachel said. "I'm moving to the utility. I'm sleeping in there, and the doors will be locked."

"Me too," Andrea said.

Lucky Joe looked up at Rick, who was scooting down the windshield onto the hood of the utility vehicle. "Sorry dad," he said, as their eyes met. "I'm not sleeping in that tepee with that bear running around out here. You didn't see how big he was. He was big. That's a big bear." The bravado in his voice, as a sentry of danger, was gone with the bear.

Lucky Joe wavered, but decided there was scant room in the utility vehicle for more than three, if that many. He would keep the flashlight and the nine millimeter under his pillow and only lightly tie the cotton straps on the canvas doorway. That way, if the bear returned, he could be outside in an instant, flashlight and gun at the ready. His family would be safe inside the utility, with the windows mostly up and the doors locked.

That plan agreed upon, the family re-arranged their sleeping bags, took one more look into the darkness of the forest, and retired again for the evening.

CHAPTER THIRTY-EIGHT

Lance slumped on the sofa in Jan's apartment in Sierra City. It was Saturday evening. Monday morning he would head back to the Three V Ranch. Tonight he was partially tired, partially bored. Apartment life was diametrically opposed to his heart-driven desire to live in the outdoors. With Jan's presence, he could tolerate it. Wherever she was held some attraction.

Jan came out of the bedroom, dressed in shorts and a form-fitting sweater.

Lance tossed on the sofa. His mind raced back to that evening in Washington, D.C., after the political reception. Jan's provocative figure in that long, clinging black dress ignited his passions. Evenings like that were evenings he wished he could experience every night.

Tonight, Jan was evasive. He wanted to hug her. She kept moving around the apartment, raising his desires and keeping a distance.

Shortly, Lance discovered she was putting off telling him about something important to her. She eventually broached the subject. Senator Walton had offered her a job on his staff.

When Lance realized she was interested in the proposal, his thoughts returned to what Lightning had said during their conversation at the Rexall drugstore. "It was obvious, wasn't it? You didn't notice?"

"He said he prefers I work in Washington, but he has an opening in Ashton. He maintains a state office there."

"And what would you be doing for Senator Walton?" Lance suggested. "Modeling?"

"Modeling! Modeling! Lance, I do believe you're jealous. That is the most ridiculous thing I've ever heard you say. Are you insinuating Senator Walton is offering me a job because he wants to sleep with me? That he has no interest in whether I'd be good at the job?"

Lance buried himself in the sofa.

"Moving to Ashton has some major pluses. Your own mother and father are going there. I would have a steady job. It would give you time to look around. We wouldn't be under any immediate financial pressure. We'd have all the government benefits. Plus you get to hobnob with a lot of important people. It could lead to a good job offer. You've told me before you like the limelight of a crowd. This move could promote you into some kind of high-profile job."

"Maybe I could find something where they would introduce me as the husband of Jan Burnett, who works for Senator Walton."

Jan ignored the sarcasm and walked to the kitchen sink, where she leaned into the job of washing dishes.

Lance walked up behind her and put his arms around her. He kissed her neck.

"Lance, a move to Ashton could mean we're together again. Wouldn't you like that?"

"Sure, and give up the ranch," Lance said. "How could I keep the ranch and move to Ashton?"

"Lance, the Three V is uneconomical. I know how much it means to you. But the reality is ranching is uneconomical. You can't make a living at it. This job with Senator Walton could open up a whole new life for us. It would open doors for you as well as me."

"What if Senator Walton wants to open up the bedroom door?"

Jan pushed away, moving toward the living room area.

"Your personal insecurity is showing."

Lance didn't answer, but walked back to the sofa and slid down in the cushions.

"You must be awfully insecure, thinking I have any interest in a man like Senator Walton. He's old enough to be my father. Or at least my older brother."

"Yeah, see, you're backing off already. Your first statement was accurate. He's old enough to be your father."

"So what are you worried about? If he's old enough to be my father, why are you concerned?"

"Young women are attracted to men in power positions," Lance said. "What about Bill and Monica?"

"That's not my situation with Senator Walton! He happens to be a smart man, who is in a powerful position, and he has offered me a good job, in a place I'd like to be, either in Washington or Ashton. I'm entitled to a career. And he's married. Did you ever think about that? He's married."

"Ho-hum," Lance replied.

"I knew I couldn't discuss this with you. You have a one-track mind. You want to be out there on that god-forsaken ranch, totally isolated from the world, spending all your time with a bunch of smelly cows. How exciting is that? And what kind of career opportunities does that leave for me?"

"Not too exciting is it?" Lance said. His face flushed red. He stood up, went to the table by the door and picked up his cowboy hat. He walked out the door, slamming it behind him.

Lance's mind swirled as he left Sierra City and headed back to the Three V Ranch. Lightning was right. There was some-

MAGIC LANCE

thing going on between Senator Walton and Jan. He pictured himself grabbing the senator by his coat lapels, drawing back and slamming his fist right in the senator's face. That would straighten things out quick. Jan needed to learn the lesson. She wasn't going to have a relationship with anyone else while she was married to Lance Burnett. He wasn't going to tolerate it, not even if it were the president of the United States. Jan was his wife, and as long as she was, no one was going to mess with her. He would see to that.

A soft moonlight drenched the countryside as Lance raced along the unpaved road leading to the ranch.

From 33 Draw, he drove twice his usual speed as he climbed the mountain to the ridge above Quail Run Creek. He knew he was traveling fast. It didn't bother him. What did he have to lose?

By the time he reached the ranch house his mood calmed. A sadness settled over him as he remembered how Pepper and Nugget customarily came rushing out to greet him. He resolved that the next week he would find two replacement cattle dogs. The quietness of the night increased his sense of caution. Following a habit he developed since finding Pepper and Nugget dead, Lance pulled a .357 magnum revolver from underneath the seat of the pickup.

He walked to the front porch and looked in all directions. Above, through the ponderosa pine tree branches, he gazed at the bright array of stars. He stopped breathing for a few moments, listening intently. There were no sounds. He pulled open the screen door. As he turned the doorknob, his eyes spotted a set of papers hanging on the door. He looked closely and saw the papers were pegged with a roofing nail.

He tried pulling out the nail. It was well secured. With a pocket knife he fished from his front pocket, he pried the nail loose.

As he entered the living room, he already had a suspicion what the papers were. Without turning on the living room lights, he walked to the kitchen, flipped the light switch and sat at the kitchen table.

The papers started with the title: "RM Mortgage Company, Plaintiff, vs. Wilfred Burnett and Mary Burnett, Defendants. Action to Foreclose Real Property."

Lance leaned back in the wooden chair, his chin resting in the palm of his left hand. Lightning was right. He was up against powerful forces. Now, on top of everything, they were going to take the ranch. Tonight, he wasn't sure how he was going to stop them.

CHAPTER THIRTY-NINE

The next day, Lance was in another place, another frame of mind. He did not worry about his relationship with Jan, his shortage of money, the unknown forces allied against him. He went through ranch chores by rote, not thinking, not being concerned. Foundations were shifting under his feet. Life was totally out of his control. He had to find an anchor. He wasn't sure what his former anchor was. Whatever it was, it was not holding. Something new was required.

Late in the afternoon, he drove up Quail Run Creek. Since the day he found the dead cows, he was anxious driving up the canyon. As best he could determine, he lost three cows, and Pepper and Nugget. That made him think the perpetrator of the animal killings was looking for a target of opportunity. The cows along the road and the two dogs were at the wrong place at the wrong time. In a way, Lance was relieved. If only three cows were lost, that would not be a financial disaster. It was a loss. The threat of more losses remained.

As he drove up canyon, for the first time in several weeks he could appreciate nature's beauty in the trees and rock formations, the pattern of Quail Run Creek, the grass mixtures and the natural colors. A few cows and two calves grazing along the creek were reassuring. Lance's mind wondered at the complexity of life. It was out of his control. It was in the hands of some power far beyond his imagination. As the sun dropped and shadows lengthened, the thought came to him that he was a steward. This land was not his. It was his for this late afternoon, for the next few weeks, possibly the next few months, the next few years, or even a lifetime. Ultimately, it would pass to others. He was but a steward.

At the trailhead, Lance parked his pickup and walked around the clearing. At the edge of the Yepa National Forest fence, he looked upstream. For a moment, he thought he saw something unusual. Perhaps it was the bleached bark of an old ponderosa pine snag. He stooped down and looked through the shinnery oak and pines. No, what he saw was something out of the ordinary.

On a whim, he walked upstream, along the path he and Lightning had taken when they walked to Chloride Springs.

He stopped. There was a whiff of smoke.

He stooped again. Was there smoke? Was someone here on the Three V? A group of hippies? Lance debated whether he should return to his pickup and get the .357 revolver from under the front seat. The concept of stewardship won out. He was a representative of a higher power. He needed no gun. Whoever was there would be confronted, advised they were on private property, and ordered to leave by daybreak or face the consequences.

Lance walked casually, without concern. On approaching Chloride Springs, he stopped on the trail, stooped again, squinted his eyes, and looked through the remaining brush between himself and the open area that adjoined the springs. At first he thought he was dreaming.

In the fading light he saw a tepee. Smoke rose from a fire in front. A man and a woman sat in two lawn chairs by the fire. A hippie group, Lance thought. Probably old ones, using a tepee.

MAGIC LANCE

He walked cautiously forward. When he was but twenty-five yards from the tepee, he called out, "Hello."

The man and woman stood up as one, facing in his direction.

The man raised his hand above his head. Lance raised his hand. He advanced to the campsite.

"Howdy," Lance said, as he approached the campfire. Lucky Joe moved several feet forward, placing himself between Lance and Rachel.

"First tepee I've ever seen up here," Lance said. "You're on private land."

"You the owner of the Three V?" Lucky Joe asked.

"Yes," Lance replied. "You sound like you know where you're at." Lance was not sure but thought this Indian man was the one whose picture he had seen in the *Sierra City Sentinel*, and was none other than the Indian Land Czar.

"We know we're trespassing," Lucky Joe said. "But we were only planning to stay a few days, then we'll be gone, leaving no trace."

"Lance Burnett," the young rancher said, extending his hand.

"Lucky Joe Cruz," Lucky Joe said, extending his own hand. "This is my wife, Rachel. Somewhere around here, I've got two kids running around."

"Don't usually let anybody camp here," Lance said.

"We'll leave," Lucky Joe said. "It's a place that has a deep meaning to our people. We were only going to stay a few days. There are some developments in the tribe that caused us to leave temporarily."

In prior days, Lance would not have given a second thought to ordering these trespassers to clear the area at once, while he waited to make sure they did so, possibly at gunpoint. Getting the foreclosure notice mellowed his thoughts. Invincible ownership was not in his grasp. And the notion of "developments in the tribe" that caused Lucky Joe's departure intrigued Lance.

Rachel looked shyly at Lance. When he returned the glance, her eyes went to the ground.

"Are you from the Grey Piñon tribe?" Lance asked, looking at the tepee.

"We're Grey Piñon, yes," Lucky Joe said, his chest rising a few inches. "This was a resting area for Wild Horse." Andrea and Rick came from behind the tepee and stood next to their parents.

"Normally, we don't allow anyone to camp here," Lance said. He looked around the camp, recognizing the four-wheel-drive utility as the same vehicle that was parked at the trailhead when he and Lightning were at the springs.

"You must have gotten the word the Three V's not for sale," Lance said. His shoulders raised and his eyes narrowed.

"Yes, we know," Lucky Joe said.

An awkward period of silence followed. A light breeze brushed through the tops of the ponderosa.

"Well, you have your family here," Lance said.

"I wanted my family to have the experience that belonged to their ancestors," Lucky Joe said.

Lance gave an expression of understanding.

"We will do as you ask," Lucky Joe said.

Lance relaxed. "How long were you planning to stay?"

"Just a day or two," Lucky Joe said. "I was in some difficulty at the reservation, and needed a place to stay for a short time." Lance immediately suspected that any difficulty in the Grey Piñon Tribe involving the Indian Land Czar might hold some opportunity, depending on what the difficulty was.

"Is anybody else planning to join you?"

"No, it's just us. And one black bear. He visited us last night. I fell out of the tent and he ran right over me."

MAGIC LANCE

Lance suppressed a laugh.

Lucky Joe grinned. Rick came up next to him and he placed his arm over his son.

"Rick here was sleeping outside. He wound up on top of the utility vehicle."

"If I'd been here, I'd have been right up there with you," Lance said, looking at Rick. "Those wild critters are scary."

"Would you join us for dinner," Lucky Joe said. "We've got some stew ready."

Lance looked around for a moment. Intrigued at this fortuitous encounter on his home ground, he accepted the invitation.

Rachel moved back to the fire and stirred the stew pot with a wooden spoon. Lucky Joe arranged a lawn chair for Lance.

"Are you that religious chief who's trying to buy this place?" Lance said.

Lucky Joe halted; his eyebrows raised. He looked right at Lance.

"The Grey Piñon would like to buy this area. It's a special place. I do not claim to be a religious chief."

"A real estate agent in Sierra City told me some religious trust group headed by an Indian chief was interested in buying the place, along with everyone else's."

Lucky Joe laughed. Rachel directed Andrea to fetch several plates. From the cast iron pot that hung over the fire, she dipped a thick stew onto each plate. Andrea took a plate to Lance, and handed him a spoon. She went to the table by the tepee door and got a salt shaker, and delivered that to Lance as well. Lance dusted a layer of salt onto the stew and started to dig in, when he realized that he was the only one who had been served. He lowered the plate to his lap, and waited for the others to be served.

Lengthening shadows reached the hillside, and gradually darkness settled over the campsite. The campfire cast a mellow light on the faces of the Cruz family and Lance.

Lance was completely in the present, at a campfire in the upper reaches of Quail Run Creek, in the camp of an Indian family, on his own private ranch, on the ancestral lands of the Grey Piñons and the resting place of Wild Horse. After the meal, Rachel and Andrea picked up the plates and stashed them at the side of the tepee. Rachel took charge of Rick and Andrea, and they moved inside the tepee. Lance and Lucky Joe remained seated at the campfire.

"I understand why you do not wish to sell," Lucky Joe said. "This place has a special feel to it."

"I don't know how long I'll be the land steward. People are coming at me from all sides, including the Grey Piñons."

"At least you are not developing it. Once they start subdividing and selling for recreation and vacation homes, it gets hard to put the land back together. Even we don't have that kind of money."

"Gambling really turned out to be the golden goose for you guys," Lance said. "Is everybody in the tribe a millionaire?"

Lucky Joe laughed. "Maybe on paper, but there are still some poor Indians. Not like it used to be. You have to try real hard to be poor, if you're a full-fledged tribe member and there's a casino."

Lance wanted to say it must be nice to be rich and not have to work for it. Rationally, he knew that applied to a lot of people, and not just Native Americans with casinos. Rationally, he knew hard work was its own reward, whether a person made big bucks or not. With the foreclosure notice nailed to the ranch house door, it was hard to rationalize it.

Lucky Joe went to the portable icebox and pulled out an orange soda. He asked Lance if he wanted a cola. Lance picked a Coke.

"Some of the old people told me this place used to be called the Broken Heart Ranch," Lucky Joe said. "They said the people who owned it looked for two generations to find the broken heart, and never found it."

"What the hell is the broken heart?" Lance asked.

"A symbol," Lucky Joe said. "It's an old Spanish warning sign."

"Warning about what?"

"That there's danger and death nearby. They used it to try to scare people away from their mine sites. Apparently there was something to it, and they were successful. The old people said to stay away from here, even if it was Wild Horse's resting place. They say if the symbol is in a mine, the mine has a curse."

"What's the curse?" Lance asked.

"It's somewhat vague. Mainly that anyone coming in contact with the broken heart sign is destined for danger and that death lurks in the mine."

"Have you ever seen any broken heart signs?" Lance asked.

"I'm not looking for silver," Lucky Joe said. "I decided to come up here for awhile to let things cool off at the reservation. My grandfather died recently. There are some old-time hostilities on the reservation. I got some indirect death threats. There are a few people who want to get even for things that happened over the years. They were afraid to act when my grandfather was chief."

"Why are they after you?"

"Revenge."

Lance shook his head. "If they had complaints against your grandfather, they should have addressed them to him."

"That's the way I see it. But that's not the way some of them see it. And I have my own adversaries. As you know, we're buying ranch lands to diversify our investments. Some people oppose that."

"Yeah, and you're talking to one of 'em right here," Lance said. "I don't want to sell this place."

"Simple," Lucky Joe said. "Don't sell."

"It's not that simple. Cattle prices falling. Expenses going up. Environmentalists running wild. Mortgage payments due every thirty days whether you sell a calf or not. And somebody's even been poisoning some of mine. You know anything about that?"

"Like who poisoned your cattle?"

"And my two cattle dogs," Lance said. "That's what makes me want to get some revenge myself."

"I can tell you that no member of the Grey Piñons poisoned anything. That's not our way. Slaughter some cows maybe, but not by poison."

"I've been suspicious some of my neighbors might have pulled that off. The Cascade is trying to buy the Three V too, and I told them the same thing I told you guys. Stuff it."

Lucky Joe smiled as he took a swig of orange soda.

Darkness settled into the forest. The light wind stopped. Silence pervaded. Smoke from the campfire drifted in one direction, then another.

"Why not sell the Three V and take the money and buy another ranch somewhere else," Lucky Joe said. "Maybe in Colorado or Utah, or New Mexico or Arizona."

"That's not for me. My parents worked this place. I've worked it ever since I was a kid. This is the place for me. Why go anywhere else?"

Lucky Joe thought he heard the faintest sound of a vehicle engine, far down the canyon. "Is someone coming?"

Lance turned his head, pointing his right ear down canyon. There was only silence. "I don't hear anything. Are you expecting someone?"

MAGIC LANCE

"Not me. What about you?"

"I wasn't even expecting you," Lance said. "How long do you want to stay?"

"A lifetime."

"No. Sorry. I can't agree to that. But if you want to camp here for a day or two, and you're the only ones, that can be worked out."

The golden light of the campfire illuminated a relieved look on Lucky Joe's face. The two men stared into the tongues of flame that sprang from the pine logs in the fire pit.

"What about a compromise?" Lucky Joe said. "On your ranch, I mean. What if you sold us a hundred acres, up here around the springs, including ingress and egress? That would give us our core area, and you would have some fast cash to improve the rest of the ranch."

The proposal hit Lance like a flash of lightning. The deep stress and fear of the mortgage payments, of the constant harassment of creditors, of providing Jan with things she wanted, with giving his parents some return, and his brother and sister as well. All those problems would be solved in a heartbeat, if he got a substantial infusion of capital from a sale of a hundred acres. He still would have seven hundred acres.

"What about my keeping grazing rights on the hundred acres," was his immediate reply.

Lucky Joe was pensive. "For how long?"

"Forever."

"Maybe forever for you and your heirs, but if you or your family ever sell, the grazing rights revert to the Grey Piñons," Lucky Joe countered. His months of horse trading on ranch lands had quickened his responses to land ownership questions.

Lance's mind turned as fast as a dentist's drill. What was his mortgage payoff? If he got that full amount for one hundred acres, that meant the Three V would be free and clear. He mentally reviewed the foreclosure complaint. Being three payments behind allowed them to call the entire amount due. That figure popped uncomfortably into his mind. It was nearly five hundred thousand.

He needed five thousand dollars per acre. No, wait. There would be capital gains taxes. Federal and state. Together, it would be about twenty five per cent. He'd have to have six hundred and seventy five thousand dollars more or less for the hundred acres, allowing him to pay twenty five per cent of that in taxes, netting five hundred thousand dollars from the sale after taxes.

"I'd have to have about seventy-five hundred dollars an acre to come out," Lance said, putting a cushion in his first expression of interest.

Lucky Joe did not respond. He was running figures through his head. The springs was the premier piece of land they wanted. In dealing with hundreds of millions of dollars, what would seven hundred and fifty thousand dollars matter? "We might be able to go five hundred thousand."

Lance shook his head. Even if he paid off only a portion of the mortgage, that would release this long-term pressure he was fighting.

He was about to make a counter offer of six hundred and seventy five thousand, when a brilliant flash sparked among the ponderosa pines. KAPOW! Lucky Joe spun off his chair and fell prone on the ground, his forearm and hand at the edge of the campfire. A second shot hit the fire pit sending sparks flying in all directions. Lance reacted instinctively. He lunged toward Lucky Joe and pulled his hand and arm away from the fire. A third rifle bullet hit the coffee pot above the fire and sent it spiraling into the air. Frantically, sitting on the ground next to

Lucky Joe, Lance used both feet to kick dirt into the campfire, snuffing out the light. He quickly lay back, getting as close to the ground as he could. Rachel screamed from inside the tepee, seeking an explanation of what was happening. "Stay down," Lance screamed back. "Somebody's shooting." As he reached over with his hand to see if Lucky Joe was moving, he knew that it was more than "somebody's shooting." Somebody was hitting.

All went quiet, although Lance's ears were ringing. After a few moments, through the forest darkness came an eerie sound, like that of a wounded animal.

Lance's body froze. His breathing halted. The forest was silent, except for the eerie sound.

"What is that?" he whispered.

Moments later, Rachel whispered from the tepee: "It's the death chant."

CHAPTER FORTY

Lance was torn between options—should he examine Lucky Joe to see how badly he was hurt, or should he pursue the person doing the shooting? "Wait about a minute, then come out here and look at your husband," Lance said to Rachel, facing the tepee. "I'm going after whoever is doing the shooting."

With a burst of speed, Lance got to his feet and dashed to the streambed that flowed from the warm springs. He crouched for a moment next to the flowing water. Hearing nothing, he sprinted down the streambed, toward the trailhead. Fifty yards out he stepped into an unseen depression in the ground and spun forward haphazardly, striking bushes and bouncing off several rocks before falling face down on the ground. For a moment, he was senseless. When his mind cleared, he decided to move forward at a reduced pace. He wasn't going to catch anyone in the middle of the night if he were sprawled on the ground. When he was within a hundred yards of the trailhead, he heard a vehicle engine start. Spinning tires threw rocks up as the vehicle sped down the narrow road. Several times, the red brake lights came on, and the headlights flashed on several times for two-second intervals. Then the vehicle was out of sight. Lance thought he had seen a light colored pickup truck, but he was not certain. It was too dark and there was too much vegetation between himself and the trailhead.

MAGIC LANCE

Lance walked to the trailhead, inspected his own vehicle, and got his .357 magnum revolver out from underneath the front seat. Disappointed, but also relieved, he turned and walked back along the stream to the campsite. As he drew near, he saw some flames suddenly shoot up the side of the tepee. In the nighttime darkness it was surreal, as sparks spewed into the air. He saw Rachel using her coat to swing at the flames, trying to snuff them out. Andrea joined in, using her sleeping bag. From the left, Rick suddenly appeared carrying a plastic bucket of water. He slung the water on the tepee and raced back toward the spring to get another load.

Lance tucked his .357 into his belt and ran the remaining distance to the campsite. There he seized the coffee pot and grabbed the iron Dutch oven Rachel used to cook the stew, and raced to the stream for water. His and Rick's efforts along with Rachel and Andrea's were hopeless, and Lance knew it when he threw his first coffee pot of water on the flames.

"The tepee's lost!" Lance shouted. "Get some more water, and start putting it on the sparks that are flying!" The water brigade resumed and over the next few minutes they circled the blazing tepee, throwing water on hot spots on the forest floor. The tepee poles made a dramatic symbol in the forest, like a skeleton burning. The pine needles collected for bedding added to the flames when the burning canvas collapsed on them.

For a moment, the fire fighters ceased their efforts and stared at the spectacle of burning logs, canvas and pine needles. Within a few minutes the fire subsided, almost as quickly as it arose. It was only then that the fire fighters turned their attention to Lucky Joe.

He had steadied himself in one of the lawn chairs, and was holding his head. Black smudges were on his face, where his forehead and cheekbones hit the ground. Rachel wiped his face with a moistened cloth and rubbed butter on his hand. Andrea and Rick stood close by, their eyes as big as billiard balls.

"What happened?" Lucky Joe asked.

"Somebody shot at us," Lance said. "Two or three times, I think. Are you hit?"

"Must have grazed the right side of my head, right over my ear. It felt like a mule kicked me. I didn't even know what happened. One minute we were talking. The next thing I knew, Rachel was helping me get up off the ground. I can feel a little streak above my ear."

Lance got up close to Lucky Joe and borrowed the flashlight Rachel was holding. He closely examined Lucky Joe's scalp. "That's about as close a call as you're ever going to get. Somebody tried to kill you."

"What about you?" Lucky Joe asked. "Maybe they were aiming at you, and hit me by mistake. Or maybe they thought I was you."

"Anything's possible," Lance said. "Know anyone who wants to kill you?"

"I know several. But how would they know where I was? I didn't tell anyone."

Lance shrugged his shoulders. Rachel looked at the ground.

"What set the tepee on fire?" Lucky Joe asked.

Lance guessed it must have been a spark from the fire pit, thrown up by one of the bullets. "Maybe you better come down to the ranch house. It's about five miles down the canyon. Don't have my watchdogs like I used to. But it'll be safer than staying here."

"Yes, that's what we need to do, at least for tonight," Rachel said. Andrea and Rick nodded their heads in agreement. Lucky Joe was wobbly when he stood up, but he was able to get to the

MAGIC LANCE

utility vehicle. Rachel, Rick and Andrea jumped in with Rachel driving. They followed Lance as he walked down the two-rut lane leading to the trailhead. "What about the rest of our stuff?" Lucky Joe asked as they fell in behind Lance's pickup.

"What good is any of that to us, if somebody is shooting at us?" Rachel asked. "We'll come back for it in the morning."

When Lance reached the turnoff at the end of the cactus flats, he stopped his pickup and came back to the Cruz vehicle. "We'll come back here first thing in the morning," Lance said, "with a camera. I'll get some close ups of the tire tracks going up over to 33 Draw. If we get lucky, there might be a distinction in the tire track. There's a place with some fine sand about fifty yards up."

Lance and the Cruzes drove on to the ranch house. Lance did the best he could to get the family arranged in his and Jan's bedroom and in the spare bedroom. Lance settled down on the sofa in the living room, which was about a half-foot too short for his six-foot frame.

The next morning, Lucky Joe slept until 10 a.m. He awoke only after Rachel put her hands on his shoulder and nudged him. She was afraid he was not going to wake up.

Lance expected him to have a major headache. Surprisingly, Lucky Joe said he felt fine. There was a mild pain along the crease over his right ear. He speculated the bullet may actually have missed him, getting close enough to leave a crease but not actually hitting him. "I suspect your coffee pot didn't fare too well," Lance said. "That thing flew up like a ping pong ball."

Lance and Lucky Joe discussed what they should do. They agreed to make an immediate trip to the road turn-off at the cactus flats, and closely examine and photograph the road to see if they could preserve the tire track evidence. Then they would return to the campsite next to the warm springs, and see if they could find a rifle shell, or any other evidence that might link the shooter to the crime.

"Whoever it was," Lance said, "they weren't out there target practicing. They were trying to kill one of us, or maybe both of us, and they darn near succeeded. We need to call the sheriff's office and see if they can help us. We also need to be careful. Whoever this person is, or whoever these people are, they could try again."

CHAPTER FORTY-ONE

Lance, Lucky Joe and Rachel discussed their next moves. Rachel reserved a flight early that evening to Los Angeles for herself, Andrea and Rick. Lucky Joe said he had pondered his situation. It was not a good idea to be gone from the Grey Piñon Reservation during the weeks after his grandfather's death. He had followed the advice of the war chief. In retrospect, he thought it was a mistake. He needed to be at the center of tribal affairs, not hiding in a traditional resting place, no matter how attractive the idea. Lance asked if he had any ideas about who shot at them. If that person sang the death chant, it had to be a Grey Piñon. That person had to have a motive. It had to be someone who would benefit from their deaths. There couldn't be many people fitting that description. Lucky Joe thought of Segundo's desire to get the hot springs. Taking Lance out could be seen as improving the chances of that acquisition. Perhaps the shots were meant for Lance. Lucky Joe was the first one hit, and there were two more shots after that.

"How about you," Lucky Joe replied. "Do you know any Grey Piñons. Jilted lover. Jealous rival. Gambling debts. Betrayal. Drug connections. Anybody fit any of those categories?"

Lance's reaction was an immediate denial. In the back of his mind, he thought of Scooter Jones. He was a hotheaded, jealous type. But he didn't think there was enough of a connection with

Lightning to generate a killing. Obviously, he was not a Grey Piñon. Could he have learned the death chant from someone else? "No one in any of those categories," Lance said.

As he filled his water bottle for the day, Lance wondered if he could be set up—if the shot fired didn't come that close to Lucky Joe at all, and he made that crease on purpose as he fell, then feigned a headache. The hand close to the fire was harder to explain. The shots into the fire and the coffee pot could have been for show. Lance suddenly was not as comfortable with the thought of Lucky Joe staying in the ranch house. Since Lucky Joe and his family were departing shortly, he decided to stay at the ranch until they departed. Later that afternoon, he intended to go to Sierra City to see Jan and bring her up to date on developments.

When Lance and Lucky Joe arrived at the road turn-off to look for tire tracks, Lance kept a close eye on Lucky Joe, to see if he really were looking for tracks, or if he was going to try some diversion and lead them in an unproductive direction. As Lance suspected, there were fresh tire tracks in the sandy area, but he could detect no unusual feature in the tracks that would allow him to make a match. Lucky Joe did nothing to raise his suspicions.

"Who knew where you were camping?" Lance asked again. "If that person was shooting at you, he had to know where you were."

"Yeah, except as I said before, I didn't tell anyone where I was going. On purpose."

"Anything going on at the reservation that pits you against anyone?"

"Yes, on that score, I have to say there is. But I can't discuss it. It involves our land program, and you're part of that. Top secret," Lucky Joe said with a smile.

MAGIC LANCE

After getting photographs of the tire tracks above the road fork, Lance and Lucky Joe headed back to the ranch house. As they drove, Lance returned to the subject of the broken heart symbol. "How did you know this place used to be called the Broken Heart Ranch?" he asked.

"Heard about it when I was a kid. There have been long-time yearnings by my tribe to get Wild Horse's old hunting grounds back in the tribal lands. The Brandenburg family that owned the Broken Heart wasn't interested in selling. They had it for sixty or seventy years, I think. After that the Burnett family got it, through some marriage or family connection. That must have been your grandfather. He changed the name to the Three V. You can call it a broken heart, or a three v. Pull over at the next place there's some sand or mud, and I'll show it to you."

Lance stopped the truck at the next Quail Run Creek water crossing. The two men walked to some wet soil at the edge of the creek. Lucky Joe found a wooden stick and kneeled down over the wet spot. He drew the three v symbol in the soil. "See," he said, using the stick to run over the top part of the symbol. "It's like the numeral three, lying on its side with the open portion toward the bottom. A lazy three, and this little 'v' below the three, makes the three v. Or you could call it a heart symbol, with a blank spot on both sides at the bottom of the heart."

"And what did you say it was?" Lance asked. "What did it mean?"

"It didn't really mean any words. It was an old Spanish warning sign. They put it in a place to warn of danger. There was a vein of gold or silver and there also was a trap. There wasn't any way to protect the mines or assert ownership in those early days. When miners went back to Mexico, they tried to mark their site so they could find it again, but also to discourage others who might try to find it."

255

"So where would you see this symbol?" Lance asked.

"I've never seen one, so I don't really know. But what they say is that when you find this symbol, you are in danger of being trapped, and you are close to a silver vein."

A great excitement engulfed Lance, but he gave no outward indication of it.

When they returned to the ranch house, Lucky Joe and Rachel gathered their goods and prepared to leave. Lucky Joe told Lance they would return to the campsite briefly to survey the damage and pick up their trailer and anything else they left. The family thanked him for his generous hospitality and support. Lucky Joe told Lance he could find him at the Magic Lance, if he had any interest in going forward with the compromise of selling a hundred acres around Chloride Springs. He raised the Grey Piñon offer to six hundred and fifty thousand dollars.

For the first time, Lance saw hope of the Three V being saved, and of his being able to preserve his ranching way of life. Whether he could interest his mother and father, and Marc and Peggy in the idea, and most of all, whether he could interest Jan in coming back to the ranch, was something he had to try. The whole thing could still blow up in his face. Most particularly, he had to come up with the full amount of the unpaid mortgage, almost five hundred thousand dollars, or everything was lost.

Lucky Joe's last offer caused his adrenaline to surge.

CHAPTER FORTY-ONE

Lance could hardly wait to find Jan and tell her about the three v symbol and the Broken Heart Ranch. It was an unexpected development. Perhaps her bad luck with the tunnel rock would turn out to be the forerunner of events that would save the ranch. When he reached the apartment in Sierra City, Jan was not there. He went to the kitchen to get some ice. He drew a long drink of water, added ice, and walked around the apartment swirling ice cubes in the glass. After sitting on the sofa for a few minutes, he got up and walked to the window, looking into the parking lot. Few cars were there during the day. Going to the refrigerator a second time, grazing for snacks, he found a piece of pressed ham, rolled it up and polished it off, licking his fingers as he finished. From the refrigerator he went into the living room, slowly walking around. He sat on one of the bar stools next to the kitchen counter that divided the living room and the kitchen.

Lying next to the toaster was a stack of envelopes. Lance picked them up. The top envelope was from the electric company. The second was a water bill. The third envelope was the one that grabbed his interest. The return address had the official-looking printing from the Office of United States Senator John Walton in Washington, D.C. It had been opened and the flap tucked back inside the envelope. The letter was addressed to

Jan Burnett. At first, Lance thought that he should not read the contents. It was addressed to Jan. He would not be eager for her to read his mail without invitation. He picked up the letter, balancing it in the palm of his hand, weighing it to determine how many pages might be contained inside.

Finally, with a raise of his eyebrows, he deftly removed the letter with his thumb and forefinger, and unfolded it. It was dated four days prior. The writing was succinct. It was a written confirmation to Jan Burnett that she was hired. Her initial job description was news analyst. She would be paid forty four thousand dollars per year, plus full government benefits. Her first duty station, as she requested, was in Ashton. Lance crumpled the letter in his fist and started to throw it on the floor. On second thought, he unraveled the letter, put it on the counter top, and ironed it out with the palm of his hand. The wrinkles were clearly permanent. It settled into Lance's mind that his relationship with Jan was in greater danger than he thought. She was getting ready to move to Ashton to work for Senator Walton. If that happened, Lance thought there would be little chance of getting her back.

Later that afternoon, when Jan returned, Lance was set to have it out with her. He had been practicing the conversation for an hour. To his surprise, when she saw him in the apartment living room, she appeared elated and eager to engage him. Her enthusiastic and charming manner postponed the showdown he was going to initiate. She proposed they go to the Yucca steakhouse. She had some exciting things to tell him. Lance immediately returned to the offensive, anticipating that when she told him how thrilled she was to join the old senator's staff, he was going to let her have it. The gauntlet was going down.

At the Yucca, Lance and Jan sat at their favorite table. Jan ordered a glass of iced tea and Lance chose a draft beer. He

MAGIC LANCE

almost opened the attack by telling her he had read the letter. Then he decided to wait for the beer. When their drinks arrived, Jan proposed a toast to their marriage. She smiled that gorgeous smile. Lance lifted his glass. His agenda was in shambles once again. Jan asked him about his activities at the ranch. Lance told her he had some house guests, an Indian family. The Indian land czar himself. They had been shot at. Jan was shocked. She prodded Lance to tell her the entire incident from start to finish. When he got to the segment where he and Lucky Joe had been shot at near the campfire, Jan couldn't believe the drama.

"What did you do?" she asked, placing her hand on the back of Lance's hand.

"Crapped in my pants," Lance replied. They both broke into laughter.

"No really. Someone actually shot at you?"

"If you call putting a bullet crease in the Indian's head getting shot at, and shots in the coffee pot and the fire right in front of me, they were really shooting at us."

"Lance, that's horrible. Have you called the sheriff?"

"I sure did. I'm supposed to go by there and make a report. They said they had a fatal car accident and a murder they were tied up on, but they would get to this problem as soon as they could."

Jan looked around the restaurant. "Do you have any idea why anyone would be shooting at you, or this Indian?"

"Not really. I've got people who don't like me. But I've never had any threats."

"It must be the Indian. And you say he was there with his family, in a tepee."

"You'd have to have seen it to believe it. Looked like something out of a Western movie. The first night, he had a bear run over him, the second night he gets shot at and then his tepee burns down. Not the kind of person you'd want to insure."

"Aren't you scared?"

"I told you how I reacted. Whoever it was peeled out of there. I didn't get a look at the truck or car or whatever it was. This guy Lucky Joe and I studied the tire tracks this morning at the cutoff by the cactus flats. That could help."

Jan shook her head. She brushed her brunette hair back and took a drink of iced tea, looking straight into Lance's eyes.

"I have some rather exciting news," Jan said. Lance started to tell her he already knew all about the senator's offer, and he was going to tell her to go wherever she wanted. It didn't matter to him, because he was going to look for someone else. The image of Lightning McClain rose in his mind.

Before he could say it, Jan said: "You're going to be a father."

Lance slid his fingers down the beer stein until they rested on the table top. He said nothing, but stared deeply into Jan's eyes. "Meaning you're going to be a mother?"

"I am," she said. Her eyes glistened. A soft smile arose.

"Jan, that's wonderful. When did you know?"

"Yesterday, I saw Dr. Allen. He confirmed it. I was suspicious before that. But I didn't want to say anything until I was sure."

"Good grief," Lance said. "Good grief."

"Are you pleased?"

"Of course, I'm pleased. Only this changes things, doesn't it?"

"Changes what?" Jan asked.

"The way we're living. I mean, I thought you were thinking of taking a job with Senator Walton."

"Yes, that seemed to be on your mind when you slammed the front door the other night."

Jan turned her head. "This does change things. I'll have to do some new thinking."

MAGIC LANCE

"What about Senator Walton's job?" Lance said. In his mind, if Jan took that job, their marriage was over.

"That's no longer on the front burner. I was thinking career. Now I'm thinking about our child."

As the evening progressed, Jan and Lance mellowed. Two other couples they knew came by the table. Jan and Lance were cordial, but their hearts were somewhere else, in a peaceful place, far from worry or pain or concern for the world.

Toward the end of dinner, Lance mentioned to Jan that there were a couple of things pending at the ranch that might dramatically change their situation. He refused to divulge what those things were, even though Jan coaxed him several times to tell her. He said he could reveal it all in a day or two, after he made another excursion to that famous tunnel.

First he needed to do some research at the library and at the newspaper to see if he could find any reports about a lost silver mine, or any mine referred to as the Broken Heart. Soon, he would have to make another excursion into the mine where her accident occurred.

"Oh Lance, promise me you're not going in that tunnel. That's crazy. You can't do that. Not now."

"I'll be careful. I have to go back. Do you remember that symbol on the wall? The one we looked at before the rock slab came down?"

"Not really," Jan said. "That's one thing I hope I never have to remember."

"Anyway, there was a symbol on that rock that may make a big difference in what happens to the ranch. I'm going back there to see if there are any more symbols like that one we saw. And I want to take a close look at that area where the slab fell. Nobody's been back in there since we left, to the best of my knowledge. I sure haven't been back."

"Oh Lance, please put that off. Wait until you have some friends or a geologist, or a miner or someone like that. Don't go in there by yourself."

"I'm not going to be moving any wooden boxes at the base of the rock, I'll tell you that. I'm just going to do some looking. If there're any more three-v symbols in there, it could mean more falling slabs, but it also could mean some rich silver veins."

"Just don't go in there by yourself. Promise me that."

"I promise I'll be careful. By this time tomorrow, we may know if I can save the ranch, or if we need to go in some new direction."

"Lance, we can't think only of ourselves now. We have another life to consider."

"That makes it all the more important that I check this thing out. Our new addition could be one of the biggest beneficiaries."

The next day, Lance visited the newsroom at the *Sierra City Sentinel*. He talked to Jim Sorenson about the name of his ranch. Jim said he had heard many stories about lost silver mines, but people located them all over the county and never knew the precise locations. The symbol of the broken heart was something he had heard about, although the newspaper had run no stories. The information came to him through an old-timer he was interviewing about the silver boom in 1979, when silver rose to almost fifty dollars an ounce. The broken heart was a Spanish symbol. It indicated there was a rich gold or silver vein nearby, but that death awaited anyone who dared look for it. The old-timer reported that the Spanish used the heart symbol for gold, and sometimes silver. But what most non-miners did not realize is that a modified heart symbol, one with aberrations, could warn of a trap.

"What kind of trap?" Lance asked.

MAGIC LANCE

"There were many. The one I remember as being fairly common, was a slab of rock placed in a mine wall. The point of the broken heart pointed to the trap. It told friends who knew the secret to change direction, to approach the gold or silver vein from a different angle. To people who did not know the secret, it was an unexpected passage to death."

"But what did the trap look like?"

"From the outside, nothing special. It was just a wooden box that acted like a dam. Behind the dam, where you could not see, was a foundation of sand. The sand was the front part of the foundation of a large slab rock. Remove the wooden box and the sand drains out. Without its foundation in the front the rock slab then falls forward. Not a place you want to be when that thing slams down."

That explanation sent expectations flashing through Lance's mind. What Jim Sorenson told was exactly what had happened to Jan. Did that mean a silver vein lay nearby?

Lance's thanked Jim for his information, and then headed to the Sierra City library. He talked to the librarian who told him the newspaper archives now were housed at the state library in Capital, on microfilm. Finding a particular story on a particular mine would not be easy. Historians were becoming an endangered species, she said. Everyone wants instant information on the Internet. The early newspaper articles eventually would be available on line, but not now, and there was no index for things like mine names.

She asked him if he had found a lost mine, since she heard Jan had been hurt in a mining accident.

"Nothing of known significance," Lance replied. It was an answer he had rehearsed several times. He knew if word got out there was a silver mine on his ranch, it would attract speculators and mining claims. Realistically, he didn't know if he had found anything significant or not. But the story of the broken heart mine symbol he got from Jim Sorenson told him the trail was getting hot.

His research at the library turned up numerous books on lost treasure stories in the Southwest, of which there were many, but none about a lost silver mine in Ladenberger County.

His next move would be an exploration trip to the mine. An anxiety rose in his chest when he imagined himself going into the mine. He remembered the tarantula crawling on Jan's blouse, the bat coming out of the tunnel, the unusual sounds from deep in the drift and the curse that spoke of danger and death lurking in the mine.

CHAPTER FORTY-THREE

Despite his concerns, Lance was eager to explore the hidden tunnel again to see if there were any indication of a silver vein where the rock slab had fallen, or if there were any more symbols in the mine that might indicate additional veins. It was something he wanted to do alone. Revealing the secret to anyone else would jeopardize the plan he was formulating to save the Three V Ranch and become its sole owner, with the full blessing of his family.

The next day, on his way to the Three V, Lance felt a new sense of responsibility and importance. There was going to be an heir. He would have to take that into consideration in future planning. He thought of the Indian family that lost their tepee. There was an intuitive confidence in his heart the family was trustworthy, and had some of the same ambitions and dreams that he himself possessed. They had a common history. They had a common appreciation of the land. They had the common openness that belonged to people who possessed the spirit of the West.

When he reached the ranch house, he saw on the steps at the front door a bundle of sticks decorated with painted symbols and hawk and duck feathers.

After tending to ranch chores, Lance could hardly wait for the next morning, when he would make his first foray into the hidden tunnel since Jan's accident. As a precaution, he called his father, told him of the tunnel, and said he'd be going into it the next morning. He told his father exactly where to find the tunnel entrance, if there was a problem. He asked his father if he had ever heard the ranch called the Broken Heart. He said he had. People had occasionally referred to it as the Broken Heart the first few years after he inherited it from his father. After that, even those few people gradually dropped the Broken Heart name and called it the Three V.

"The Three V is what your grandfather called it before his death," his father said, "so that's what I called it. Earlier, your grandfather called it the Lazy Three V, but his ranch friends hazed him about it. They called his ranch the Lazy Three, and they called him the Lazy One. So your grandfather dropped the Lazy part, and called it the Three V. The brand, as Lance knew, was three small 'v's in a horizontal row.

The next morning, Lance had a breakfast of three fried eggs, six pieces of bacon, three pieces of toast and two cups of coffee. He was full when he drove the road along Quail Run Creek. When he reached cactus flats, he was surprised to see a beige-colored truck of the Cascade Ranch parked at the road fork. His excitement peaked when he saw the sole occupant in the truck was Lightning McClain. He drove slowly to her parking spot. Without a word being spoken, Lightning and Lance got out of their vehicles. Lightning came over to Lance's truck, and stood before him. Lance leaned back on the truck's front fender near the front wheel.

"Morning, Lightning." Lance was in an adventurous mood before he saw Lightning. She pushed his energy level up another notch. That Lightning had good looks was a given fact, but Lance realized her sensuality was something beyond that, communicated to men in some unknown way.

MAGIC LANCE

"I need to talk to you, Lance."

"I'm all ears," Lance said. He noticed Lightning had a red area on the left side of her face.

"I don't know how to start this. I guess it really started at the springs. There must be something in the water." Lightning moved over next to Lance and leaned on the pickup fender. He was four inches taller than she and she looked up when she talked to him at close range.

Lance was enthralled with her beauty.

"I'm telling Scooter I'm leaving. My heart is somewhere else. It's no longer at the Cascade Ranch."

"Oh?"

"It probably sounds strange. The glamour and the money and the power are what attracted me to the place, and to Big Bob's world. That's what I wanted. But now that I have it and I've lived it, from the inside out, it doesn't mean that much anymore. The thrill doesn't last, like I thought it would."

"That's surprising. You seem like you have the world wrapped around your finger."

"It looks good. Great clothes, jewelry, servants, big house, social activities, fancy cars, or a fancy truck, I guess. I can go anywhere, do anything I want. But something sure is missing. I didn't realize it until we had that meeting at the springs. Now I realize there're other things that are more important."

Lance shifted his feet and crossed his arms on his chest.

"Do you have any of those feelings?" Lightning asked.

If Lance had been honest, he would have told her he would have given the whole ranch to have had her on that day at the springs, or any day thereafter. Now, something was different. Lance wasn't sure what it was. He did know the opportunity to have a relationship with Lightning had passed. A week earlier he would have grabbed for it. Now, his thoughts were elsewhere.

Lightning moved closer to Lance. "I don't get the feeling you completely share those thoughts," she said, looking into his eyes. She ran her hand up and down his right arm. She moved her lips closer to his, looking into his eyes. Lance was mesmerized. She put her arms around him, placing her body next to his, kissing him, pressing her lips to his.

Lance pulled back. Lightning put both of her hands on Lance's face, guided him to her, and kissed him again.

Lance felt the surge of passion, from his toes to the top of his head.

"Lightning." Her lips were warm and moist and he had rarely felt such a pleasure.

"Lightning," he began again. "Something has changed."

She looked into his eyes.

"Lighting, Jan's pregnant," Lance said. "I'm going to be a father, and that changes everything."

"Oh, my," Lightning said, her face flushing red. "Oh, my. Exciting news." The corners of her mouth dropped and her shoulders sagged.

"You must be pleased," she said, stepping back.

"Yes, I am," Lance said.

Lightning stepped to the side and leaned against the pickup truck. She looked into the trees, then upward to the clear sky. After several moments, she drew in a deep breath.

"Maybe I should reconsider telling Scooter I'm leaving," she mused.

Lance did not reply.

"No, I've made up my mind," she said after another pause. "I'm leaving the Cascade Ranch. For the first time ever last night, Scooter slapped me, hard. Can you see it?"

Lightning ground her boot in the road dirt. "The magic is gone. I need to move on. I need to find me a really nice guy, set-

MAGIC LANCE

tle down, have a family. For a fleeting moment, I thought you might provide something like that. Life is full of illusions."

"Scooter hit you?"

"Nearly knocked me down. I've never experienced anything like that. It scared me. I don't really want to go back. That's part of the reason I came here."

"I don't blame you. Do you have family somewhere?"

"Oh, don't worry about me. I'm used to taking care of myself. But I don't think I'll be staying much longer at the Cascade."

Lance shook his head.

"I understand," Lightning said. "In this crazy world of male and female, your whole life can change on you in sixty seconds. It wasn't right for me to get interested in a married guy anyway. I should have known better. I thought since you didn't have any children, and Jan had left the ranch, you might be fair game. That obviously has changed."

"Some guy is going to think he's died and gone to heaven when you give him that look of yours," Lance said.

"But not you."

"Not the way things are now."

"Before I start getting all teary-eyed, I need to get on back to the Cascade. I've got a lot of thinking to do. I'll tell you this, Lance. You've sure given me some great thoughts during the past few months. And I'll always thank you for that. Jan's a lucky girl."

With that, Lightning walked to her pickup truck, gave Lance a goodbye wave, and headed up the hill toward 33 Draw.

Lance leaned against the pickup truck, wondering if he had done the right thing, wishing on one level that he had taken Lightning to the spring. On another level, what he told her was the truth. Things had changed. Finally, he got into his pickup and resumed his drive to the spot on the road closest to the hidden mine.

When he reached the site, he walked the fifty yards to the piñon tree that hid the mine entrance. His thoughts were distracted. The image of Lighting was fixed in his mind.

Peering through the piñon branches, he saw the mine entrance once again. As he worked his way through the piñon branches, he sensed no cool air flowing on this occasion.

Lance carried a nine-volt battery flashlight, to ensure he had plenty of light. Ten feet past the mine adit a bat flew by his face. He ducked, and remembered how horrified Jan had been. He was cautious this time. Before with Jan, he'd been aggressive; now, alone, all his senses watched for danger.

He wasn't sure how far back in the mine the rock slab was located. In the months since Jan's accident, his memory of the details had faded. When he reached the eighteen-inch wooden support beams, he remembered nearly knocking himself out on it during his speedy return to the tunnel to reach Jan with the pry bar. He moved slowly, flashing the light in all directions, to the floor, then to the ribs and finally to the back of the tunnel.

Nothing had changed since his last visit. He thought of the two tarantulas crawling on top of the rock and how he had scraped them off with the brush of his hand. No wonder Jan didn't like this place.

Lance reached the fallen rock slab. He made a thorough search to make sure there were no more tarantulas. He stood for a moment, looking at the hole he had dug with the pry bar to allow Jan's foot to drop down. The pry bar lay where he had left it. He examined the sides of the slab and compared them to the sides of the indenture in the rib of the tunnel, noting how precisely they had been cut. At the base of the slab, near the floor, he saw remains of the wooden box he and Jan had worked on,

MAGIC LANCE

thinking it contained silver ore. In fact, it must have been a crude kind of dam like the one the newspaper editor had described. When the box was removed the sand drained out and the slab fell forward on Jan.

Lance flashed the light onto the rib of the tunnel, previously hidden by the rock slab. There was a glint. A six-inch section of white quartz rock ran up and down in the indenture. In the middle of the quartz section was a two-inch silvery vein. Lance took out his pocketknife and stuck the point into it. The point went in a quarter of an inch. He felt an elation he had never experienced.

This was a momentous discovery, and consistent with what Lucky Joe and Jim Sorenson had told him about early Spanish mining secrets. The symbol told of the trap; the trap guarded the silver, but only for those who knew the symbol's secret. Obviously, he and Jan were among those who learned the secret the hard way. Lance sat on the rock slab that had crushed Jan's foot, and thought about his situation. Initially, he could not digest it. He thought of Jan, now the expectant mother of his child. And he thought of Lightning, the woman who so thoroughly aroused his passion. He still savored her kisses.

After a time of thought and reflection, Lance decided to explore further. He scooted to the far side of the rock slab and walked deeper into the tunnel. As he advanced, his eyes followed his light around the tunnel. On the opposite rib, he caught sight of the symbol. It was about even with his eyes on the opposite side of the tunnel from the first slab. The symbol was the outline of what appeared to be a heart, but with a two-inch break near the bottom, several inches above the bottom point of the heart. That gap explained the name, the broken heart.

And then, in one of those revelations that turn a puzzle from a frustration to a clear understanding, he visualized the top of the heart as the numeral three, lying horizontally, the open portion of the numeral facing down, the lazy three. The bottom point of the heart, separated from the upper part, was the letter "v." The Three V. The Broken Heart. They were one and the same. Just as Lucky Joe had shown him in the mud along Quail Run Creek.

Instinctively, he stepped back from the symbol on the rib of the tunnel. He looked at the base, where the rib met the floor. There it was. A long, narrow, wooden box, identical to the one he and Jan had worked on under the first symbol. Did this mean there was a second silver vein, or a continuation of the first? Was he in another Comstock lode? After all, this was the silver belt. Lance shined the flashlight on the rib to either side of the symbol. Although it was filled with dust and dirt, upon close examination, he detected a vertical slice in the rock, showing a slab had been wedged into a rib cut. When the wooden box was removed, he was sure a fine layer of sand would drain out removing the notched foundation of the rock slab above, and the slab would come slamming down, just as the first one had.

Lance fetched the pry bar from its place next to the first slab. He returned to the second symbol and pushed the pry bar under the wooden box. Remembering the deadly fall of the slab, he stepped to one side as he prepared to pry the wood box from its base.

At that moment, he decided to return to the pickup truck and leave a written message telling where he was, and what he was about to do. That way, if anything went wrong, whoever found his pickup would know exactly where he was and what he had been doing. He left the pry bar wedged between the wooden box and the mine floor and returned to the pickup.

After writing out his message, he put the note under the windshield wiper blade. He was about to return to the tunnel when he heard the sound of a vehicle coming up the ranch road behind him.

Lance assumed it must be his father, checking up on him. To his surprise, when the approaching vehicle came along the road that ran among the cedars and piñon, it had the beige color of the Cascade Ranch. His heart leaped as he thought of Lightning McClain. It leaped a second time when the pickup stopped and the driver's door opened. A large man with wide shoulders and a bull's neck stepped from the cab.

It was Scooter Jones and he was fighting mad.

CHAPTER FORTY-FOUR

When he returned to the Grey Piñon Reservation, Lucky Joe was a changed person. His visit to the warm springs, being with his family, his meditations and visions, his attitude toward his role in the tribe and his new abiding and fellowship with the spirits, had changed him. It was not his own will that mattered, but the tribe's will. He had to give himself up; he had to put aside his desire for worldly things, for sensual pleasure, for security, for honors and for praise from other tribe members. His old self was the Lucky Joe self, driven by his own ego, seeking everything for his own benefit. It was not the good of the tribe that was driving him. It was the good of the old self: self-focus, self-reward, self-control, self-discipline, self-enjoyment, self-first and selfishness. Now, the old Lucky Joe would be snuffed out, his own ego, his own sense of self, disavowed, abandoned. In its place would be the will of the Grey Piñons, the will of the spirits, the Kachinas directing him.

This transition caused him to relax and to feel a deep peace, a deep rest. A subliminal fear that he was inadequate, incompetent, failing, unqualified, undeserving and guilty left him. It was when that fear departed that he realized for the first time what that fear had been doing to him, what hold it had had on him. When that perennial, subliminal fear was gone, a total relaxation engulfed his body and soul. It no longer was Lucky Joe

MAGIC LANCE

Cruz striving, driving things. It was the spirits. Their energy and their will would work through him. He was responsible only to follow their lead and their guidance, not the wishes and commands of others, and not his own.

The thought that someone on the reservation was trying to kill him no longer caused anxiety. He would try to find out who that person was. In the meantime, he would rely on the spirits to protect him. He had taken the digital photo disc from Lance and stopped in Sierra City at a fast photo booth and had prints made. It was not exciting photography, close-ups of tire tracks in sand. He had a half dozen prints made of the two best pictures.

When he returned to the reservation, his first stop was at tribal police headquarters. His friend Ralph Jojola, a member of the tribal police department, agreed to take the tire photos to some friends at the State Police office and see if they could send them to someone who could identify the make and type of tire by the tread pattern. That mission accomplished, he headed directly to the dugout.

He had been gone for three days. He needed to find Segundo and learn what was happening with the land acquisitions, and the tribal discussions of who would assume the leadership role of the tribe, as community chief. The medicine society, the war society and the tribal council all would be working on it. And so would the word-of-mouth network throughout the entire tribe. Some movement toward picking a new leader would be well underway. In fact, they may already have made a new selection. As he thought of it, Lucky Joe realized he had left the reservation at precisely the wrong time. His absence at such a crucial time may well have been interpreted as abandonment.

He debated whether to say anything about the offer he made on the warm springs; getting that particular tract would be a major victory in their land campaign. But to date, it was only an offer. Lance had not accepted it, and it was not certain what he was going to do. Finally, he decided it was best not to mention his offer until he received some kind of response from Lance.

When Lucky Joe reached the dugout, telephones were ringing, fax machines were pumping papers and people were coming and going. He checked in with Anita Martinez. As soon as he saw her, Lucky Joe remembered his earlier attraction. His blood surged as she came up to him. "Lucky," she said with wide-eyed surprise. "Where have you been? We didn't know where you were. Everyone has been looking for you, asking about you. I didn't know what to tell them." She wore a perfume that seemed to go right into his bloodstream.

"I had some family business to take care of," Lucky Joe said. "Any emergencies?"

"Only that people thought something might have happened to you. El Segundo said you might have left for good, or maybe you had met foul play."

"Have there been any announcements about who will take my grandfather's place?"

"Would I be the first to know?" Anita said. "You know better. You'll have to ask the men. They don't tell me anything."

Lucky Joe walked to the coffee bar in the utility room and poured a cup, adding a container of half-and-half. He moved on to the war room and studied the state map. He wasn't sure, but he thought a couple of new ranches had been added to the acquired areas.

"El Segundo told me to call him immediately if you showed up," Anita said, sticking her head into the room. "He said he's coming right over."

Lucky Joe tensed. With this new motivational force he felt, he no longer was responsible to Segundo or to anyone else. The

awe and fear of Segundo he had felt was gone. Whether he could control those feelings in Segundo's actual presence was something he was going to test. The old man's earlier invincibility now was not so certain. Lucky Joe felt a trace of concern, a deep-rooted animal feeling that Segundo could have an agenda that was not in the tribe's best interests, perhaps an agenda that was dangerous for him. The feeling was vague but he could not dismiss it. His dealings with Segundo were on a different basis, a different level now. How that would work in real life was yet to be determined.

Segundo came into the war room almost at a run. His eyes expanded when he saw Lucky Joe. His mouth dropped open. His hands shook as he tried to light a cigarette. "That was a short trip," he said.

"It was a rewarding experience," Lucky Joe said. "I'm not the same."

"What do you mean you're not the same?"

"It's an inward thing. Nothing on the surface," Lucky Joe said. He really did not have words to describe what had happened. He could feel it, but he could not communicate it. He wasn't sure he would trust Segundo, even if he could communicate it.

"The situation has not changed," Segundo said. He walked around in a circle in front of Lucky Joe's desk. "It is now more dangerous than ever, as much for your family as for you. Are you sure it was wise to return?"

"I had not heard anything," Lucky Joe said. "It wasn't that safe where I was. Somebody shot at me."

"Shot at you. Who?"

"We've got some evidence, but we have to have it analyzed."

"What kind of evidence?"

"Tire tracks, a cartridge shell, things like that."

"Oh," Segundo said. "That can be hard to link. Did you see whoever it was?"

"It was night. Not that clear."

Segundo rubbed his chin with the three good fingers on his right hand. "That just goes to show what we're up against. Where are Rachel and your kids?"

"California."

"At least they should be safe that far away."

"How is the chief selection going?" Lucky Joe asked. As war chief, he knew Segundo would be on the inside of considerations.

"It's always unpredictable. As you could probably guess, I am in the top rung of those being considered."

"I would assume so." He watched Segundo scratch his left chest area with his right hand, then rub his right ear with the same hand, then rub both hands together.

"If I were you, I would leave at once," Segundo said, looking Lucky Joe in the eye. The magic that was in his personality was gone. Lucky Joe took the remark as that of an old man, rather than the power figure that Segundo represented before.

"I'm not leaving. It was a mistake to have gone earlier. I am not leaving again."

"Very well," Segundo said, tightening his lips and baring his teeth. "But I will not be able to guarantee your safety."

"I will guarantee my own safety."

Segundo spun around and left the room. Lucky Joe sat back in his swivel chair, hands folded on his chest, staring at the ceiling. He would continue to do his job on the land acquisitions. Segundo's overall idea for the land acquisitions was brilliant. But before, it had been setting goals and celebrating acquisitions. Now it was the deep pleasure, peace and rest of glorifying a higher will. Nonetheless, they had to tighten up on the execu-

MAGIC LANCE

tion. The death of his grandfather, and someone trying to snuff out his own life, had distracted him too long from the land acquisition plan. He must return to that task immediately. As Lucky Joe pondered his next moves, Anita Martinez stuck her head into the room and caught his eye. "Roberto Maestas is here to see you," she said.

Roberto Maestas was head of the Obsidian Society, head of the medicine men and as such a key to the selection of a new community chief. Lucky Joe was on his feet when Roberto entered the room.

Roberto was exuberant to see him. They had known each other for decades, although Roberto was twenty-five years his senior. He was a tall man, with long grey hair pulled back in a ponytail, wearing traditional native clothing as he did every day on the reservation.

"We have been looking for you," Roberto said. "Even your family didn't know where you were, or at least they weren't telling."

"At least one person knew," Lucky Joe said. "And I don't know how he knew."

Roberto passed over the remark. "Your return is a blessing, a favorable sign," he said. "The Obsidian Society, the war society and the tribal council all have been discussing you."

Lucky Joe's eyebrows raised. For a moment, his thoughts sped back to the campsite and the place by the hot springs where they arranged the prayer sticks. On his brief return to that spot on the day they departed, he saw that in their efforts to get water for the tepee fire, Lance and Rick had stomped all around the earth circle in the darkness. Even the bear had passed over the spot. And through it all, the prayer sticks remained untouched, straight and tall.

"How me?"

"There has been unusual activity regarding a successor to your grandfather. As you know, the selection process of the next community chief is somewhat mysterious. Those powers at work are not supposed to be manipulated by outside influence. But this time, a certain individual in the tribe has been making it clear he is entitled to the position, and that you in particular are neither entitled nor competent."

Lucky Joe's interest jumped at the declaration someone was saying he was incompetent to lead the tribe.

"The tribe's will, will prevail," Lucky Joe said. "There is no need for me to promote myself, or to discredit anyone else."

"Clearly, that is the traditional way," Roberto said. "Until now."

Roberto and Lucky Joe stood for a moment, looking at each other, each waiting for the other to speak.

"What does all this mean?" Lucky Joe asked at last. Roberto stepped back, looked into the adjoining office where Anita Martinez and another girl were sitting. He closed the door and moved close to Lucky Joe.

"With your return, there is a good chance you will be appointed community chief to replace your grandfather. The other contender is not liked, and not trusted. He is the one who is saying unfavorable things about you, and who is trying to win the appointment for himself. His aggressive behavior, while consistent with what he is, is not favorably received by most of us. It is not for oneself to declare oneself chief; it is for those persons who will be served to declare a person chief."

"You are looked upon as a succession of the spirit of your grandfather. As you know, he led the Grey Piñons admirably for a generation. We are hopeful this same spiritual tradition will be continued."

"What do you wish me to do?"

"There will be a gathering tonight at the place of honor. Come to that gathering, and be prepared to speak and answer questions. Tomorrow, you may well be the community chief of the Grey Piñon Tribe."

CHAPTER FORTY-FIVE

Late in the afternoon, Lucky Joe went to the river, to the base of the cottonwood tree that grew at the river's bank. Lowering himself off the river bank, he dropped next to the exposed roots of the tree, where he could not be seen from his side of the river. From that vantage point, he could see upstream and downstream, and across the river and into the village on the far side. It was a place he visited often. It was near home. It was private. Today, his level of anxiety was considerably below what it had been for the past four months, since the time Segundo started the land acquisition effort. Abandoning his own will, abandoning his own reliance on what others thought of him and what he was doing, abandoning his own ambitions to acquire things, and the merging of his own will with the tribe's will, gave him a new goal, a new guidepost, and a new boldness. For the first time in his life, he felt the promises of the spirits. More important, he acknowledged his own lack of power, his own spiritual weaknesses.

He also understood that while he no longer relied on members of the tribe for approval, he was committed to their welfare and their well-being. A sense of humility ran through his thoughts and took charge of his will. He picked up several cottonwood twigs, snapped them and tossed them into the current. He gazed into the swirling water. What would happen tonight

MAGIC LANCE

at the gathering? Would he be appointed community chief, the position held by his grandfather? He thought of Alfredo. He could talk to him now, without words, as though he were here. If the tribe selected him, it was the work of the spirits. If the tribe rejected him, it was the work of the spirits. His job was to serve the higher will, not to control.

Lucky Joe smiled as he thought of his name, not his real name, not his tribal name, but the name that was his daily fare. He remembered the day twenty five years earlier, when he was but seven years old, standing outside the casino doors, waiting with his mother and sister for his father to leave the Magic Lance. A lady tourist came out the glass doors, waving an arm, celebrating a five thousand dollar slot machine jackpot. She was ecstatic. The big black eyes of an Indian child's face caught her fancy. She reached into her sack of money, pulled out a hundred-dollar bill and handed it to the youngster. "You're one Lucky Joe," she said, patting him on the head and not missing a step as she whisked on to the parking lot.

His mother and sister immediately picked up the moniker. "You're one Lucky Joe," they said, half-chiding and half-congratulating him as he stood clutching a hundred-dollar bill in his little fingers. In those days, a hundred dollars was a lot of money, especially for a seven-year-old. From that day on, as the story made its way around the reservation, people started to call him "Lucky Joe." The name had a ring that people liked, whether they knew how he got it or not. Because of his nickname, other tribal members began anticipating he would be lucky, and each time he did appear to have a run of good luck, the name became more ingrained.

Lucky Joe laughed to himself. He liked the name. It made him feel lucky. As he pitched another twig into the swirling river, he confirmed to himself that he was not relying on luck now. Relying on luck, or even on his own efforts, brought nothing but stress and worry. Relying on the spirits gave him confidence, courage, assurance. And that was what he needed for the tribal gathering tonight. It was a time of commitment.

That evening, when Lucky Joe arrived at the rock overhang at the place of honor, he drew in a long breath of piñon smoke. He looked into the night sky, cloudless that night, with thousands of bright stars. While still in the dark, away from the glow of the fire pit, the stars and the piñon smoke seemed to provide a sign, a sign that all was aligned.

Below the rock overhang, Lucky Joe took a minute to allow his eyes to adjust to the dim light of the piñon fire and the haze of smoke. He spoke to numerous tribe members he knew well and took a place against the sandstone wall.

Farther along the wall, he spied Segundo, that tell-tale porcupine hair standing straight up.

Shortly talks began, with one tribe member after another talking about the tradition of the tribe, about the qualities of its leaders over the centuries, how they had resisted their tribal enemies, then the Spanish, then the Mexicans, then the Americans, and now the powerful cultural forces that opposed them, and through it all, they survived, and now they not only survived, but prospered. The past was not assurance they would prevail in the future, but it was encouraging that by following their own traditions, their own spirits, they now were on the verge of regaining some of their former independence and freedoms. This would only be done by selecting the right leader, by respecting traditions, by carrying on the successes of the past generation.

One leader after another spoke along that theme, without proposing who the next leader should be.

When it came time for Segundo to speak, he talked of the qualities needed for the tribe's new leader. It also was time for change, Segundo said. A man of vision must be selected. A man who is not afraid to act. A man who will seize the initiative and execute. It will not do to select a person who lacks will power. When he made that statement, he paused, looking directly at Lucky Joe. Words are not what is needed now, Segundo said. A man of action is required. The only way to pick a man of action is to rely on what a man has done. Who has shown vision? Who has shown willingness to act on his visions, who is decisive?" Segundo said. "In all modesty, I describe myself."

Other speakers gave their views. When it was the turn of Velasquez, he spoke eloquently, but as his speech wore on, he shifted to a discussion of Segundo, and his commitment of two hundred and fifty million dollars of the tribe's funds on real estate options.

"Think of it," Velasquez said. "Two hundred and fifty million dollars of the tribe's money. At high risk. Possibly gone forever. And I need not remind you of what this leader of vision has done to me and my family. He withdrew my grazing allotment, after over a hundred years in my family, and with the grazing allotment went my share of Magic Lance sharing. Consider your own situation. How would that kind of action affect you? How long could you subsist if your major income was withdrawn arbitrarily. And for what reason? Because I suggested that committing two hundred and fifty million dollars of the tribe's money on a high-risk proposition might not be a good idea. Is this the kind of visionary we wish to reward?"

"And we have just learned that the very first land purchase, the Peterson Ranch, was not put in the tribe's name, not at all," he continued. "It was put in the name of an individual. Paid for with tribal funds, but titled in the name of our esteemed war leader. And that same esteemed war leader is getting kickbacks from the real estate agents who are arranging these land deals.

One of our own agents, Earl Wallace, complained to me that part of his commission had to be given back to our esteemed war chief, to assure he would get future business. I tell you that this man should not only be rejected from any leadership position of the tribe, but he should be banished. It is an extreme remedy, as we all know. In this case, it is justified. It is demanded. As Grey Piñon leaders, we must act. It is as though the water well is poisoned. What is the source of the poison? In this case, the source of this poison sits among us tonight. It is imperative we act tonight, not only to pick a new leader but to remove an old contamination."

Segundo cut off the talk by raising his fist into the air and shouting a string of personal insults and threats at Velasquez. Two tribal councilmen joined him, both members of his family. Several tribal members demanded to know if the accusations about the Peterson Ranch and the kickbacks were true. Segundo said the accusations were desperate attempts by desperate men to malign him. High-pitched shouting and threats flew back and forth.

Lucky Joe shifted on his feet, anticipating violence would erupt.

When a semblance of order was restored, Abeita followed Velasquez, reciting a similar history and demanding the same resolution as Velasquez. In one last shot, Abeita reported that their war leader was offering to pay Anita Martinez for special favors, tribal money for personal pleasures.

Finally, Roberto Maestas began to speak. He recited substantial elements of Grey Piñon tradition. In particular, he extolled the leadership of Alfredo Cruz. With that subject concluded, he spoke of how the spirit of a man is often passed to his children and grandchildren. It is not automatic. We have all seen times when the spirit was not passed on, in fact, the contradiction of the spirit was passed on. Fortunately, in the case of their former leader, that spirit still was with them. He acknowledged that the plan of acquiring land, of establishing a Native American state, of converting ink-on-paper to land was indeed a visionary one, a goal they should pursue and bring to a successful conclusion. The person who had the vision was to be recognized, but that same person has not developed an adequate program to accomplish the vision, and beyond that, had become enamored of his own powers and personal prowess and had looked to his own betterment instead of the betterment of the tribe. While committing two hundred fifty million dollars of the tribe's money, this person at the same time failed to acquire the piece of land that was most important to the tribe: Wild Horse's hunting grounds and spiritual home. Roberto said that same person, if given supreme power, would continue to misuse power and violate the tribe's trust.

No doubt other members of the tribe who dared question his decisions would be treated as Velasquez and Abeita had been treated. And by failing to get Wild Horse's preserve, he had demonstrated his inadequacy. From a visionary who generated respect, that person became lost in the illusion of his own self-importance. Roberto recalled how Segundo had treated Louie Jinza, a tribe member with debt and alcohol problems, but nevertheless a tribe member. Louie was degraded and humiliated by the war chief.

All in all, Maestas concluded, our Segundo has betrayed the most important values of the tribe and has become the chief hindrance to the fulfillment of the tribe's land acquisition plan. And for that he should be banished. The task of carrying out the vision should be assigned to others who truly embodied the will of the tribe, who had the daring, the humility and the wisdom to sacrifice themselves and accept the higher calling. They were fortunate,

Maestas said, to have such a person in the tribe. That person had the spirit of his grandfather. He turned and stared at Lucky Joe. When Maestas sat down, silence settled over the meeting.

Lucky Joe was shocked to hear the allegations against Segundo. In secret, the tribe's trust had been betrayed.

Segundo slumped on his seat against the sandstone wall and placed his forehead in his hands.

For a quarter hour there were intermittent discussions among members. After another period of silence, Maestas rose and spoke for the consensus. Lucky Joe Cruz was to succeed his grandfather as community chief, cacique of the tribe. El Segundo, the former second-in-command, for having put two hundred and fifty million of the tribe's money at risk, for having abused his power to take revenge against two respected tribal members, for having personally used tribal funds for his own personal land acquisition and personal pleasure pursuits, for degrading tribal members in trouble, for having demanded kickbacks from a real estate agent for tribal business, for violating tribal traditions, and for failing to acquire Wild Horse's favorite lands, was to be banished from the reservation and denied contact with the tribe.

Segundo's body slumped further down on the seat along the wall. The omen of the dual names, the Magic Lance and Lance Burnett, floated through his mind.

Had fate been in control since his efforts began? Instead of personal glory, as chief of the Grey Piñons, his efforts had made him an outcast, rejected by his tribal brethren.

No one consoled Segundo as the meeting ended.

They knew that for him the race was over, and that from the tribal leaders' decision there was no appeal.

The new cacique was Lucky Joe Cruz.

CHAPTER FORTY-SIX

Lucky Joe was the last to leave the honored place. His mind swirled with thoughts of his newly acquired responsibilities. The piñon fire in the pit had settled into glowing, pulsating coals. A hint of piñon smoke filled the air, but dissipated quickly as Lucky Joe climbed up the sandstone cliff, in the centuries-old stair steps carved in the rock.

When he reached the top steps, near the flat area overlooking the river where he had parked his utility vehicle, he turned and gazed into the fire pit below, allowing his thoughts to go blank, merging with his environment, feeling a spirit, placing no boundaries on his spirit. The soft murmur of the river relaxed him.

As he turned to climb the final step to the overlook, he saw a dark figure above him, peering down. In a second, although it was too dark to see individual features, he knew it was Segundo. Lucky Joe's breathing paused and all his senses tensed.

"So, here's the new big chief," Segundo said derisively. "How does it feel to have all of the power, all of the popularity?"

'I haven't had any thoughts like that."

"Oh, no thoughts of glory. How patriarchal. Do you imagine yourself one of the Kachinas?"

"I don't imagine myself at all."

"You're lying. You've been after this position for as long as I can remember. You are good at disguising your ambitions. I give your credit for that."

Lucky Joe took a step up the rock stairway to reach the mesa level. As he did so, Segundo took several steps toward him, blocking the pathway. Although a foot shorter than Lucky Joe, Segundo occupied the high ground by a foot.

"I have nothing to lose now," Segundo said. "You have banished me, you and your friends. An entire lifetime spent promoting the interests of the Grey Piñons, and suddenly I'm banished. For what? For nothing. I have done nothing that those who voted against me have not done themselves, or wanted to do and were too faint-hearted to do. I must admit I expected your support. Did I not support your grandfather, and you too, for decades? And now you return that loyalty with betrayal."

"Life has changed," Lucky Joe said. "You have lost perspective. Your ways are no longer the ways of our people."

"My ways! How can you say such lies? Everything I did was working. The tribe is prospering. It is recovering land that was stolen centuries ago. My ways are receiving national attention for brilliance and daring. Other Indian tribes are looking to the Grey Piñons for direction, for leadership. And now a cowardly clique has banished me. There are afraid of me. They fear my spirit will dominate their timidity. They are like frightened little lambs when the wolf appears. Where am I supposed to go? Now that you are the big chief, and I am banished, tell me where I'm supposed to go. The reservation has been my life and my home all of my life. These people are my people. Now I am cut off. Betrayed. Double-crossed.

"You have done things that are not acceptable to the tribe, things that have never been acceptable."

"Like what?"

MAGIC LANCE

"Can you tell the truth? Was that not you on the Three V Ranch? Those shots in the dark?"

"What are you talking about?"

"You know all too well what I am talking about. Around the campfire. You saw the teepee. Somehow, I don't know how, you found out where I was. Under cover of darkness, you snuck up and shot at me, and the rancher. And when I went down, you shot at him. The only reason we are not dead is that you are a sorry shot."

Segundo shifted his feet. "When you betray someone who has been your supporter and friend, you deserve to die," he said.

"Obviously, if I had been killed, that would have left you open to be named chief. But what about the rancher? Why shoot him?"

"He isn't going to sell. He wouldn't sell to me, and he won't sell to you. I'm the only one who had the guts to move forward with our vision. With the rancher dead, the Three V would be easy pickings. You'll have to do the same thing, to get that ranch. And you haven't got the guts to do it. You don't know the difference between murder and war. This has been a war from the day we started our land acquisition drive. It isn't going to change. If you don't realize it is a war, you're going to lose. With my leadership, the tribe had a chance to win. Now, they have chosen defeat. And you are the weak-hearted one they have chosen to negotiate the surrender."

Lucky Joe began to move along the path, closing the distance between himself and Segundo.

"Stay back," Segundo shouted.

"Get out of my way," Lucky Joe said as he moved directly at Segundo, pushing the smaller man in the chest to clear the path. Segundo swung his fist and struck Lucky Joe in the right eye socket. Lucky Joe grabbed his former mentor to wrestle him to the side. Segundo kneed him in the groin, then placed his right foot behind Lucky Joe's left foot and ripped it forward, slinging Lucky Joe on his back to the ground. Segundo then made a free fall onto Lucky Joe's chest, landing with both knees.

Lucky Joe was shocked at the velocity and ferocity of Segundo's attack. It took him only a second to change fighting modes, from under-estimation to survival.

Lucky Joe had powerful arms and as Segundo landed on his chest, he reached up and grabbed Segundo's foot and twisted it, throwing the older man to the side. Lucky Joe was up like a cat, and jerked Segundo to his feet.

"You tried to kill me!" he yelled at Segundo.

Segundo realized his surprise attack had failed.

"All right, all right, I'll go," he said, trying to slink away. At first Lucky Joe was not inclined to release him. Then, he changed his mind and opened his grip, giving the old man his freedom. Segundo moved slowly away, but still gripping Lucky Joe's shirt.

After only a couple of steps, Segundo fell to the ground. As he fell, he pulled Lucky Joe downward toward the edge of the mesa ledge overlooking the river. With his foot placed in Lucky Joe's stomach, and with both hands now grasping Lucky Joe's shirt, he tried to catapult the bigger man up and over, and off the mesa cliff.

Lucky Joe was too heavy. Segundo raised him off the ground a couple of feet, but not enough to gain leverage. After Lucky Joe came down almost on top of Segundo, he struggled to his feet and instinctively jerked Segundo up, and threw him in a wrestling move away from him. In the lightning fast action, Segundo went sailing off the mesa rim, and fell into the darkness.

Lucky Joe heard Segundo's body hit the flowing river and only then realized what he had done.

His body shook. Carefully, Lucky Joe moved to the edge of the cliff and looked down to the water below. The quite murmur of the river was all he heard. He strained his eyes, staring into the darkness, hoping to see Segundo's head appear. He saw nothing. The horror struck that he had killed him.

For several minutes, Lucky Joe stared at the river.

Then, silently, on the far side of the river, he saw a man rise from the water near the bank. The figure waded to the far shore, and slowly and haltingly walked downstream along the sandy bank. There was no sound except the water whispers.

Lucky Joe took in a deep breath. For all his faults, Segundo was a survivor.

CHAPTER FORTY-SEVEN

A sinking feeling engulfed Lance's stomach. Scooter Jones was big. If he were here now, it was related to Lightning. A trace of guilt caused Lance to expect the worst. There would be no reasoning with Jones. Not when it came to Lightning. The problem was that Jones had reason to be jealous. Lance had craved Lightning. When she responded, it was his earlier commitment to Jan, and now to his own expectant child, that caused him to rethink. That earlier desire could not be reasoned away. An hour ago, he was kissing her. That fact remained. Now he was facing an irate, jealous lover—the worst kind.

Scooter looked as though he had thought it through and knew what he was going to do. He approached Lance cautiously, looking in all directions for possible weapons, possible defenses. Lance thought of his .357 under the seat of his pickup truck. Scooter was between him and the truck. Lance looked for an open area where he could not be trapped. There was a spot near the front of the pickup. As best he could judge it, Lance maneuvered to the middle of it. There was sand and gramma grass and some unevenness. The slow approach gave Scooter time to check out the surroundings; it gave Lance time to adjust to the surprise factor.

"Hey, Burnett, I got something for you," Scooter said as he drew near, holding up Lightning's Indian bead belt. In a quick and

MAGIC LANCE

unexpected move, he swung the belt like a whip and lashed Lance across the neck. The sting was intensely painful and sobering.

When it was clear a fight was coming, Lance's demeanor changed. From initial fright he shifted to calculation and resolve. Scooter pressed toward Lance, twirling the belt in a menacing manner. He reached out with his thick left hand and tried to grab Lance by the shirt. At the same time he loaded his right fist like a cannon shell, and shot it forward, belt, fist and all. Lance anticipated the first punch, and was able to duck to his left so that Scooter's powerful fist grazed his right cheek. Even the partial blow turned him around. The flashlight he was holding spun to the ground.

The two men sparred for a moment. Then Scooter tucked Lightning's belt under his own and moved in for a knockout. He threw his fists in rapid succession, some striking Lance in the face and side of his head, and several in his stomach. Lance tried to defend himself, and threw a half dozen counterpunches, all ineffective. His lack of offense caused Scooter to relax a notch, thinking there was no danger. In an instant, Lance threw a left jab that hit Scooter right between the eyes. If Lance could have followed up with a right, he might have gained an advantage. As it was, Lance was so shocked when he connected with the left, he drew back a moment to admire what he had done.

The lucky hit enraged Scooter. He charged Lance and grabbed him in a tackle that drove Lance backward and to the ground. Scooter used his superior weight to fall right on top of his opponent. He began smashing Lance in the face with both fists. For a moment, Lance thought he was gone. He took a savage pounding. Then, to his shock, Scooter looped Lightning's belt and slid it over Lance's head and started to tighten it on his neck.

Deciding all was lost, Lance grabbed for whatever he could on the ground, and came up with some sand and a miniature cactus plant about the size of a lemon. Not even knowing what he had, he jammed it into Scooter's face just above his right eye. The cactus spines stuck in Scooter's skin and caused him to cry out in pain. Lance released the cactus and pounded it into Scooter's forehead with his closed fist. Lance also felt the intense pain of the cactus spines that penetrated the flesh of his own hand and fingers.

Scooter still was on top of Lance, but he had to use both hands to pluck the cactus spines from his face. In that moment, Lance was able to turn over and push himself up, throwing Scooter to the side. Once free, Lance swore that he would not let himself be taken down again. Both men regained their footing.

Lance jerked the belt from his neck just as Scooter charged again. This time, Lance met the charge by sidestepping slightly and planting his feet firmly in the sand. He threw an upper cut that caught Scooter in the throat. Both men threw every punch they ever imagined. It was a wild, free-for-all swingfest. It took only a minute, but the free-for-all sapped the energy of both fighters. They separated, and Lance did a few boxing steps to separate them.

Lance knew that he would not last if he met Scooter head on. He needed a strategy. He danced to his right, then his left, making sure he was on the move so Scooter would not have a stable target to charge. Lance ran his stinging right hand over his face, and it came down bloody. As he moved in a tight circle, Scooter recuperated, devising a new strategy to put Lance away. His forehead was on fire with cactus spines sticking out and the punctures starting to ooze blood. His nostrils flared. He rolled his fists in the air, looking for an opening while regaining strength.

Lance glanced at his pickup truck. It was twenty yards away, and still on the other side of Scooter. If he made a run for the

MAGIC LANCE

truck, Scooter would be on him before he could get the truck door open. Realizing his best chance was to keep out of Scooter's reach, Lance started retreating along the trail that led to the piñon tree in front of the mine entrance. Scooter advanced as Lance retreated, maintaining a distance of only a few feet. This tactic went on for several minutes, Scooter maintaining a steady advance as Lance fell back.

When Lance reached the piñon tree in front of the mine, he pulled a branch with him as he back-pedaled, and then let it pop back. Scooter let the branch strike him without flinching and without slowing down. When he reached the adit, in a sudden burst of energy Lance turned and ran into the tunnel, disappearing into the foggy darkness of the mine.

Scooter Jones stopped. He stood startled. What was this? An old mine? He ventured but a few feet into the tunnel. "Come out of there you damn weasel!" he shouted. Lance stopped a dozen yards into the tunnel. He could see Scooter's silhouette in the light of the tunnel adit.

"You may have found a little ole mine but you're never going to enjoy it!" Scooter shouted. "Big Bob's going to get it. And I'm foreclosing on everything else you got, right now."

Scooter was taller and wider than Lance remembered. Although he could see Scooter, Lance surmised Scooter was having a hard time seeing him in the blackness of the tunnel. Lance made no reply to Scooter's taunts. He crowded against the rib to further reduce Scooter's ability to see him. Perhaps Scooter would hesitate to come in after him. He thought of his own distaste for these pitch-black tunnels.

Lance looked deeper into the mine, anticipating how he would move if Scooter came after him. He could see nothing. From his recollection, he knew the wooden beam would be somewhere down the tunnel. He could put his hand up in the air and move slowly, waiting until his hand struck the beam. That would tell him exactly where he was. The fallen slab was not far past the beam.

To his relief, Scooter Jones disappeared from the tunnel entrance. Lance eased, and leaned against the rib. Perhaps the darkness of the mine had discouraged him. Then he considered whether Scooter Jones somehow could cave in the entrance and bury him alive in the mine. The thought caused him to consider running to the adit to see what Scooter was doing. Maybe he had had enough, and would consider the matter temporarily settled. If Lance heard the pickup engine start, he would know Scooter was leaving.

Lance walked back toward the adit, looking into the piñon branches on the outside. He stood attentively, hoping to hear the start of the pickup truck engine. He heard the pickup truck door open, then close. He anticipated the engine starting.

Several moments passed. Then he saw the figure of Scooter Jones coming toward the piñon. He back-pedaled again, moving further into the mine. Shortly, Scooter Jones was in the mine. A light beam circled the tunnel. Twice, the light shone square in Lance's eyes. He turned and moved more quickly into the mine, raising his hand to feel for the supporting wooden beam on the back of the tunnel. When he reached that, he knew the fallen slab was not far beyond.

Then the thought hit him. At the second slab, the pry bar was sticking under the wood box. He could get the pry bar and use it to defend himself. His spirit soared. If he could reach the pry bar, he could defend himself in the tunnel. As he moved deeper into the tunnel, all trace of light disappeared. He put the palm of his left hand up to his nose so that it touched. He could not see it. When he looked behind him, he could see Scooter's flashlight coming. It was closing on him.

MAGIC LANCE

"You're finished!" Scooter yelled. "Do you hear that, Burnett? You're finished! You ain't never gonna touch that woman again!"

Lance did not respond. He was heading for the pry bar. Could he find it without the use of his eyes?

With his hand raised in the air, Lance found the wooden beam. He knew where he was. Scooter was getting closer. Quickly he moved beyond the beam, shuffling his feet along the mine floor, moving steadily, anticipating the rock slab that had fallen on Jan.

"Hah! I see you!" Scooter hollered triumphantly, as his flashlight beam caught Lance moving into the tunnel. "I see you, you sleazy little maggot! You ain't never coming out of here! This hole is going to be your grave!"

The light beam showed Lance the slab on the mine floor. When he reached it, he jumped up on the slab and skittered over it. He knew the pry bar was only a few yards beyond. To his horror, as he jumped off the slab, he sensed Scooter Jones was on top of it, only few feet behind him. In his shock, he raced along the tunnel.

Suddenly, he realized he had gone past the pry bar. He turned and saw the hulk of Scooter Jones a few yards behind him, no longer charging but moving resolutely, sensing his prey was within reach. Lance saw the pry bar sticking up from the mine floor from its leverage point under the wooden box. At the same instant, Scooter came even with the pry bar.

"Well, look what we have here," Scooter said. "Looky here."

Lance bent down instinctively, trying to create as small a target as possible. He anticipated Scooter charging him.

Scooter put his left hand on the pry bar and tried to lift it from its holding position. It would not budge. He kept the light on Lance to make sure he did not get away. He shifted the flashlight to his left hand and took hold of the pry bar with his right. He worked it back and forth, and finally pushed it down.

When he moved the pry bar in a downward direction to dislodge it, the leverage popped the wooden box out of its centuries-old placement. Enraged, Scooter raised the pry bar in the air with his right hand, like a spear drawn back, and began a thrust forward to ram it into his cornered prey. In the instant the pry bar started forward, driven by Scooter's powerful right arm, the rock slab from the rib of the mine tunnel came slamming down like a trap door. Nothing slowed its descent.

On its crushing fall to the mine floor, the monstrous slab smashed down directly on top of Scooter Jones.

Lance stood in shock. The flashlight vanished. Absolute darkness and silence prevailed. Lance could not remember where he was. He could not see. He could not hear. He could not think. A musty smell rose from the mine floor.

Lance teetered with the realization that something horrendous had happened to Scooter Jones, and whatever that something was, it probably saved the life of Lance Burnett.

CHAPTER FORTY-EIGHT

For several moments Lance stood with his mouth open, barely breathing, in shock. In the blackness of the mine tunnel, he had no idea where he was—or which way led further into the tunnel and which way led out. He was disoriented. Finally, a perception of his location crept back. He still was hazy on what had happened. He stretched his hands out as far as possible. He felt nothing. Slowly, he inched his way into the inky black, pushing his right toe forward a distance, then his left toe.

After a few steps, his right toe struck a solid object. He reached down with his hand, to feel what it was. The object was solid rock, about two feet high. Although he wasn't sure, he thought the object must be the slab that fell from the rib, just like the one that hurt Jan. If it were the second slab, it marked the direction to the tunnel entrance. He should climb over it, and get back to the mine floor. The first slab then would be several yards beyond. He inched forward. In a way, he hated to leave the second slab. At least there he thought he knew where he was. He crawled over the slab and moved forward for an unknown distance.

A sense of panic crept into his mind. What if he were going in the wrong direction? What if he were going deeper into the mine? He stood for several moments, straining to see even a trace of light, in any direction. There was none. The darkness was absolute. It was as if he had no eyes. He moved forward again, slowly. Finally he bumped into a rock. He sighed with relief. It must be the first slab. He remembered the tarantulas that had been on it before. His hand jerked back reflexively. He could imagine those hairy creatures hanging from the back, or crawling up the ribs of the mine. From the slab, he knew his next identifier would be the wooden beam. How far, he could not remember.

For some period of time, which he could not calculate, he inched his way through the darkness. Occasionally he would touch the ribs or side of the tunnel. That would cause him to angle slightly in the opposite direction. Then he realized he had neglected to keep his hand above him. He could have passed right under the wooden beam, and not known it. Should he go back? Well, if he passed it, what difference did it make. If he were going in the right direction he would soon see light from the tunnel adit. His eyes were relaxed, wide open and seeing nothing. He moved forward again, this time with his hand in the air.

After going what seemed a long way, Lance suddenly felt the wood beam. He was going toward the tunnel entrance. He could move forward with assurance. In a matter of steps, he would see some light. Shortly, in a strange limbo between reality and illusion, he imagined he could see some light. He pushed one toe forward, then the other, scooting each one along the mine floor, making sure he had a solid footing for the next move.

Finally, he was sure. There was a speck of light ahead. His spirit took flight. He picked up his pace. If he got out of this pitch black hole, he was never coming back. He had been inside the whale's stomach, like Jonah. And now he was coming out. It was a horrible dream. He would spend the rest of his life in the sunshine, never inside this man-made intestine.

When he stepped into the sunlight, Lance raised both hands to the sky and shouted.

It was only after he fully confirmed his salvation that his thoughts turned to Scooter Jones. A rescue effort had to be made. Lance knew Scooter had tried to kill him For reasons unknown, Lance prevailed. Even if Scooter survived the slab, Lance wondered if he might be better off to let him die, to delay a rescue effort, to let nature take its course.

That thought was short-lived. Lance knew he had no choice. He had to find his own flashlight, dropped in the open area as the fight commenced, and return to the tunnel he had just sworn never to re-enter, to find out what happened to Scooter Jones. If the man could be saved, Lance had an obligation to do it. He went to the pickup and took out the .357 revolver. He spun the cylinder to check the shells, then stuck the weapon into his belt. With a flashlight and the .357, he threw his shoulders back and returned to the mine.

The flashlight beam swung around the tunnel as Lance progressed. He recognized smaller landmarks now, a rock outcropping, a column formation on the right rib twenty yards from the adit. He ducked under the wooden beam support this time, and anticipated the first rock slab. When he reached it, he flashed the light onto the rock quartz with the silver vein. He climbed over the slab and moved cautiously to the second one.

It was tilted, but only a few inches. Lance knew Scooter was under that slab. His body must be smashed and compressed. Lance flashed the light along the slab. There was no sign of Scooter. He climbed up on top of it and crawled to the far side. There, extending out from underneath the slab, was the pointed end of the pry bar, perhaps three feet long. Running parallel to it was a wide ribbon of dark substance. It took Lance only a moment to realize that it must be blood.

In repulsion, he pulled back. Near the tip of the pry bar and at the edge of blood was a tarantula, legs bent and furry, with a fat spongy body. Lance frowned in disgust. He stepped down from the slab intending to stomp the tarantula with his boot. Instead, the deft creature leaped onto Lance's lower leg and started up the inside seam of his pants leg.

Lance shouted in fright and slapped the tarantula with both hands and the flashlight, then spun in a circle trying to see where the hairy horror had gone. He flashed the light in all directions, on the mine floor, on the ribs and on the back above him. The tarantula vanished unscathed as quickly as it had appeared.

When he resumed his investigation, he focused on the narrow space between the bottom of the slab and the mine floor. If he could get down on the mine floor, with his face right on the floor, he might be able to flash the light into the space to confirm that Scooter was there.

The thought of blood, the elusive tarantula, and the nausea that suddenly started to rise in his stomach, caused him to stop. It was time to go, time to call the authorities, time to let someone else take over this situation. If Scooter Jones was under the slab, as Lance was sure he was, there was nothing he could do for him now.

The curse of the broken heart had been fulfilled.

CHAPTER FORTY-NINE

There were plenty of things to talk about at the apartment in Sierra City. Jan was staggered when she saw Lance. His face was bloody, bruised and cut. His left eye was swollen almost shut. Bumps and welts stood out on his forehead. And worst of all, his nose was broken, although the doctor said it would heal on its own. When he said he had been attacked by Scooter Jones, Jan assumed at once Scooter was after Lance to force him to sell the Three V to Big Bob McCoy.

A new current of fear ran through her heart when Lance told her Scooter Jones was dead. She was afraid to ask what caused his death. Whatever happened, she realized how close to death Lance must have been. The thought of going on without him shot through her mind. The child she bore would have no father. She coaxed Lance to sit on the sofa and give her a full report.

After describing the fight, and how Scooter died, Lance said he had called the sheriff from the ranch and waited at the cactus flats' cutoff. The sheriff came himself, along with a half-dozen deputies, state police investigators and the Sierra City police chief. What the city police chief was doing there, thirty-five miles from his jurisdiction, irked Lance. After thinking about it, Lance understood what it meant for the ranch foreman of Big Bob McCoy to be injured, probably killed. A full explanation was going to be required at all levels. They asked Lance if he wanted an attorney. He told them he didn't need one. He hadn't done anything wrong. The slab falling on top of Scooter was an accident, something caused by Scooter himself, a totally unexpected event that probably saved Lance's life.

The sheriff wanted to know why he and Scooter were fighting. Lance had thought about that for the entire hour it took the sheriff to arrive. At first, he didn't really know. As soon as the fight started, it didn't matter. Then it came to him. The way Scooter followed Lightning around, he must have seen them on the road near cactus flats. He couldn't handle that. He was coming for Lance in a jealous rage.

Notwithstanding Lightning's improvised explanation about how Lance happened to have her Indian bead belt, Lance knew his fate was sealed that day at the Cascade Ranch when he threw the belt at Scooter. Scooter would have thought it over and concluded there was only one way Lance had gotten that belt. He got Lightning to take it off. The belt held a special significance, which is why Scooter tried to strangle him with it.

Fortunately, before the sheriff arrived, Lance had picked up the belt from the sandy ground where he and Scooter fought near the pickup trucks, and tossed it into Scooter's truck cab. No mention of it was made during the interview.

A savage jealousy over Lightning was what triggered Scooter's rage, Lance decided.

But was there more? Did Scooter resent Lance for being his own boss, handling his own operation, defying the super-ranch operation of Big Bob McCoy, thumbing his nose at the economics of cattle ranching, irrationally refusing to sell his red-ink operation that Big Bob wanted, that Big Bob was willing to pay an outrageous amount to get? Was all that galling to Scooter Jones?

MAGIC LANCE

More likely it was Lightning, Lance concluded. But that explanation of the fight had some difficulties. Sierra City was a small town. The slightest mention of an involvement with Lightning McClain, even though it had not developed, would spread to every person in the county within twenty-four hours. It would reach Jan within forty-eight hours, even if she was the last one to hear it.

Better to stay with the simple truth, Lance decided. He wasn't sure what incited Scooter Jones to attack him. His suspicions would stay with himself. How he described the possible motives of Scooter Jones would be handled with discretion and caution. He wasn't Scooter Jones. He could only guess, as could anyone else, what motivated Big Bob's foreman.

In truth, Scooter had said little before the attack began. Had he mentioned Lightning? Sort of, Lance admitted to himself, assuming Lightning was "that woman." He remembered Scooter saying something about never touching that woman again. If he were jealous of Lightning, he must have been jealous of half the men in Ladenberger County. He didn't know what Scooter had seen, and he didn't know what Scooter was thinking as he prepared to run him through with the pry bar. All he knew for sure was that Scooter's motive died with him, and the rock slab ambush that had been laid centuries earlier, by Spanish miners unknown, proved incredibly deadly. That is what Lance told the sheriff.

Even with Jan, Lance was guarded with his report of events. Better let a sleeping dog lie. The less said by Lance, the less room for rumors based on his own testimony or first-hand reports. It would be clear Scooter was killed by a falling rock slab, and that he had a pry bar in his hand when it happened. That would be consistent with what Lance said, because it was what actually occurred. Beyond that, why Scooter found himself next to the rock slab with a pry bar in his hand, and why the rock slab fell at precisely the time he was there, after remaining in place for hundreds of years, would be left to the forensic guys. They would recreate what happened. They could only speculate on why it happened.

The strongest evidence would be the words of Lance Burnett, the only eyewitness. And Lance had already given his story. It would not change in the future, because as best he could, he had told the truth. The memory of those events would remain with him for a lifetime. Of that he was sure.

In a telephone call, his father told him that the stories of Scooter's death and the discovery of a lost silver mine had sped through Sierra City with the speed of two tornadoes. A friend of his at the title company called and said a lawyer for the Cascade Ranch had called looking for any legal descriptions of the mine's location, that might support a mining claim.

His father told Lance they should meet at the mine site that very evening and make sure no one came onto the place. He would witness Lance put up some rock monuments on the four corners of the mining claims they were filing, and he personally would see that the paperwork was filed immediately.

Lance told his father of the Grey Piñon offer to buy a hundred acres around the hot springs for six hundred and fifty thousand dollars, enough to pay off the mortgage. His father said he found the offer hard to believe, but it if were true, Lance should call the Indian at once and tell him their offer was accepted. The mortgage would be paid off out of the closing funds. Lance made no mention of the foreclosure action. Perhaps he would miss that bullet.

That night Lance and Jan talked of what lay ahead for the Three V Ranch. Lance told her of the Grey Piñons' offer to buy a hundred acres around Chloride Springs and of his parents'

MAGIC LANCE

acceptance. That would leave them with seven hundred acres for ranching. And on top of that, the discovery of a silver vein in the Piñon Tree Mine, as Lance had decided to name it, would mean a mining operation might start. With the royalties they would receive, they could use their share to buy the seven hundred acres from his parents. Bottom line they would wind up with title to the Three V Ranch, his parents and brother and sister would be paid from the silver mine operation, and the place would be theirs debt-free.

Jan was elated. Their financial worries were over. They would own the Three V free and clear. With the silver profits they could build a modern ranch house and use the old homestead as living quarters for the family of the mine foreman. They would no longer be alone. Perhaps they could even operate a bed and breakfast, building several cabins along Quail Run Creek between the ranch house and cactus flats. That would provide a flow of people to the ranch, and in the summer, perhaps they could have a children's camp, to show city kids how a working ranch operated. Her friend at the library told her of a national organization that encouraged ranchers to turn a portion of their operation into a living ranch museum, that allowed all kinds of people to come from the city to see and experience the ranching life.

"And Lance, I've been going by the animal shelter lately. Yesterday I saw the cutest pair of border collie pups, a male and a female. Jack told me he would hold them until you could come see them. They look just like 'Silver' and 'Lady.' Do those names sound all right to you?"

Lance sat back on the sofa, his arms folded, listening to Jan. He could hardly believe what she was saying. He reached over and took her hand, and pulled her from her chair to the sofa so she was next to him.

"I've been thinking," Lance said. "I think I'm getting tired of this cattle ranching operation. Maybe I'll move into Sierra City and work for the bank, and then run for the U.S. Senate, so I can attract all of these gorgeous young women who are attracted to political power."

Jan punched him on the arm with her fist. "You do, and you'll wind up impotent!"

Lance and Jan looked into each other's eyes and slowly drew together, kissing each other as passionately as they had the night they spent in Washington, D.C.

CHAPTER FIFTY

Lucky Joe lowered himself off the dirt bank, next to the exposed roots of the cottonwood tree at the river. There was a rock next to the roots, and he sat down on it, as he had many times before. He inhaled the aroma of the cottonwood leaves and the freshness of the flowing water. Across the river, he watched smoke from home fireplaces curl into the evening sky. The church silhouette attracted his eye. For several minutes, his mind was a total blank; he let nature stimulate his senses—the smell of the leaves and water, the panorama of earth colors from the trees, bushes, grasses, rocks and soil, the low walls of the reservation buildings, the blues and oranges and yellows of the sky, the grey, charcoal and white of the smoke, the dark greens of the junipers and piñons, the light greens and golds of the cottonwoods.

His private sanctuary by the cottonwood and the river was a refuge from stress; tonight it was a sanctuary for meditation, a monastery for contemplation, for giving thanks and for praise and prayer. Lucky Joe sensed a merger of spirits. The Kachinas were foremost in his mind, but the Church and Jesus Christ also influenced him. Often those thoughts were in conflict.

Tonight, he felt no conflict. The Kachinas and the Church could abide together, as far as he was concerned. He knew the priests did not agree with that. And neither did most of the tribal elders. You had to choose. Lucky Joe was not in a mood to think a decision was required. He felt comfortable this evening, at rest in both spiritual camps.

He remembered his promise to Father O'Grady. If the Lord got him through his difficulties, he promised the priest he would have the biggest church on any reservation in the state. It was clear now that his difficulties temporarily were over. Therefore, his oath would have to be fulfilled. He was the community chief, the cacique. In some form or another, a portion of the tribe's revenues was going to be used to build the biggest Indian church in the state on the Grey Piñon Reservation. He would see to that. After all, there was so much money coming in, they no longer counted it, they only weighed it.

Lucky Joe snapped a twig and tossed it into the river. He watched it sail downstream until it was lost from sight in the ripples and foam of the river. He rejoiced that Rachel, Andrea and Rick had returned to the reservation, confident their husband and father could protect them.

He gazed into the sky. The thought of his former mentor El Segundo was foremost on his mind. On the way to his river sanctuary, he had stopped by the reservation police station. There he talked with his friend Ralph Jojola. A report had come back on the tire tracks. They were made by a Goodyear Wrangler tire. There were millions of those tires in circulation. As a matter of interest, the set of tires on the tribal utility vehicle turned in by El Segundo before he left the reservation were Goodyear Wrangler tires. Evidence, or a coincidence? Two reservation police utility vehicles also had Goodyear Wranglers.

Segundo had known where he was. Rachel confessed to him she told her mother by cell phone on the day they left where they were going, in case of emergency. And her mother said she told no one they were near the chloride springs, except for one evening when El Segundo dropped by her house and said it was

MAGIC LANCE

imperative he get hold of Lucky Joe, and did she know where he could be found. She knew Lucky Joe would want El Segundo to know where he was, for emergencies. The two were looked upon almost as father and son, almost as close as Lucky Joe and his grandfather Alfredo, who were seen as one person, one spirit.

Was the shot at the campfire a warning shot? Or was it a killing shot that missed? If someone sang the death chant, likely it was a killing shot that missed.

Lucky Joe decided to make no judgment.

In the quiet by the river, he thought of life's complexities. He thought of the perfidy of Earl Wallace. The real estate agent confided that he had poisoned several cows on Lance Burnett's ranch, and had killed a couple of his cattle dogs "to encourage him to sell." He also wanted to get even with the dogs that bit him on an earlier occasion when he was chased by a bull named Igor. Had he found Igor, he would have poisoned him too. Wallace thought Lucky Joe would appreciate his perfidy as a clever incentive to force a sale, where a sale was not forthcoming. For his own part, Wallace anticipated the real estate commission.

Lucky Joe pondered if he were compelled to let Lance know who had done the poisonings. As it was, Lance could be suspecting everyone, probably the Grey Piñons and Big Bob McCoy. It is doubtful he would suspect Earl Wallace. If he told Lance, Earl Wallace's life might be in jeopardy, and Lance might commit an act of revenge that would ruin his own life. Earl Wallace had also suggested a portion of his commission might belong to Lucky Joe, if future real estate commissions were guaranteed. At a minimum, Lucky Joe knew that Earl Wallace would never handle another real estate deal for the Grey Piñons, and he would guarantee he wouldn't get five cents out of the deal between Lance Burnett and the Grey Piñons.

Lucky Joe inhaled a deep breath of piñon smoke coming from the village. Now that he was the Grey Piñon community chief, he would guide the tribe according to the spirits. The first momentous decision was whether they would move forward and conclude the purchase of ranches, comprising about two million acres. Although El Segundo was discredited and banished, his vision was worthy. The tribe would be better off in the long run with land ownership rather than ink-on-paper. Although many tribe members opposed the commitment of two hundred and fifty million dollars in land options, the better course now was to follow through with the purchases, even if they had to raise hundreds of millions more to do it. The alternative was to forfeit the two hundred and fifty million, which was unthinkable.

Lucky Joe knew all the difficulties had not gone away. State legislators and city and county officials would recognize the impact on tax revenues. All open private land areas of the state could become depopulated. The environmentalists, instead of celebrating, would turn on them, since Indian land would be out of their orbit of influence. Congress would try to wipe out Indian gambling since the proceeds were being used for a purpose that no one envisioned when the Indian Gaming Regulatory Act was passed. Still the situation was not hopeless. And his own confidence had been replaced by an understanding that by himself he was weak, incompetent and undeserving. Only as Lucky Joe Cruz was lost, and the spirit of the tribe within him was found, could he perform the leadership role that had been entrusted to him.

As the sun settled on the horizon, Lucky Joe returned to his utility vehicle. From the cab he withdrew a long lance from its protective covering. He held the lance in both hands and returned to the bank above the river.

MAGIC LANCE

While singing a chant, Lucky Joe raised the tip of the magic lance skyward, holding it in front of him. Following the chant, he gave praise and said a prayer to the spirits. He acknowledged he was the steward of the vision of a Native American state, and if it was their pleasure, he would bring that vision to reality. They were the vine, he the branch. He asked that they return open land to the Grey Piñons, that the lands of the West be filled with deer, antelope, elk, bear, beaver, fox, lions and turkey, and that the lands to the East be filled once again with rolling herds of buffalo. He further asked that the spirits be filled with understanding when he fulfilled his promise to Father O'Grady to build the largest Catholic church on an Indian reservation in the state, and he asked their continued guidance, directing his will to do what was needed to establish the first Native American state in the United States of America.

He confessed that earlier he thought that if the Grey Piñons obtained enough money from the Magic Lance, all would be well with them. In his prayers he acknowledged his mistake.

Now he understood that the spirit of the tribe was supplied and replenished, not from stacks of money on the casino tables, but from deep within the blood.

Another Great Novel of Suspense by Hal Simmons
DEADLY GOLD
272 pp., 5-1/2 x 8-1/2 (paper) $14.95
ISBN 1574160605

"A novel with murders and mystery, but no dull moments." (Tony Hillerman)

"This must-read book is 261 pages long and makes for an enjoyable, fast-paced read." (Rio Rancho Observer)

"I started to read this mystery story one Sunday after lunch. Except for a mid-afternoon snack break, I didn't put the book down until I finished it." (Santa Fe New Mexican)

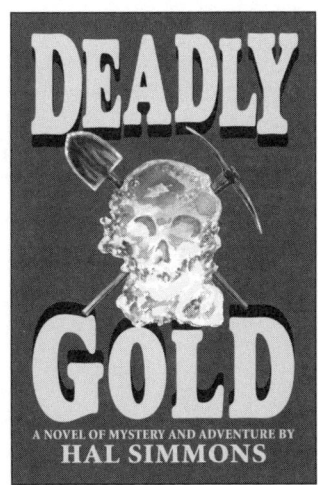

Deadly Gold is an adventure story of a young newspaper reporter from a metropolitan daily as he journeys to a small Colorado town to begin his quest for fame and fortune as owner, publisher and editor. Along the way he meets threats, romance, greed, betrayal and even murder. From precarious moments tottering in his old pickup at the brink of plunging over the edge of an icy cliff in the opening pages—to fighting desperately to avoid being thrown into an old mine hopper and being pulverized along with the ore, near the end—both the hero, Marc Young, and the reader are barely able to catch a breath. Along the way, Young matures from an ambitious yet likeable, somewhat naïve and clueless young man to one who exemplifies qualities of true heroism in the modern West—a man who understands a complex situation and takes a stand for the truth as he sees it, even knowing the potentially grim, perhaps deadly, consequences.

Available at www.clearlightbooks.com
or toll-free at (800) 253-2747.

ABOUT THE AUTHOR

HAL SIMMONS worked as a news reporter for metropolitan dailies before and after military service as an officer with the U.S. Army in Europe. As an attorney, he has been a legal counsel for the New Mexico Press Association and the New Mexico Broadcasters Association. His free-lance articles have appeared in such magazines as *Field & Stream, New Mexico* and *Wild West*. For several years he wrote an outdoor column for the Associated Press in New Mexico, and he was an adjunct professor of news media law at the University of New Mexico.

Simmons's first mystery-adventure novel, *Deadly Gold*, was well-received. He and his wife, Ina, live in Albuquerque, New Mexico.